"Trent?" Chelsea said

He kept walking. His anger was like a pool of molten lava in the pit of his stomach and he just wanted her to leave him alone. Forever.

If he ignored her, she might do exactly that. Right. This was Chelsea Everett he was dealing with. Being ignored wasn't going to deter her.

"It's my fault Amy's gone," she said when he looked at her. "So whatever the kidnapper wants, whatever you're going to try to do, you have to let me help."

"Thanks, but you can't. It's a one-man job."

Good. He was feeling *controlled* anger. He hadn't been sure he could manage that.

"You said the kidnapper has to be someone who threatened revenge and—"

"I'm not certain about that anymore."

"Why not?"

"Chelsea, I can't talk ab̶̶̶̶̶̶̶̶̶̶̶̶̶

He looked at h̶̶̶̶̶̶̶̶̶̶̶̶̶̶̶̶̶̶̶̶̶̶̶re was any concei̶̶̶̶̶̶̶̶̶̶̶̶̶̶̶̶̶g aside the fact th̶̶̶̶̶̶̶̶̶̶̶̶̶̶̶̶̶s help and accepting the̶̶̶̶̶̶̶̶̶̶̶̶̶̶ded it. *Chelsea*—a woman he'd th̶̶̶̶̶̶̶̶̶̶̶, he'd been scared right down to his sho̶̶̶̶̶̶e might end up falling in love with her.

Dear Reader,

Sometimes an author discovers that she's put her characters into an almost impossible emotional situation, and that's what happened to me with *Finding Amy*.

Trent Harrison and Chelsea Everett were perfect for each other, a fact they both recognized virtually the moment they met.

They were well on their way to falling in love—or perhaps they were already beyond the falling stage—when the unthinkable happened. Trent's nine-year-old daughter was kidnapped while she was in Chelsea's care.

In the blink of an eye, Trent's heart turned to stone and Chelsea was consumed by guilt.

The only chance they had of finding Amy lay in working together toward that end.

But how could Trent accept help from the woman responsible for what had happened?

And how could Chelsea bear to be with the man she loved, when his love for her had turned to hatred?

As hard as it was for both of them, they did their best to ignore their feelings and focus on the only thing in the world that really mattered. Finding Amy.

I hope you enjoy the story of how they succeed in attaining a happy ending, *despite* their impossible situation.

Warmest wishes,

Dawn Stewardson

P.S. Please come and visit me at www.superauthors.com.

Finding Amy
Dawn Stewardson

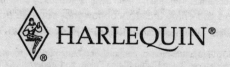

HARLEQUIN®

TORONTO • NEW YORK • LONDON
AMSTERDAM • PARIS • SYDNEY • HAMBURG
STOCKHOLM • ATHENS • TOKYO • MILAN • MADRID
PRAGUE • WARSAW • BUDAPEST • AUCKLAND

ISBN 0-373-71107-7

FINDING AMY

Visit us at www.eHarlequin.com

Printed in U.S.A.

To John, Always.

With special thanks to Constable Craig Coleman,
who helped paint an accurate picture of Rikers Island.

CHAPTER ONE

RISK CONTROL International was in the "survival business." At least, that was the phrase the company's director preferred.

He'd decided, Chelsea assumed, it sounded better than saying people came to them because they feared for their lives.

But semantics aside, the world was becoming a more dangerous place—practically by the day. People were clamoring for the sort of top-quality bodyguards and chauffeurs that RCI provided. And the demand for sophisticated training programs in personal security was growing at an unprecedented rate.

New companies, eager to meet that demand, seemed to be popping up all the time. RCI, however, had been around for almost twenty years and had a reputation as one of the very best. Its instructors were all top-flight professionals who'd demonstrated their skills in real-life situations—which translated into the company having as many clients as it could handle.

Many of them were accustomed to special treatment, so before each new tactical driving course began, Chelsea reviewed her prospective students' files—which generally helped her tailor her teaching to their specific needs.

Today, however, one of the files was doing nothing

but puzzling her. Trent Harrison simply wasn't standard RCI material.

Oh, he wasn't *entirely* different from most of the individuals they trained. The vast majority were males, and she hadn't needed more than a glance at the snapshot clipped inside his folder to decide there was no doubt he fit into that category.

In fact, she was thinking she might have to create a subcategory reserved for men who looked enough like Antonio Banderas that they'd blow the top off a hunk-a-meter merely by walking within ten feet of it.

Regardless of that, though, why did Harrison want to learn what her dad always called guerrilla driving? For that matter, why had he already taken five other RCI courses?

Typically, RCI students were celebrities, high-level government officials or corporate executives whose work landed them in hotbeds of terrorism. Or they were people *employed* by individuals at high risk.

The other major category was comprised of folk in law enforcement of one sort or another. She'd taught members of police and sheriffs' departments from half the states in the nation, as well as FBI agents and CIA types.

But when it came to law professors, Trent Harrison of Ridley University was her first. Actually, he was her first *any* kind of professor.

Her gaze slipped down to the line on his application form that asked his reason for taking her course. *Interested in expanding the scope of my skills,* he'd written.

Uh-uh. She wasn't buying that he was simply a run-of-the-mill Joe Public wanting to be a better driver.

She might have—just maybe—except for the records of those five previous courses. He seemed to have taken one every time there was a break between terms.

Of course, he could merely be looking for some excitement in his life. And since the little town of Ridley wasn't much more than a half hour's drive from the outskirts of Hartford, where the RCI training center was located, getting here wouldn't require a lot of effort.

But *six* courses?

She set his current application aside, then flipped through the older ones. He'd begun with Defensive Tactics. Next had come first- and second-level Handgun Training. Then he'd done both basic and comprehensive Personal Protection Training.

He looked to be working his way through RCI's entire range of offerings, and on each of the forms he'd simply claimed to be interested in expanding the scope of his skills.

She couldn't help wondering if that was a euphemism for "I'm paranoid to the max," then she began sincerely hoping it wasn't. Courses went far more smoothly when all the students were sane, rational people.

TRENT STOOD on the edge of the track, waiting for the instructor to show and making small talk with the others.

It wasn't the easiest thing to do, given that confidentiality was the watchword at Risk Control International, but he had no problem with the *first names only* rule.

People who needed the sort of training RCI provided didn't want anyone flagging them as potential kidnap or assassination targets. And even if that wasn't the case, he wouldn't be interested in telling three strangers who he was and why he was there.

He glanced at his new classmates in turn—Al, Mike and... The other one's name had slipped his mind but—

At the sound of a door opening, all four men turned toward the building.

"Not bad," Mike said.

To Trent's mind that was a distinct understatement.

The woman who'd stepped out into the warmth of the June morning was tall and slender, with sun-streaked hair the color of pale honey and the sort of natural good looks that would make any redblooded male take notice.

She headed across the track, flashing a terrific smile as she neared them.

"I'm Chelsea Everett," she said, then waited a beat before adding, "I teach the tactical driving course.

"So let's start by getting the obvious questions answered," she continued, her amused expression telling Trent that her new students had done a poor job of concealing their surprise.

"I've completed every course RCI offers, as have the other instructors here, and I'm qualified to teach several of them."

Which, he thought, had to make her *extremely* capable of taking care of herself.

"But I feel most comfortable with this one," she went on, "because I've been driving for almost as long as I can remember.

"My father is Howie—'Slick'—Everett. Retired race-car driver?"

Trent nodded that he recognized the name, although he figured *champion* would have been a better choice of words than *driver*. In his prime, Slick Everett had been at the top of the heap.

"Well, when I was eight years old my dad stood me between his knees at the wheel and taught me to drive. I was racing a Ford Galaxie on dirt ovals in Indiana before I had a driver's license.

"And beating all the boys," she added with another smile.

Then she pointed along the track to where orange cones had been set up, creating an obstacle course. "We're going to begin with a test drive so I can see what level you're starting at. After that, we'll spend the rest of the morning in the classroom—not just talking technical stuff, but studying real incidents and discussing how deaths could have been avoided.

"This afternoon, we'll get down to some practice work with our driving simulators, then I'll do individual sessions with each of you on the track. And that's primarily where you'll spend the rest of your time here—driving those training cars." She gestured toward the half-dozen that were parked nearby.

"They've been specially modified for safety. In addition to the roll bars, they're equipped with racing-style seat belts, fire suppression systems and special hydraulic brakes."

"Not exactly what we drive in the real world," Al said.

"No. But we don't want to risk injuries while you're learning. And by the end of our week together you'll have the skill to keep from getting into trouble—and know maneuvers that'll get you out of it. Regardless of what you're driving.

"Any other comments or questions?"

As the four men shook their heads, she said, "Fine, then let me explain how the test works. You'll start at the far end, drive the course, turn around and drive back. I'll be timing you, and each cone you knock over adds ten seconds to your time.

"This is Bob," she added, introducing a man who'd materialized while she was speaking. "He resets the course after each run, and I should warn you that he gets a little snarly if you make him work too hard."

She shot Bob a grin before looking at the rest of them again. "We'll do the test a second time on Friday afternoon, and you'll be amazed at how much better you are."

"And if we're not?" Al asked.

She smiled once more. "I'll be looking for a new job. So, who wants to go first?"

Since no one else volunteered, Trent did—mostly because he hated the hung-out-to-dry feeling that came when you got no response from your students.

A few minutes later, he was regretting having opened his mouth.

He'd always considered himself a pretty good driver, yet he'd sent enough cones flying that he'd probably made Bob as snarly as a half-starved cougar.

By the time the others had completed their runs, though, he felt better. As bad as he'd been, his three minutes fifty seconds was the second-best time.

"Now do you show us how it *should* be done?" Mike, who'd gotten the worst score, asked Chelsea.

His tone was more than a little challenging, but if she noticed she gave no indication.

"Sure, I'll take a run if you'd like. But then we

have to hit the classroom. Why don't you time me," she added, handing Mike her stopwatch.

When she started off, Trent found himself watching the enticing sway of her hips, and feeling the sort of stirring inside that he'd almost forgotten he could experience.

It took him by surprise. As great-looking as she might be, in the three years since Sheila's death he'd seldom felt the slightest whisper of attraction to a woman. And the few times he had, he'd done absolutely nothing about it. Precisely what he'd do this time around.

Maybe, way off in the distant future, he might be able to lead a normal life again. But not yet.

Oh, he realized some of his friends thought he was simply suffering from a case of "once hurt, twice shy," but they didn't know the whole story. They had no idea why the idea of getting involved in a relationship scared the hell out of him. Even if it was with someone who'd apparently been raised on adrenaline.

Shutting a mental door against the *relationship* thoughts, he realized his gaze had returned to Chelsea's hips.

He adjusted it upward and watched her put on her helmet. Then she climbed into the car and proceeded to impress the devil out of them by practically flying down the track and back up.

As she reached the far end of the course again, Mike checked the stopwatch. "I don't believe it," he muttered. "A minute forty-five seconds."

Her time clearly ticked him off, which struck Trent

as so childish he couldn't resist saying, "And she didn't hit a single cone. Talk about inheriting good driving genes."

CHELSEA HEADED for her office, glad the morning's preliminary instruction session was over.

Classrooms had never made her list of favorite places, and sitting on the teacher's side of the desk did nothing to change her feelings about them. She far preferred to be where the action was.

Once she'd reached her destination, she sat gazing at the little stack of student files, resisting the urge to have another peek at Trent Harrison's—to read through the personal information section she hadn't looked at earlier.

She didn't usually bother with that, partly because it wasn't really relevant to her job and partly because the sections were so darn lengthy.

Actually, she wouldn't be surprised to learn that RCI required more information from prospective students than the Feds did from prospective special agents. But being careful about whom they accepted had always been a necessity, and at this point...

Well, if they inadvertently trained some wannabe terrorists, they'd lose the endorsement of the World Security Organization. Not to mention getting kicked out of the International Association of Counterterrorism and Security Professionals.

She didn't imagine the FBI or CIA would exactly be smiling in their direction, either.

After eyeing the stack of files for another few seconds, she decided she was being silly by resisting. There was absolutely no reason she shouldn't satisfy her curiosity about Harrison. Especially since he'd turned out to be even better-looking than his snapshot. And when he seemed like a nice guy, too.

Not that she viewed her job as an opportunity to meet men. But with the driving course spanning a mere five days, her students became ex-students quickly enough that she had no rule against dating the occasional one.

Actually, she'd always figured a rule like that would be pretty dumb, considering the "dating" seldom amounted to more than a single dinner or a movie. RCI's students came from all over the country, and once they were gone it was usually for good.

Trent Harrison, however, lived virtually just down the road. Which made it only sensible to see whether his lack of a wedding band was significant.

She reached for his file, dug out the most recent application form and checked the line that asked his marital status.

Widowed, he'd written.

Ah. Maybe that explained all the courses he'd taken. They could be his way of filling a void.

Reading further, she learned he was thirty-five years old, had a nine-year-old daughter and had been teaching at Ridley University for the past three years. Before that, he'd been a prosecuting attorney in New York City.

Quite a drastic change in lifestyle, from the D.A.'s Office in Manhattan to teaching in sleepy little Ridley, Connecticut.

Of course, since Ridley was a college town, there were *some* things to do. And it had enough trendy restaurants that one or another of her friends would sometimes suggest driving over for dinner. But Ridley

was a universe away from the sidewalks of New
York.

She spent a couple of seconds speculating about
what might have prompted Trent Harrison to go from
one extreme to another, then her mind jumped tracks
and she began to wonder whether he'd felt the same
chemistry between them that she had.

Given the way she'd noticed him looking at her a
few times, she suspected he had. Or maybe that was
only wishful thinking. Recently, things had been awfully slow in the Department of Attractive Males.

Oh, she'd been seeing a little of Shawn Madders,
an FBI agent who'd taken her course about three
months ago. His home base was in Boston, though, a
hundred miles from Hartford, and...

But was she trying to kid herself?

A two-hundred-mile round trip would hardly be a
major obstacle if the attraction between them was really strong.

And although he was nice enough, there were a few
things about him that she suspected would bother her
in the long term. Especially that when he got talking—and he *loved* to talk—he tended to go on forever, giving her far more details about whatever he'd
done than she had any real interest in.

That was unusual in a special agent. Most of the
Feds she'd met were so careful when it came to what
they said that she'd always assumed a philosophy of
"better too little than too much" was drilled into
them during their training.

But regardless of any of that, the fact she and
Shawn had had exactly four dates in the past three
months said the spark between them was far more
likely to sputter out than to flame into something se-

rious. Which was standard when it came to her and men.

She'd always been…

Well, according to her mother, she scared men off. *If you'd just make an effort not to intimidate them…*

She'd bet, since she'd first begun to notice boys, that her mom had repeated that phrase two zillion times. And every single time she'd said it within her husband's hearing, he'd countered by saying that any guy who was intimidated by Chelsea obviously just wasn't good enough for her.

Her dad, though, had always been proud that his only child didn't conform to most people's expectations of how women should behave; whereas her mom…

Her mother loved her. There wasn't any doubt about that. But she'd have been a lot happier if Chelsea had preferred ballet lessons and frilly dresses to sports and jeans. And if, as an adult, she'd chosen a conventionally feminine occupation.

Then there was the issue of marriage and children.

Her mother was dying for grandchildren, and was growing more and more worried that her daughter would never find Mr. Right. Or that if she did, she'd frighten *him* away, too. Just like all the others.

But as much as Chelsea adored kids, she wasn't unhappy with her life the way it was. Far from it.

She loved the freedom of being able to do what she wanted when she wanted, which was one reason she enjoyed her contract arrangement with RCI. It let her pretty much pick and choose when she wanted to teach a course, and she rarely did two back to back.

That way, she could lock her apartment door and

take off virtually whenever the desire seized her—not something that would be possible if she had more responsibilities. So if she never fell madly, insanely in love…

Well, settling for less wouldn't be something she could do. It wasn't in her nature.

Absently, she looked at Trent Harrison's picture again, thinking he didn't strike her as the type who'd frighten easily.

Then she tucked his application form away and headed for the cafeteria. There was barely enough time left to grab a salad before she had to get back to her students.

UNTIL TODAY, Trent had never given much thought to the "theory" of driving. He'd always just climbed into a car and blithely turned the key.

But by the end of this morning's session, his head had been so full of facts about weight transfer and traction, steering geometry and braking techniques, that he'd hardly been able to think straight. And he'd felt certain that if he did the visual-rotation-sequence exercise many more times his neck would freeze up.

Then, this afternoon, he'd quickly developed a deep respect for driving simulators. If he and his classmates had been sitting behind the wheels of actual cars, they'd probably all be graveyard dead by now.

He just hoped that enough of what he'd learned transferred to the real thing, because he'd prefer not to make a fool of himself in front of Chelsea Everett.

Watching her get out of the training car after her third one-on-one—with the fellow named Ross—he started thinking that the other guys probably felt the same way he did.

Whether it was fact or fiction, the majority of American males figured they were better drivers than women. And while a man would have to be delusional to believe he was better than Chelsea, none of them would want her deciding he needed training wheels.

And then there was the other element that came into play. Chelsea Everett was the sort of woman whom most men…

Hell, the way Ross looked—as if he'd like to crawl across the hood of the car toward her—said it all. Not only was she over-the-edge gorgeous, she had a wry sense of humor and seemed as smart as it got.

While Ross was saying a few final words and removing his helmet, Trent reminded himself he had no intention of trying to start something with *any* woman. Not in the present decade, at least. Which meant that this particular one's opinion of him really didn't matter in the slightest.

He'd barely finished putting together that bit of logic when she smiled over at him—and he went back to hoping he wouldn't make a fool of himself.

"Your turn," she said, gesturing him toward the driver's side before climbing back into the passenger's seat.

As he slid in beside her he could smell her perfume. He'd been aware of it a couple of times in the classroom, then again, after lunch, when she'd leaned close to adjust his hands on the simulator's steering wheel. The haunting scent put him in mind of a soft Caribbean evening, the fragrance of night-blooming flowers in the air.

But instead of thinking about how good she

smelled, he'd be wiser to think about how you kept from understeering or oversteering at high speed.

Wiping out on the simulator was one thing. Not handling a fast curve properly on the track would be something else.

"Okay," she said. "With the simulator, you can never get a really good sense of road feel, so we're going to begin with a few laps. And I want you to concentrate on being aware of the car.

"Think of it as an extension of yourself, because that's actually what it is. It only does what you tell it to, so getting it to respond the way you want is a matter of learning to tell it the right thing."

"You sound like my dog obedience instructor. He always said he was teaching the owners, not the dogs."

She smiled at that, and when she did he was alarmingly conscious of how lush her lips were. It almost started him wishing that someone else were teaching the course.

Almost, but not quite.

He liked being around Chelsea, even though the fact that he did made him uneasy.

"Is your dog any particular kind?" she was saying.

"A Bouvier."

"Named?"

"Pete."

"Ah."

"My daughter's choice," he added when she looked as though she didn't consider that much of a name for a dog.

"And it could have been worse. He was still a little guy when we got him, and at first Amy was intent on calling him Tiny."

That made Chelsea smile again. "But you were thinking ahead, to a hundred-pound dog with an identity crisis."

"Exactly," he said. He *also* liked her sense of humor.

"And you chose such a big breed because…?"

"Because of Amy. I'd been told Bouviers were great with kids."

Chelsea merely nodded, which was fine with him. He had no desire to elaborate further, to say that he'd researched all the large breeds and had decided on a Bouvier because, aside from being reliable around children, they were excellent watchdogs and protective as hell.

"Okay, let's get going," Chelsea said.

"Hands at three and nine o'clock," she added as he started the engine.

"That much I remember."

"Good. Then we're off.

"Now, what I want you to do," she added as he shifted out of Park, "is focus on your physical reactions while you're picking up speed. The faster you go, the more your body will want to tighten up, so you have to work at not letting it.

"Keep your arms flexed and don't let your hands get stiff. As soon as they do they lose half their feeling, and feeling is control."

"Right."

"Okay, now speed up so you're going about ten miles an hour above your comfort level as we hit the first curve. And remember what I talked about this morning.

"As the car takes a corner, the weight transfers to the outside and front while you're braking and to the outside and rear when you accelerate out of the curve."

He nodded. "And you avoid fishtailing by making that transfer go as smoothly as possible."

"Exactly. So even though you feel you're going too fast, make sure you *ease* off the accelerator and onto the brake. If you lift off the gas rapidly you'll also hit the brake hard. That's just the way the body works."

"And I don't want to twist the wheel too abruptly," he said, glancing at her and trying to shake the sense that he was back in grade three.

"Good," she said, shooting him a smile. "You were paying attention."

He focused on the track again and managed to negotiate the curve without skidding.

"*Very* good," Chelsea told him.

Then, just as he was starting to feel a little more relaxed, she said, "Now, by the time we reach the next curve, I want you going *fifteen* miles an hour above your comfort level."

CHAPTER TWO

AFTER HER STUDENTS had spent forty-five minutes on the accident simulators, Chelsea decided they'd better hit the track. This was their final day, and before lunch she wanted to demonstrate the reverse one-eighty-degree spin, a maneuver that could prove a lifesaver for someone being pursued.

If she got the demonstration and their questions out of the way now, they could begin practicing as soon as they'd eaten, so she told them to head out to the training cars.

"I'll be right behind you," she added.

But as they walked toward the door, she found herself simply standing where she was, utterly unable to take her gaze off Trent Harrison's broad shoulders.

Closing her eyes solved the immediate problem. In her entire life, though, she'd never met another man who...

Well, when it came to the subject of Professor Harrison, she didn't even know where to start.

Should it be with the way she was so ridiculously attracted to him that she found herself smiling when she took her birth control pill in the morning?

Usually, she was more likely to frown and wonder why she bothered with them, given that her sexual encounters were so few and far between.

But, of course, she took them because years ago

she'd promised her mother she would. The result of
a particularly embarrassing mother-daughter talk, during which her mother had made clear that she worried
immensely about what she'd referred to as her daughter's "frequent spontaneity."

Shifting her thoughts from her mother back to
Trent Harrison, she began musing that the pull she
felt toward him seemed to grow stronger with every
passing hour.

But there was more involved than pure and simple
lust. She liked the man. *Really* liked him. He was
intelligent and level-headed, yet fun at the same time.
And he seemed genuinely interested in her as a person. Which wasn't a common trait in men. Not the
ones she met, at any rate. Trent, though…

She let her thoughts drift back to the conversation
she'd had with him during their break this morning.

"You know," he'd said, "I can't help wondering
why you didn't go into pro racing yourself. I mean,
you've mentioned your father always encouraged
your interest in driving, so…"

She'd shrugged and said, "He's far from the most
practical person in the world, but when it came to the
idea of my trying to make it as a race driver his take
was totally realistic."

"Meaning?"

"Meaning that when *he* started out, women weren't
even allowed around race tracks. They were considered bad luck. And even though they've gradually
been breaking in, racing is still very much a male
sport and the good ol' boys' network is as strong as
ever."

She shrugged. "I guess in the end it came down to
two things. The first was whether I really wanted to

spend twenty or thirty years banging my head against the proverbial brick wall.''

''And the answer was no.''

''Well…it might not have been, except for the economics of the picture. You can't be a serious competitor without major financial backing. And while sponsors are willing to throw money at a man who shows enough potential, it's a different story with a woman.

''Even with Slick Everett as my father, I'd have had to start winning at top levels before I'd have gotten any support from a sponsor. And the cost of getting to the stage of qualifying for something like the Indy…''

''Kind of a Catch-22 situation?''

''Exactly.''

''So you decided on this job, instead?''

''Uh-huh. I'm not the most practical person in the world, either, but I'd rather enjoy my life than spend it chasing dreams that are… Well, probably not impossible, but close to it.''

Trent hesitated, then said, ''No regrets?''

She smiled. ''The occasional one. On a really bad day, when a student flips a car or something.''

That had made *Trent* smile. And just recalling the hot shiver his smile had sent through her turned her thoughts back to the way his mere presence had become enough to seriously interfere with her concentration.

All it took was one of his smiles to make her heart skip half a dozen beats. And as if he'd decided that the days weren't enough, he'd been wandering around in her dreams for the past four nights.

Plus, he had her totally confused, never mind seriously doubting her intuition, which until now she'd considered eminently reliable.

But maybe she'd been deluding herself on that count. Because her instincts had been insisting from the outset that Trent felt the same dynamite chemistry between them as she did.

Yet if that was so, why hadn't he said or done anything to indicate that he *did* feel that chemistry?

Of course, this *was* the twenty-first century. Women no longer had to sit on their hands until a man expressed interest. However, in her situation...

Well, she might not have a rule against dating students, but she *did* have one against making the initial move.

After all, she was the instructor. And even though it was hardly the same as being a high-school teacher, even though she taught adults, she just wouldn't feel right about...

Probably, the best way of summing it up was to say she wouldn't want to risk putting someone on the spot.

Having brought that thought to a satisfactory conclusion, she firmly told herself—for the nine hundred and third time—that obsessing about Trent Harrison like some lovesick teenager was ridiculous. And not the sort of behavior that had *ever* been her style.

It also couldn't be good for a person's mental health. So if the man was content to walk out of here at the end of today, without a backward glance, she'd simply forget about him.

Once she'd silently repeated that a few times to ensure it sank in, she left the simulator room and headed down the hallway.

When she opened the door to the outside world, the situation with Trent suddenly made more sense.

The attractive woman standing on the edge of the track and talking to him explained a lot.

She looked a few years older than Chelsea, probably mid thirties, like Trent, and their body language said they knew each other very well.

Trying to pretend she wasn't feeling a sting of disappointment, she reminded herself that she'd been aware all along that a man's being widowed didn't guarantee there was no female in his life.

But since, in this instance, she hadn't wanted that possibility to be reality, she'd pretty much ignored it. However, she couldn't ignore a flesh-and-blood human being.

Forcing her eyes from Trent and the woman, she focused on the cute little girl with them—Trent's daughter, she imagined, given the casual way his hands were resting on her shoulders.

The child was gazing up, listening to the adult conversation with a somber expression.

Neither Trent nor his girlfriend seemed happy, either. Actually, the woman looked downright grim.

But whatever they were discussing was none of her business, so she started toward the cars, where her other students were waiting.

She'd only taken a few steps before Trent called, "Chelsea?"

When she paused, he strode rapidly over and said, "I'm sorry, but I won't be able to finish out the day."

He nodded toward his girlfriend, adding, "My daughter's nanny has a family emergency, so I have to take Amy home."

His daughter's nanny?

Not that she couldn't be both that *and* a romantic interest, but maybe she wasn't.

Chelsea turned her attention back to what Trent was saying in time to catch that it was something about the woman heading for Philadelphia.

"And the neighbor who sometimes looks after Amy wasn't home," he added. "Which meant Lizzie had to stop by here with her. So I guess I'll just have to hope I never need to do a reverse one-eighty."

"Ah, but hoping isn't always enough," she said, glancing over at the little girl and thinking that no one would object to her being here for a few hours.

Then she looked back at Trent and said, "Why doesn't Amy spend the rest of the day with us?"

"Well," he said slowly, "Lizzie's going to be gone for a while, so I'll have to make some arrangements. Although, I guess I don't have to get on it right this minute."

He hesitated, then added, "But if Amy stays here, there'd be nobody to watch her while I'm on the track."

Watch her? Lord, when *she'd* been Amy's age…

Her father, however, believed that children should become as independent as possible, as quickly as possible. Whereas that wasn't the way Trent seemed to think.

Reminding herself that his early parenting experience had been in New York City, which would go a long way toward making *anyone* overprotective, she said, "We can all keep an eye on Amy. And I'll bet she'd get a kick out of seeing you practice."

"Well…"

He hesitated longer this time, before saying, "You don't think she'd be in the way?"

"Not at all. And if she gets bored she can go inside and help our receptionist. Esther's great with kids."

When that didn't seem enough to convince him, she added, "Hey, you aren't thinking that leaving now would get you out of retaking the driving test, are you?"

"Of course not."

"Good, because if you don't face up to something like that, it can leave psychological scars."

He smiled at that, making her heart do one of those half-a-dozen-beat skips she was almost getting used to.

Then he said, "Chelsea, is there *anything* you can't turn into a challenge?"

TRENT SHOT another glance in Amy's direction, but she was oblivious to him.

She hadn't taken her eyes off the car Chelsea was using for her demonstration, obviously fascinated that his "special driving" teacher had proven to be a woman.

He hadn't mentioned that, hadn't gone into any more detail about this course than about the others he'd taken at Risk Control.

His daughter couldn't have a perfectly normal childhood. Their circumstances simply wouldn't permit that. But he did his best to make it as close to normal as possible, and he didn't want her putting together enough facts to frighten herself.

With that in mind, he'd referred to his handgun training as "target practice," and to the defensive tactics and personal protection courses simply as "exercise workouts."

He turned his attention back to the track, where

Chelsea was just finishing up a series of reverse hundred-eighty-degree spins. That completed, she climbed out of the car and delivered a minilecture on how to execute the maneuver.

"Which is about all I have to say," she concluded.

"After lunch, there'll be lots of time to practice—before the dreaded driving retest," she added with a smile. "But does anyone have questions now?"

There were only a couple, and once she'd finished answering them, she caught Trent's eye and nodded toward Amy.

When he mouthed a "Sure" in response, she turned and started over to where the girl was perched on one of the benches alongside the track.

While the other fellows headed for the cafeteria, he trailed after Chelsea, uncertain whether he liked the idea of her introducing herself to his daughter.

But that was hardly surprising. When it came to Chelsea Everett, he was uncertain about an awful lot of things.

Despite knowing that letting a woman into his life would be extremely unwise, he just couldn't shake the thought that it might be safe to make an exception with her.

Well, no, *safe* was hardly the word. Downplaying the risk involved would be stupid. But when it came to someone like Chelsea…

Like Chelsea.

Now, that was funny.

In the first place, he truly doubted there was anyone else in the world like Chelsea. Her uniqueness was one of the things he found so appealing about her.

And in the second place, he realized he was trying to rationalize a foolish idea. He also realized why.

In a single week, Chelsea Everett had... Would "mesmerized him" be a good way of putting it?

It had to be, he decided, because when she was anywhere in his field of vision he simply couldn't keep his eyes off her.

Even when the two of them were doing a practice session in the car and he should be concentrating solely on his driving, he'd find himself sneaking glances at her, while his thoughts would be drifting in all kinds of crazy directions.

He'd be wondering what she thought of him. Whether she really liked him or just made a practice of acting as if she liked *all* her students.

Then he'd start wondering whether she was even marginally as turned on by him as he was by her.

And, hell, it wasn't just when he was around her that he couldn't shut her out of his mind. Regardless of where he was or what he was doing, she'd been front and center in his head since practically the first moment he'd seen her.

He'd be playing a board game with Amy, and suddenly an image of Chelsea would be right before his eyes.

Or he'd take the dog for his after-dinner walk and find himself speeding up, thinking some woman ahead of them bore enough resemblance to Chelsea that it might be her. Which was absurd when she lived in Hartford, not Ridley.

Man, it was a good thing this was the last day of the course. Because his willpower had been fading fast, and if he had to spend much more time around her...

He caught up to her just as she reached Amy and was saying, "Hi, I'm Chelsea."

"Hi." Amy gave her a smile.

"I guess you're ready for lunch, but I was thinking that if you're not too hungry you might like a little tour first. I'm sure your dad's told you about our simulators, and I could let you try one out."

Amy shook her head. "He didn't tell me about them."

Chelsea seemed surprised; Trent fought the urge to explain that he *did* talk to his daughter, that he just didn't talk to her about *everything.*

After a few seconds, Amy filled the silence by saying, "But I'd like to try one."

"Good," Chelsea said. "Then let's go.

"Should we see you in the cafeteria?" she added to him. "In twenty minutes or so?"

"Ah…sure."

He watched them walk away together, an all-too-familiar tightness in his chest—even though he knew nothing awful was going to happen to Amy here in the RCI compound.

Hell, he'd bet that with Chelsea looking out for her, she'd be perfectly safe in the New York subway system.

AMY WAS an enthusiastic, fun-to-be-with little girl, and so enthralled by the driving simulator that Chelsea found it tough resisting the temptation to let her try the accident simulator, as well. But the lunch break was half over and they hadn't eaten.

As they started for the cafeteria, Amy gave her a huge grin and said, "That was *way* neat."

Chelsea smiled. "I'm glad you enjoyed it."

"It's just like a video game. Only bigger and better."

"And you were good at it, too."

That made Amy grin again. "I wish I could play with stuff like that all the time."

"Oh, I bet you get to do lots of good stuff."

"Only sometimes."

"What about this weekend? Have you and your dad got anything exciting planned?"

The minute she asked the question she regretted it. Amy's expression went from sunny to dark in the blink of an eye.

"We *did* have," she said. "We were gonna celebrate, cuz school finished last week."

"Already?"

"Uh-huh. It's a private school and we get out a little early."

"Ah."

"So we were supposed to take Pete, our dog, to a dog-sitter tonight. Well, not a *real* dog-sitter, but a friend of my dad's who was gonna take care of him."

"And then?"

"Then, early, early in the morning—at the crack of dawn, my dad said—we were gonna drive to Boston. And stay until Sunday. In a hotel.

"But now my dad's going by himself. And coming back tomorrow night."

"Why the change of plans?"

"Cuz Lizzie had to go home. Lizzie's my nanny."

"Right. Your father said there was some sort of emergency."

"Uh-huh. Her mom's in the hospital. In Philadelphia. And I think she must be *real* sick," Amy continued in a confiding tone. "Cuz Lizzie was crying."

"Oh. That's sad, isn't it."

"Uh-huh. But her boyfriend said he'd drive her, and that made her feel better. Some better, anyway."

"Well, that's good."

Boyfriend. The word lingered in Chelsea's mind long enough to whisper that Lizzie *wasn't* a romantic interest as well as the nanny.

Focusing her attention an Amy once more, she said, "But couldn't you still go to Boston? With just your dad?"

"No. Cuz he's gotta give a talk. At a conference. And me and Lizzie were gonna do stuff while he was busy. But now that she won't be there he's gonna get someone to look after me at home. Probably Mrs. Wilson, our next-door neighbor."

"Ah. You must be disappointed."

Amy nodded. "We had tickets to a baseball game tomorrow night. And on Sunday we were gonna go whale watching, and everything."

The girl was silent for a minute, then said, "Have you been to Boston?"

"Sure. Lots of times."

The thought flitted through her mind that the last couple had been because she'd had dates with Special Agent Shawn Madders. But since there was no reason to say anything about him to Amy, she went with, "It's not a very long drive."

"I know, but I've never been there. Do you like it?"

"Yes. It's a neat place."

She didn't elaborate beyond that, even though Boston was one of her all-time favorite cities. Saying wonderful things about it would just make Amy feel worse.

Yet...why wasn't Trent still taking her? If he was

only going to be tied up for part of the time, then canceling their plans entirely seemed extreme, Lizzie or no Lizzie.

But she'd better not raise that thought with Amy. In fact, she wouldn't utter another word on the subject.

Then, not more than three seconds later, she found herself saying, "You know, I think most hotels can arrange for someone to stay with kids when their parents are busy."

Amy shook her head. "My dad would never let me stay with a stranger."

"Oh." Not even a stranger vetted by hotel management? When the alternative was leaving her home, disappointed?

The word *overprotective* popped into her head again—this time in capital letters. But it simply wasn't her place to voice an opinion about parenting to Trent.

She could just imagine how much he'd appreciate an unsolicited two cents' worth from someone who didn't have even a single child of her own.

They reached the cafeteria, where the man in question was sitting at a table with her other students.

When he spotted them, he seemed almost relieved to see that his daughter was safe and sound.

But Chelsea assumed she had to be misreading that. Nobody who'd known her for even five minutes would worry about leaving a child in her care.

He rose from the group table and walked over to the counter to buy Amy some lunch. Then, as the three of them sat down at one of the other small tables, he asked Amy how she'd liked the simulator.

"It was awesome," she told him. "I wish I could have come here with you all week."

She slowly ate a bite of her sandwich, her gaze flickering from her father to Chelsea, then back to Trent.

"Chelsea likes Boston," she said at last.

Trent nodded. "We'll go another time, honey. I promise. Just not this weekend."

"But—"

"Amy, we'll do it soon. Not tomorrow, though. I got hold of Mrs. Wilson while you two were off having fun, and she'll be happy to look after you."

Amy sat staring at the table for a long moment, then said, "Daddy?"

"Uh-huh?"

"Why can't Chelsea come with us? Then I could do stuff with *her* while you're giving your talk."

Chelsea glanced at Trent in time to catch him looking more than a little flustered.

"Well…" he said. "I imagine Chelsea already has plans for the weekend."

"Do you?" Amy asked her.

She gazed at the girl, thinking about a bit of advice her father always used to give her.

You don't get what you want by waiting for it to fall into your lap, darling, he'd say. *You have to speak up. Reach out and grab opportunities before they can slip away.*

"Do you?" Amy repeated.

She thought rapidly. She could end this, right here and now, by saying that she *did* have plans. And then…?

And then she'd probably never see either of the Harrisons again.

After weighing her options for a couple of seconds longer, she said, "You know what, Amy? I don't have even the ghost of a plan."

TRENT AND AMY picked Chelsea up so early that they were only half-awake, and initially all three of them were subdued.

However, Amy had soon begun asking questions from the back seat.

"Chelsea and me are gonna have two beds in our room, right?" she continued after pausing for breath.

"Chelsea and *I*," Trent said automatically. "But right."

"And our room's gonna be next to yours?"

"That's the plan."

And hotel rooms next to each other often had an adjoining door.

The moment that thought snuck into his head he ordered it back out.

Chelsea would be in the next room *with his daughter.*

Besides, things hadn't changed overnight. There was still no way he was going to let himself get involved with a woman.

Yet even while he was reminding himself of that, his gaze strayed across the car to Chelsea, and he couldn't help thinking she looked even more gorgeous than usual.

She was turned half around so she could see Amy, and the morning sunlight was catching strands of her pale hair, transforming them into spun gold.

"And when we get to Boston, the very first thing we're gonna do is check into the hotel?" Amy said.

"Uh-huh, I specified an early-morning check-in,"

he told her, starting to wonder if he'd only dreamed that she'd made him repeat all the details at least three times last night.

"Then you go to the conference and Chelsea and I go see stuff, right?"

"You've got it," Chelsea agreed.

"And what *else* can we do? Besides what you already told me about?"

"Oh," said Chelsea, "there's just way too much for us to choose from. There's the aquarium. And Chinatown. And, if we're lucky, the Boston Pops will be giving a concert on the Esplanade."

"What's the Esplanade?"

"It's an open stretch along the river. Then there's Faneuil Hall. That's a huge marketplace you'll just love, and—"

"Hey, I'll only be tied up for part of the morning," Trent teased. "You don't really figure you can cover all those things, do you? Half of them won't even be open when you get going."

Chelsea smiled, making his heart thud against his ribs.

"Well," she said, "I just want her to know what all our options are."

When he nodded and turned his attention back to the road, she began telling Amy about how many great restaurants there were in Boston. And his daughter, whose interest in food rarely extended beyond peanut butter and ice cream, seemed utterly fascinated by every word Chelsea spoke.

Or maybe she was just utterly fascinated by Chelsea.

He'd never seen her take to anyone this way before. Chelsea was all she'd talked about the entire way home from RCI yesterday. And she'd not very subtly pointed out that since Chelsea hadn't had any plans for the weekend, she probably didn't have a boyfriend.

Hoping Amy wouldn't be too disappointed when this didn't develop into anything more than a one-shot deal, he tuned back into their conversation.

"And the hot dogs we'll get at the game tonight," Chelsea was saying, "are going to be the best you've ever eaten."

"I've never been to a real live baseball game before," Amy said. "Except for kids' ones, I mean."

"Oh, you'll love it. You can't beat a Yankees–Sox game. The Sox are my favorite team. But did you know they were originally called the Pilgrims?"

"Honest?"

"Uh-huh. They were renamed for the color of the players' socks, way back in 1907."

Amy giggled. "That's so silly. To name a team for their socks. Why would anyone do that?"

As Chelsea said she really didn't know, Trent glanced over at her again.

She rewarded him with another smile—a somewhat sheepish one this time.

"Sorry," she said. "I get carried away now and then. My father didn't have any sons, just me, so he made sure I became a serious sports fan."

He shrugged, told her that you never knew when sports trivia might come in handy, then began to reflect, yet again, that he was probably crazy to have gone along with Amy's idea that the three of them make this trip.

Or maybe that should be *undoubtedly* crazy.

If his attraction to Chelsea was only physical...

Well, if things were that simple he'd hardly be concerned. It would just mean that he'd recovered enough from Sheila's death to be seriously noticing other women.

Things *weren't* that simple, though. There was more to what he felt toward Chelsea than the merely physical. A lot more. For starters…

But, no. He wasn't going to let himself dwell on the subject, because the fact there was more made him damn uneasy.

After all, those other feelings had developed awfully rapidly, and given the way they kept getting stronger, voluntarily spending more time with her sure didn't qualify as one of the smartest things he'd ever done.

But what choice had he had once she'd said she was free for the weekend? Especially when Amy was so taken with her?

And now…now Chelsea and Amy would be on their own together.

He'd been avoiding thinking about that part, but he'd have to have a talk with Chelsea before he headed for the conference. And he wasn't going to enjoy it.

He hated explaining what had happened. It forced him to relive the horror, which even after so long always left him in a down mood. And it also made the person he was telling uncomfortable.

There'd be an uneasy expression, a break in eye contact, followed by a few mumbled, sympathetic words that never made him feel even marginally better.

It was the same each time, and he certainly wasn't looking forward to playing the scene with Chelsea.

Especially not right before he had to stand up in front of a room full of lawyers, plant a smile on his face and try to be both informative and entertaining.

And it would put a damper on her day, as well. She wouldn't enjoy herself half as much when...

For a few seconds, he tried to ignore the thought wriggling up from the bottom of his brain. Then he gave in and began to consider it.

Did he really have to tell her?

CHAPTER THREE

THE THOUGHT LINGERED, repeating itself in his head. Did he really have to tell Chelsea the story?

He'd just automatically been assuming he did, but could be he'd simply grown so accustomed to...

Ever since Sheila's death, he'd made sure that everyone who took on any responsibility for Amy knew the situation. Maybe, though, with Chelsea, he could make an exception.

Hell, he couldn't have asked for anyone better than an RCI instructor to look after his daughter. So would it be enough to merely make her understand that she had to keep a close watch over Amy?

He could say Amy had a bad habit of wandering off or something, and...

Feeling that familiar, gnawing worry, he reminded himself that nothing at all had happened in the past three years. Which might mean the threat had been an empty one. From the very beginning.

He'd always known that was a possibility. In fact, at the time the police had told him it was a *good* one.

And even though he'd never taken a chance on that being the case, he realized the older Amy got the less he'd be able to monitor her. Sooner or later, he'd have to begin easing up. So maybe this was the time and place to start.

As unsettling as he found the prospect, he knew

that the odds against something going wrong—within the space of any specific few hours—had to be astronomical. And filling Chelsea in wouldn't stop him from worrying.

He didn't imagine anything would do that. He'd be worrying for years yet. But when it came to the other…

Considering things again, he arrived at the same conclusion. Both logic and the odds said that everything would be just fine today. Whether he confided in Chelsea or not.

And if by some remote chance anything *did* happen, she'd likely deal with it better than he could. Or than Lizzie could, regardless of the fact that she was a trained bodyguard.

That had been a primary requirement when he'd hired her. He'd wanted far more than a mere nanny.

But given Chelsea's extensive training at RCI, Lizzie would qualify as an amateur in comparison, so…

Just as he made his decision, Chelsea said, "I think we want the next exit."

"Right."

He flicked on the turn indicator and changed lanes. Then, as they left the Massachusetts Turnpike behind, Chelsea said, "Do you know exactly what time you'll be free? What time we should arrange to meet?"

"Well, I'm the opening speaker. And I know they're expecting me to stay through the morning break. But I should be able to escape after that.

"So why don't I call you then. I'm guessing it'll be around ten-thirty. Eleven at the latest."

"Okay. You've got my number tucked away?"

"Uh-huh." They'd exchanged cell phone numbers yesterday, after deciding that Chelsea would come along.

"Then we're all set."

"And after this morning," Amy said, "you'll be spending the rest of the weekend with me and Chelsea—right, Daddy?"

"With Chelsea and *me*."

"Chelsea and me," she repeated. "And you won't make us wait around while you do something on your laptop, right?"

"You brought a computer along?" Chelsea said.

He shrugged, feeling a little geekish. "I always take it when I travel. I'm an early riser. And sometimes…

"But, no," he said, focusing on Amy again. "To answer your question, I won't make either of you wait around. We'll spend every minute just enjoying ourselves."

"Sounds good," Chelsea said.

Good. Yes, in one way it sounded *incredibly* good.

But in another way, the prospect of spending the best part of two days with Chelsea Everett scared him half to death.

Given the rate at which his willpower had been fading, by the end of the weekend it might be gone completely.

And then where would he be?

INITIALLY, CHELSEA had hardly taken her eyes off Amy. After all, the impression Trent had given was that if she so much as blinked the girl might vanish.

But Amy must have left her tendency to wander away back home in Ridley, because she hadn't made the slightest attempt to head off on her own. In fact, she'd been clinging to Chelsea's hand ever since they'd left the hotel.

Of course, they were having a great time together, which could explain why she was content to stay close.

"Look!" she said, tugging on Chelsea's arm.

"Look at what?"

"That bear wearing the policeman's uniform." Amy gestured in the direction of a portly teddy sitting behind a window they were passing. "Isn't he neat?"

"He sure is. Do you want to go in and see what else they've got?"

"No, that's okay."

Chelsea glanced at her watch, thinking Amy might be getting tired of the market. It was almost ten-thirty, though. And since Trent had figured he'd be free then—or shortly after—it didn't make sense to start for anywhere else until he'd called.

"I don't suppose you like ice cream, do you?" she said.

"I love it!"

"You do? Really?" she teased.

"Yes!"

"But I'll bet you're not allowed to have any in the morning, are you?"

"Sure I am. It doesn't matter."

"You're positive about that?"

As Amy nodded enthusiastically, she said, "Okay, then let me guess. Your favorite flavor is…"

"Chocolate."

"I was *just* about to say I bet you're the chocolate type. And it's such a coincidence, because they have some of the best chocolate ice cream in the world at a little stall down this way. So I think we'd better get some. Sound like a good idea to you?''

Amy happily nodded again and they started off.

When they neared the stall, they could see people were packed three deep, waiting their turns.

''Looks as if I'm not the only one who knows how great this place is,'' she said.

''Chelsea?''

''Uh-huh?''

''Is it okay if I just wait here? I don't like it when there's so many people.''

''Well, maybe we should come back later then. It's not usually this busy.''

''But it's almost time for my dad to phone, isn't it?''

When she nodded, Amy said, ''And he might want to meet us somewhere else. Then we won't be able to come back. But, look.'' She pointed at an empty bench. ''I can sit right there, where you can see me. And I won't move.''

''Not even an inch?''

''Nope. Not even half an inch. I promise.''

''Well…''

Suddenly, the absurdity of her hesitation struck her.

It was high noon—more or less—in the middle of a tourist haven. What on earth did she imagine would happen to Amy when she was ten feet away and in plain sight?

Lord, it hadn't occurred to her until this minute that Trent's overprotectiveness might be contagious.

''Okay,'' she said. ''You stay right there and I'll be back in no time.''

She joined the crowd at the stall, keeping one eye on Amy, not because she was being overprotective, but just in case the child *hadn't* left her tendency to wander off back in Ridley.

"What can I get you?" the kid behind the counter finally asked her.

"Two chocolate cones, please."

Glancing at Amy once more, she gave the girl a thumbs-up.

As she did, a familiar voice said, "Chelsea!"

She'd barely turned toward Shawn Madders before he wrapped his arms around her in a big hug.

"Your cones, lady," the kid behind the counter said when Shawn released her.

"Right." She dug out money and paid him.

"What are you doing in Boston?" Shawn asked as she reached for the cones.

She looked at him, thinking he didn't seem quite as attractive as he used to. But that was silly. His appearance hadn't changed a bit. He was still the tall, blond, Nordic type who didn't at all fit the image of a special agent able to blend right in with any crowd.

"And why didn't you tell me you were coming?" he demanded when she didn't answer his first question.

"Oh, it was one of those last-minute things," she said, not really certain whether she was glad to see him. Or that he'd seen her, would be a more accurate way of putting it.

Since she'd met Trent, her sense that she and Shawn weren't on their way into a serious relationship had pretty well evolved into a feeling of certainty.

Not that she was an expert when it came to the man-woman thing. Her own mother would be the first to attest to that.

But surely, if Shawn was Mr. Right, or even Mr. Right-for-the-Moment, the merest glimpse of Trent shouldn't make her heartbeat accelerate the way it did.

However, she'd just as soon avoid hurting Shawn's feelings. And telling him that she was in town with another man, even if she explained the circumstances…

Attempting to sidetrack him, she said, "But what are *you* doing in Faneuil Hall?"

"Hey, even special agents have to buy birthday presents. And you can always find something good here. You changed the subject, though. How come you're in Boston?"

Rats. She should have known he wouldn't forget about his question. The Feds trained their people better than that.

"Actually, I'm baby-sitting," she said. "A friend is speaking at a conference here, and he suddenly needed someone to come along and watch his little girl while he was tied up."

"A friend?"

The appraising look Shawn gave her made her wonder if he was more fond of her than she'd realized. But since that wasn't something she wanted to get into, she simply turned toward the bench, saying, "His daughter's name is Amy and she's sitting just over there."

Only she wasn't. She was nowhere in sight.

Telling herself the girl couldn't have gone far, Chelsea tried to ignore the shiver of uneasiness she felt and said, "She's taken off. I'd better find her."

"I'll help," Shawn volunteered. "Describe her."

"She's nine. Cute. With long dark hair pulled back

in a ponytail. And she's wearing a red T-shirt and denim shorts.''

"Shouldn't be hard to spot," Shawn said.

Chelsea sincerely hoped he was right, but Amy could have darted away to a hundred different places.

They headed over to the bench and looked carefully in all directions. When neither of them spotted the girl, Chelsea felt a twinge of panic. And she never panicked.

She stepped up onto the bench, but even from that vantage point she couldn't see Amy.

"She's nowhere," she said, hearing that the panic had crept into her voice.

"All right, don't worry," Shawn said. "She has to be around someplace. So we should head in opposite directions, and if I find her—"

"No, she'll know better than to talk to a strange man. You'd only frighten her."

"Then we'll stick together. Which way do you think she'd have gone?"

"I'm not sure. We came from that direction, so she'd probably head where we hadn't been yet. Unless…she was looking at a bear in a window back there and—"

She stopped midsentence and swore under her breath when her cellular started ringing. Then she began to pray it wasn't Trent calling. But this was about when he'd said he'd call, so who else was it likely to be?

She dug the phone out of her purse and answered it.

"Chelsea, it's Trent."

She silently swore again, vaguely aware that she

wouldn't have been sure it was him if he hadn't told her. He hadn't sounded quite like himself.

"Chelsea, is Amy with you?"

"Well...yes, of course."

"She's right there? You can see her?"

"Ah...not exactly. I mean, I could see her a minute ago, but—"

"Oh, God," he whispered.

"Trent, we're in the Faneuil Hall marketplace. And she wandered off like you warned me she might, that's all. She—"

"No! Chelsea, someone's got her! He just phoned and told me!"

"What?" she whispered.

"Someone *has* her!"

Every thought in her head vaporized into a white-hot surge of horror. Then the panic was back—not a mere twinge this time, but so strong it threatened to swamp her.

She couldn't let it. She had to deal with this.

"Trent, listen," she said as calmly as she could. "Amy's been gone no time at all. Really. Not long enough for them to even have gotten out of the building."

Oh, Lord, she prayed that was true.

"And there are always police officers around here, so—"

"No! No police."

"What? But that—"

"No police! It would be the worst move you could make. This isn't a straightforward... Chelsea, it's complicated and there's no time to explain now. But if I involve the police the guy will kill her."

"What?" she said again. This was so ghastly she almost couldn't believe it was happening.

"Don't say anything to *anyone*," Trent was telling her. "Understand?"

"Yes, but—"

"Just start looking for her. Don't do anything else. I'll be there as soon as I can. Twenty minutes. Tell me where to meet you in twenty minutes. Someplace I can find easily."

Forcing herself to think outside the box of fear surrounding her, she said, "The front door of the smallest building. The one with the grasshopper weather vane on top. And I'll have her by then, Trent."

He clicked off without another word, leaving her feeling sick and frantic. What if she *didn't* have Amy by then? What if they never saw her again?

"Okay, fill me in," Shawn demanded.

Don't say anything to anyone, Trent had said. But how could she not tell Shawn when he'd already heard her side of the conversation? And when he could help?

She took a deep breath and exhaled. It had almost zero calming effect, but she managed to say, "Someone's taken Amy."

"What?"

"In that few minutes I wasn't watching her. While I was getting the cones and talking to you. Then he called her father's cellular and said he had her. Shawn, we've got to find her."

"Do you have a gun?"

"No. It's back in Hartford."

"Well, I do, so we'll stick together. Let's go."

As they started off, half running, scanning the crowd, Shawn fished a phone from his pocket.

"What are you doing?"

"Calling 911."

"No! You can't."

"Chelsea, don't be ridiculous."

"I'm not! He said…"

She took another deep breath, hoping to regain more self-control.

"Amy's father told me not to bring the police into this," she explained, still moving fast and trying to see everything and everyone around them. "The guy said he'd kill her if we did."

"Look, Chelsea, abductors always say that. But the sooner the police are in on it the more likely they'll find her."

"No!" she said so sharply that people turned toward them as they hurried past.

"This isn't… Shawn, I don't know exactly what's going on. There was stuff Amy's father didn't take time to tell me. But we can't do anything except search for her until he arrives. That much I got. Loud and clear."

Shawn obviously didn't think that was a good plan, but he stuck his phone back into his pocket and they continued on, her terror growing with each passing moment.

"How did this guy know the father's number?" Shawn said after a few seconds.

She glanced at him. She was so upset she hadn't even wondered about that. But, of course, *she* wasn't a special agent.

"Did the girl tell him?" he asked. "Or did whoever grabbed her already have it, in which case this wasn't a spur-of-the-moment thing. It would mean she was targeted."

"I don't know," Chelsea said, both her heart and head pounding.

All she knew was that either way, it was *her* fault that Amy was gone. And that she'd never be able to live with herself if Trent didn't get his daughter back safely.

TRENT TOSSED a handful of bills through the open Plexiglas divider, then bolted from the taxi and took off running for the building's entrance.

The Boston traffic had been torturously slow—barely crawling by the time they'd reached Faneuil Hall. But during the entire trip he'd clung to the hope that Chelsea had found Amy—despite being virtually certain she'd have called him if she had.

The slim hope vanished when he spotted Chelsea standing outside the front door. Alone.

His heart sank to the pit of his stomach and his entire body turned to ice. His worst fear was now reality. He could no longer even try to deny it.

Chelsea started toward him, her face a portrait of fear and remorse.

But what good was regret after the fact? And how could she *possibly* have let this happen?

"I'm so, so sorry," she murmured as she reached him. "I know that can't be any consolation at all, but…

"Oh, Trent, if you pulled a gun and shot me dead, I wouldn't blame you. I think I'd even welcome it."

He said nothing. He couldn't let himself respond to that when, deep down at gut level, the prospect of murdering her was far from repugnant.

Had he really spent an entire week unable to think straight because of this woman?

That seemed totally unbelievable when, at the moment, merely looking at her was like twisting a knife into his heart. He'd trusted her with the most important person in his life, and now Amy was...

Which made trusting Chelsea the worst thing he could have done. And as painful as it was to admit, that made what had happened his fault as well as hers.

If he'd left Amy at home with Martha Wilson, the way he should have... Or if he'd told Chelsea that his daughter might be in danger and why...

Dammit, all he'd been trying to do was spare both of them a tough conversation. It had been a terrible mistake, though. Now he just had to pray it didn't prove a deadly one.

"Trent?" she said.

He forced himself look at her again, but before she had time to say anything more, a man appeared at her side and she focused on him.

When he shook his head, she pressed her lips together for a second, then said, "Trent, this is Shawn Madders. He was still in there searching for Amy, but...

"He's a friend," she continued just as Trent was going to ask how this Madders even knew about Amy.

"We ran into each other only seconds before I realized that Amy had disappeared. And I know you told me not to say anything to *anyone,* but he was standing right there when you phoned, so...

"At any rate, he helped me try to find her."

Trent managed to string together enough coherent words to thank Madders. Then he was at a loss about where to go from there.

Raking his fingers through his hair, he did his best

to stop his mind from racing and get his emotions under some semblance of control. His best wasn't much, though.

Usually, he was good in a crisis situation, but not today.

For three long years, he'd lived with the knowledge that something like this could happen. He'd conjured up a thousand awful variations of exactly what evil might befall Amy, and had planned how to deal with each and every possibility.

Yet now that the unspeakable had happened, a sense of helplessness had him by the throat. Helplessness so overpowering that he felt as if all the connections in his brain had been unplugged.

He'd tried so bloody hard to keep his daughter safe, but he hadn't succeeded. As a result, she was in the hands of some monster.

"Trent?" Chelsea said. "*Please* tell us exactly what's going on. Explain what you didn't have time to when you called. If you fill us in, we'll be able to help."

Help? Hell, the last thing he wanted was *her* help. He wanted nothing more to do with her. Wished he'd never laid eyes on her.

If he hadn't enrolled in her damn driving course, if he hadn't gone along with the idea of her taking care of Amy...

Some *care* she'd taken.

"Oh, Lord," she murmured. "I know you must be wishing I'd just drop off the face of the earth, but you *have* to let me help you get Amy back."

"Look, Trent," Shawn said, "I'm a special agent with the Bureau. I've been trained in dealing with kidnappers. So...

"Well, Chelsea told me that whoever has Amy warned you against involving the authorities. But that's something I think we should discuss."

"Shawn, this isn't—" He stopped there. Discussion was futile, so he simply said, "There's no point getting into the details. The bottom line is that I can't involve authorities of any kind. Period."

"Okay. I hear you. But let's just—"

"No. I *can't* handle it that way."

Shawn eyed him for a moment, his expression unreadable.

"In that case I can't help you," he finally said. "Not *officially*. But *unofficially…*"

Once again, Trent tried to get his brain fully into gear. He might not want Chelsea's help, but he could definitely use someone's.

Shawn Madders was a total stranger, though. Plus, he was Chelsea's friend. So since *she'd* turned out to be unreliable…

"You know," Shawn said quietly, "I think you're in shock. And that talking to us about this might help you pull out of it."

Would it? He wasn't sure. But if Shawn had been trained to deal with kidnappers, didn't that make talking to him a good idea? Only then Chelsea would hang in, too.

Dammit, he was starting to think in circles again, and he had to focus on what was most important. He could worry about getting rid of Chelsea later.

Right now, nothing in the world mattered except finding Amy. Because if he didn't find her…

He warned himself not to go there. Negative thinking wouldn't help.

Besides, he *would* get her back. He just wasn't confident he could do it alone. He wasn't even...

No matter how badly he wanted to stay positive, in truth he wasn't even confident he could do it with help.

The old saying about two heads being better than one whispered in his ear, at the same time that Shawn was asking whether, when the kidnapper had phoned, there'd been a number on the caller ID screen.

Trent shook his head. "There was the *caller ID blocked* message," he said, half surprised he remembered noticing that. His brain definitely wasn't working on all six cylinders.

"So he was probably using a cellular," Shawn muttered. "Damn. I wish all the criminals in the country weren't onto that trick. When they used pay phones, even if they cut the call short a trace would sometimes at least narrow the location down to a neighborhood.

"But did your guy make any demands?"

"Uh-uh. He didn't say much more than that he had my daughter. And that she hadn't been harmed."

"Thank heavens," Chelsea murmured.

"That's what he *said*."

Chelsea made a little noise in her throat, but he didn't look at her.

"The next time he calls, make him put Amy on the phone," Shawn advised. "That way we'll be certain she's okay. And ask her some questions.

"He'll probably be listening in and cut you off, but it's worth a try. Maybe he's a screwup. And any clue about where he's got her would be a starting place."

"Right." If his head had been working properly he'd have done all that the first time.

"He said he'll get back to me in an hour or so. Tell me then what he wants me to do."

Glancing at his watch, he saw that an hour or so had become less than *half* an hour or so.

"Do?" Shawn repeated. "You mean you don't think he's just after ransom money?"

"No. That won't be it."

When Shawn eyed him curiously, he said, "Trust me. It won't be money he's after. But until he calls again…"

"While you're waiting," Shawn said, "you could take Chelsea's suggestion and fill us in. Unless we know what's going on, we'll have a hard time coming up with any good ideas."

Okay. Shock or no shock, he had to stop vacillating. Which way was he going to jump?

He rapidly considered the question, then said, "Yeah. Yeah, I guess that makes sense. Let's find someplace quiet to talk."

CHAPTER FOUR

THE THREE OF THEM ended up in an almost deserted tavern just over on North Street, sitting, with three coffees, at a little table in the back.

Chelsea hadn't opened her mouth since they'd left the marketplace, afraid that if she said anything it would be the wrong thing—because all she could think about was the excruciating pain she could see Trent was in, and that wherever Amy was, whatever was happening, she had to be absolutely terrified.

Swallowing hard, she wondered yet again how she could conceivably have let something so horrendous happen. It went without saying that if there was any way in the world she could undo what she'd done, she would.

But there wasn't. The only thing she could do now was try to help. Yet she was growing more and more afraid that Trent had changed his mind, that he wasn't going to confide in them after all. And if he didn't...

She began willing Shawn to think of something to say that would make Trent start talking. Unfortunately, though, he was a lot better when it came to talking about himself than getting other people to talk about themselves.

Just as she was starting to feel a sense of desperation, Trent cleared his throat.

Her gaze flashed to him.

"All right, here's the deal," he said. "Someone took Amy as a way of getting revenge against me."

Chelsea exhaled slowly. His voice was still on the shaky side, but he sounded a whole lot more together than he had fifteen minutes ago.

"Revenge for what?" Shawn asked.

Trent shook his head. "I don't know. Not exactly."

"But more or less?" she prompted when he paused.

He didn't so much as glance her way, making her feel even worse, which she wouldn't have believed was possible.

"I have several ideas," he finally continued. "That's the problem. There are any number of people who…"

He paused once more, then looked across the table at Shawn and said, "I'd better start at the beginning.

"I'm a lawyer. And I went straight from law school to the New York City District Attorney's Office.

"It's always unbelievably short staffed, so they had me in the courtroom within weeks. And I turned out to have a real knack for prosecuting work.

"That meant I got assigned tougher and tougher cases, until I was prosecuting the Teflon guys—the ones who were well enough connected they almost never did time. Only, I managed to ensure that a fair number of them did."

"You're talking organized crime," Shawn said.

"For the most part. I made a lot of enemies that smart people wouldn't want to make. Enemies who swore revenge."

"But you told yourself those sorts of threats just went with the territory," Shawn said.

"Exactly. Basically, I laughed them off. I was

pretty cocky in those days. Young and invincible. I figured nobody was actually going to hurt Trent Harrison.

"And no one did. Not directly. But..."

Chelsea waited, telling herself she wouldn't say a word this time.

Then, after the silence had stretched for so long that she felt certain he was never going to complete his sentence, she heard herself whisper, "But?"

Trent stared at the table for an eternity before he said, "But they killed my wife."

TRENT HAD BEEN FORCED to recount the story so often that he'd pared it down to the basics. That way, it didn't hurt as much in the telling. Today, however, he knew it would hurt like hell.

Having to talk about what happened always brought back the horror of it. And this time...

Man, with Amy gone he was at a level of reality he'd prayed he'd never reach.

There wasn't the slightest doubt in his mind that the same man who'd murdered his wife now had his daughter. And if Amy ended up dead it would kill *him,* as well.

But she wasn't going to end up dead. She just couldn't.

Not taking his gaze from the table, he made himself begin.

"It happened a little more than three years ago," he said.

"My wife's name was Sheila, and we both worked in Manhattan. But when Amy was small, we bought a place in Connecticut and started commuting.

"We had irregular hours, which meant we needed two cars. And the day it happened...

"Sheila was leaving early. I was supposed to drop Amy off at school. So the two of us were still in the house when Sheila left.

"Amy was dawdling over breakfast. I was trying to get her to hurry up. And then..."

He had to pause. This was always the hardest part.

"There was an explosion," he went on at last. "I rushed to the front of the house and...it was Sheila's car. Someone had planted a bomb in it."

"Oh, Lord," Chelsea murmured.

"I thought, well, the only reason that made any sense... It had to be related to one of the cases I'd prosecuted. And at first I figured the perp had made a mistake. That he'd mistaken Sheila's car for mine.

"Then, a few days after her funeral, I got an anonymous letter explaining what he was up to.

"He said that just killing me wouldn't be good enough. That he hoped I lived to be a hundred, because he intended to make the rest of my life a living hell.

"Murdering Sheila was only the beginning, he said. From then on, terrible things were going to happen to anyone I ever loved."

"Oh, Lord," Chelsea murmured again. But why on earth hadn't he told her this before?

She'd assumed he was overprotective, when in reality...

If she'd known why he actually worried so much about Amy, she wouldn't have taken her eyes off the little girl for a second.

She had, though. Regardless of what she'd known or not known, it was her fault Amy was gone. And every time that fact pounded itself against the inside of her head she wanted to cry.

"The note didn't give the police any leads?" Shawn was asking.

"No, not really. I mean, the most obvious people were the ones who'd openly threatened me with revenge. So they interviewed all of them. As well as their associates. But the authorities couldn't find hard evidence pointing at anyone.

"And when it became clear the case would probably remain unsolved, I had to decide what I was going to do. How I was going to keep Amy safe.

"I considered creating a new identity for myself, but if a major crime figure is serious about tracking somebody down it really isn't very hard."

Shawn nodded. "That's one of the problems with witness protection programs."

"Exactly. So rather than give up my profession and cut myself entirely off from my family and friends, I opted for a low profile and an ultracareful lifestyle, and hoped to hell this guy would eventually decide that killing Sheila had been enough.

"I left my job in New York, took a faculty position at a small law college. In Ridley, Connecticut," he added, remembering that Shawn didn't know some of the things about him Chelsea did.

"It wasn't a hard move to make?" Shawn said.

"Well, getting the job wasn't hard. I'd been a teaching assistant all through university, so I'd had exposure to working with students. Plus, I had great real-life experience and good references. And there aren't a whole lot of people hammering down the door to teach at a little place like Ridley.

"At any rate, I moved there and hired a bodyguard for Amy."

"Lizzie?" Chelsea asked.

"Uh-huh. As far as Amy knows, Lizzie's just the woman who helps look after her. I figured I'd wait until she was older to explain, but..."

Chelsea knew why his words had trailed off. He was terrified that now Amy might not *get* older.

That made her want to cry, too.

CHELSEA TOOK another sip of her now-cold coffee, thinking that if the tension at their table grew any thicker none of them would be able to breathe.

A good fifteen or twenty minutes had passed since Trent had finished telling her and Shawn about some of the other precautions he'd taken—installing an alarm system, getting his big dog, sending Amy to a private school and doing RCI courses whenever he had time off from teaching.

At this point, the conversation had run down and they were simply waiting for the kidnapper to call again. Waiting and worrying.

She felt positively sick with fear. For Trent, this had to be pure torture. And she was the one responsible for it.

Swallowing hard, she snuck another peek at him. The lines of anxiety etched into his forehead appeared even deeper than they had the last time she'd checked.

"Trent?" Shawn said, breaking the silence.

The sound of his voice had almost made her jump, telling her that, as impossible as it seemed, she was even more on edge that she'd realized.

"You've got *no* idea what this guy could want if it's not money?" Shawn continued.

She looked at Trent once more, waiting to see whether he'd have an answer this time.

Shawn had posed the question before. Slightly different phraseology, but the same basic question. And Trent's only response had been to shake his head.

When he did the same thing again, her gut feeling was that he really didn't have any clue what the demands might be. But sooner or later they were going to find out.

Assuming the man *did* phone back. Assuming his plan wasn't to torment Trent by saying he would and then not following through.

Oh, Lord, she desperately hoped that wasn't it. If Amy didn't come out of this okay...

Chelsea was trying not to imagine all the horrible things people could do to children, when Trent's cellular rang.

"Trent Harrison," he answered, his voice sounding almost, although not quite, normal.

He nodded that it was the call they'd been expecting and said, "No. Wait. Before you tell me *anything* I want to talk to my daughter. Unless I'm sure she's all right, we have nothing to discuss."

Seconds dragged by, then he finally said, "Amy, honey, are you okay?"

That wanting-to-cry feeling swept through Chelsea yet again—twice as strong as it had been the previous times.

"Oh, baby, I know you're scared," Trent said. "But are you all right? Nobody's hurt you?"

She held her breath until he said, "That's good, darling. And this lady? Is she nice?"

Please let her be nice. *Whoever* she is.

"That's good," he said once more.

Thank heavens.

"Amy, listen, you'll be fine. I promise. And I'm going to get you back here with me just as soon as I can. But right now I have to ask you a few questions. And you answer with a yes or no. Don't say anything else, understand?

"Good. Now, are you in a house?

"No? In an apartment, then?

"Okay, good. And when the man made you go with him, was it a long drive to where you are?

"Yes. Does that mean you think it was more than half an hour?

"No? Less, then. Okay, terrific. Now… Amy?… Dammit, will you put her back on so I can finish what I was saying?"

The kidnapper apparently ignored that, and Chelsea sat gazing at Trent as he listened to whatever the man was telling him.

He looked as if the stress of the past couple of hours had totally drained him, leaving him operating on adrenaline and nothing else, which made her desperately wish she could think of some way to make him feel even a little better.

But nothing was going to make him feel better except getting his daughter back, so she had to do everything in her power to help ensure he did.

If he let her, that is. If he didn't decide that having her around was more than he could bear.

She knew he had to hate her for what had happened, although it couldn't be any more than she hated herself. She was positively consumed with guilt.

"I can't do that," he said at last. "There's just no conceivable way."

Her throat went dry. If it would mean Amy's return, he had to do *whatever* the kidnapper wanted. No matter what it was.

But if he really couldn't...

"Okay, then," he eventually said. "Here's the deal. I'm not sure he'll even consider it, but I'll give it a try—on one condition. As long as you have Amy, I talk to her every day.

"I don't hear from you by nine o'clock and I'll assume the worst. Then every cop in the country will be looking for you."

There was a brief pause before he said, "Of course I know what you mean about keeping my mouth shut *forever*. And what you'll do if I don't.

"So. We're agreed, then. I'll...

"Gone." He clicked the phone off and set it on the table.

"But you did well," Shawn told him.

"Only because the guy must not have been listening in."

"The reason doesn't matter. And from your side of the conversation, I gather she's in an apartment within half an hour of Faneuil Hall?"

"Yeah. Some woman's place."

"That's good," Shawn said. "I know how far half an hour takes you in Boston traffic, so we can draw a circle on the map. It won't get us close to pinpointing the location, but it'll be a start."

Trent nodded. "The woman must be his girlfriend. Or...oh, hell, she could be anyone, for all I know."

"Whoever she is," Chelsea said gently, "Amy probably won't be quite as frightened with a woman there."

"I hope not. She sounded awfully scared, though.

She was managing to keep from crying, but just barely."

Chelsea had no idea what else to say, and she resisted the urge to reach across the table and rest her hand on his. She was positive he wouldn't appreciate any gesture of reassurance from *her*.

"What does he want you to do?" Shawn said.

After a moment or two of silence, Trent said, "I can't tell you."

"What do you mean?" Shawn asked, more than a touch of annoyance in his tone.

"I mean, look, thanks a lot for the help you've already given me. But I've got to handle the rest of this on my own."

Without another word, Trent rose and headed off.

As Chelsea watched him walk away there was no doubt in her mind that she was going after him. She couldn't not, regardless of how much he wouldn't want her to.

"Pretty rough," Shawn said quietly. "But, I guess there's nothing more we can do. So…are you up to some lunch? We could stay here or go someplace better."

She forced her gaze from Trent and simply stared at Shawn, wondering how he could possibly have gone from concerned to cavalier in mere seconds. Just the thought of food had started her stomach churning.

Of course, he was probably damn insulted that Trent had refused to confide in him. But even so, how shallow could someone be?

"I didn't mean to sound as if I don't care," he said, his expression guilty. "I do. But when someone flat out turns down an offer of—"

"Shawn, I *have* to help him," she said, pushing back her chair.

He shook his head. "You can't force help on someone, you know."

"Well, I'm sure going to try." She rose from the table and started for the door.

"Chelsea?" Shawn called after her.

She paused and glanced back.

"Look, I care how this turns out. Really. So call if he changes his mind. If there's any way I can help."

"I CERTAINLY APPRECIATE this, Matthew," Trent said into his cell phone.

"I've been telling you," Matthew said, "any time you feel like a change we should talk about it."

"Well, hopefully, I'll be there around four. If not, it shouldn't be much after."

"Don't get any speeding tickets. I'll be in the office till at least seven."

"On a Saturday?"

"Hell, I'm here all day Sunday, half the time. You know how it is."

"Yeah, I remember. Well, I'll see you sometime between four and seven, then."

He clicked off, thinking he'd been lucky to get hold of Matthew so easily—and wishing he believed in omens.

He didn't, however, and Matthew's agreeing to see him was only the first in a long series of steps.

As he continued walking rapidly down North Street, it struck him that he'd never felt more alone in his life. Not even during those almost unbearable months after Sheila's death.

Then, he'd had Amy to focus on. And he'd spent

as much time as he could with her. Trying to explain. Trying to help her cope with the fact that her mother was suddenly gone.

But now, it was Amy who was gone. And if he had any hope of getting her back he was going to have to do something that went against everything he believed in. Everything he'd been taught at law school. Everything he taught his own students at Ridley.

He was being forced to do something so far across the line that he'd never have even conceived of himself...

Hell, talk about a rock and a hard place.

He didn't have a prayer of getting Amy back unless he went along with what the kidnapper wanted. But if he did and the authorities found out, he'd end up in prison and Amy would be dead. Simple as that.

He made a major effort to banish that awful truth from his head and reminded himself there was one possible way out. He could pretend he was following the creep's orders, then double-cross him.

But he had no idea whether that would prove a realistic option or not. And he couldn't possibly try it as long as the guy had Amy. There was no way in the world. So for the time being, at least, he was just going to have to set his principles aside, ignore his conscience and—

He swore under his breath as Chelsea fell into step beside him. He'd thought he'd made good his escape, but he'd obviously thought wrong.

"Trent?" she said.

He kept walking. His anger was like a pool of molten lava in the pit of his stomach and he just wanted her to leave him alone. Forever.

If he ignored her, she might do exactly that.

"Trent?" she repeated.

Right. This was Chelsea Everett he was dealing with. Being ignored wasn't going to deter her.

"It's my fault Amy's gone," she said when he looked at her. "So whatever the kidnapper wants, whatever you're going to try to do for him, you have to let me help."

"Thanks, but you can't. It's a one-man job."

Good. He was at *controlled* anger. He hadn't been sure he could manage that.

She was silent for a minute, then said, "Shawn's still prepared to pitch in. He told me all we have to do is call him. And it seems to me that he might be able to learn who the guy is.

"I mean, you said it has to be someone who threatened revenge and—"

"I'm not certain about that anymore."

"Why not?"

"Chelsea, I can't talk about this, okay?"

He picked up his pace, even though he'd already been walking fast, but she stuck right with him and said, "Do you trust this guy?"

"The kidnapper?"

"Yes."

"Of course not."

"Yet you're just going to do…*whatever* it is he wants and trust that he'll give Amy back?"

"No."

"Then…?"

He simply shook his head, partly because he was still trying to work out exactly what he *was* going to do.

But he certainly knew he couldn't naively assume

that his little girl would be safely returned to him. Regardless of what he did. As foggy as his thinking might have been for the past few hours, that was one thing he'd been clear about from the start.

He looked at Chelsea again, trying to decide if there was any conceivable way...

It's my fault Amy's gone, she'd said. And she was right. Which more than justified the fact that—as she'd guessed—he wished she'd simply drop off the face of the earth.

Yet his daughter was in the hands of a kidnapper and Chelsea wanted to help get her back. And now that taking Shawn Madders up on his offer was out of the question...

Dammit, he wished the guy didn't even *know* about the kidnapping. That alone would start him putting bits and pieces together if he heard anything more.

What were the odds he would, though?

Not high. Not unless Chelsea said something.

But would she? If he *did* let her help?

Oh, man, he could barely believe he was even considering that as a possibility. But as badly as he didn't want her around, his feelings weren't the most important consideration here. Not by any stretch of the imagination.

Which meant that even if she was the devil incarnate, he'd probably be wise to give the whole situation a little more thought before he sent her packing.

Just as the saying about two heads being better than one whispered to him again, she said, "Look, Trent, we *have* to find Amy. We've got to learn who took her and where she is. And Shawn is FBI, for heaven's sake. So—"

"No," he snapped. "I *cannot* confide in Shawn."

Chelsea went quiet for a long moment before she said, "Then confide in me. I'll do anything to help you get her back. *Anything*.

"I'm not scheduled to teach a course next week, and even if I was…I'd book off work entirely until we found her. That's the only important thing right now."

He stopped walking, took a deep breath and exhaled slowly. He knew he was close to falling apart, which he couldn't let happen. He'd promised Amy he'd get her back and that was exactly what he was going to do.

But it would mean locking away his fears, ignoring the horrible emptiness he felt inside and refusing to let his imagination wander down the dark path that ended at failure.

It would also mean setting aside the fact that he didn't want Chelsea's help and accepting the reality that he needed it.

Okay, then. Right this minute he'd start thinking only with his head, not his heart. He'd rationally weigh the pros and cons, and—

"Do you want to sit for a minute?" she said, gesturing toward a bench in the parkette they'd ended up by.

CHAPTER FIVE

WORDLESSLY, Trent followed along after Chelsea and sat down on the far end of the park bench from her, still trying to get his head completely around the idea that he was going to have to accept her help.

But what other choice was there when he had to at least *seem* to be doing exactly what the kidnapper wanted?

There just wouldn't be enough hours in his days to do that and try to learn where Amy was. Which meant that he definitely needed *someone*.

Besides, this was going to be a risky operation, so how many people could he turn to? People who just might be able to pull off the impossible.

Were there really any? Aside from Chelsea?

He had a dreadful feeling she could be the only viable candidate. So as much as he'd rather not spend another minute of his life with her...

Yet even if he resigned himself to the necessity of that, had she truly meant she'd do *anything* to help? And if she had, could he trust her this time?

He finally met her gaze and said, "How close are you and Shawn?"

"Not very," she said slowly. "Why?"

He was tempted to just come right out and tell her he'd get thrown in jail if Shawn learned what was going on. But he held back, still hoping he could somehow manage to think of an alternative to her.

At his lack of response, she said, "Trent, look. Shawn took my course about three months ago and we've seen each other precisely four times since then.

"We're not…an item. And you don't have to worry about me filling him in. If you feel you can't confide in him, you must have a reason. And that's good enough for me. I won't repeat anything you tell me. Not to a soul."

He sat staring at nothing, just letting his mind drift back over the past week.

Before that creep had grabbed Amy, he'd figured Chelsea was the most competent woman he'd ever met. Figured there was probably very little she couldn't do if she put her mind to it and…

Oh, hell, why didn't he just be honest with himself? He'd thought she was so terrific he'd been scared right down to his shoes that he might end up falling in love with her. And he'd have trusted her with…

But he *had* trusted her. And whatever his feelings toward her had been, well, they sure weren't the same now.

"I won't screw up again, Trent," she murmured. "I swear I won't."

He looked along the bench at her. She was desperate to help. Nobody else would be.

Hell, maybe even she wouldn't be once she knew what the situation was.

"Trent?"

He rapidly weighed the pros and cons once more, then focused on her. "You said you thought Shawn might be able to learn who the kidnapper is."

She nodded.

"Well, there's no way I can even let him try. But do you think *you'd* have any chance of doing it?"

The expression that flickered across her face told him she hadn't actually believed he'd let her be part of this. All she said, though, was, "I know a lot about the unsavory types in the world—courtesy of RCI.

"We've done workshops on how terrorists and kidnappers think. How they operate. What sort of legwork it takes to track them down.

"That doesn't make me an expert, but I've got most of the basic theory. And I'd put two hundred percent into learning who the guy is."

He hesitated, then made himself say, "How would you feel about spending the next little while in New York?"

"New York? But Amy's here. Somewhere in Boston."

"Yeah. And the plan might or might not be to keep her here. But whoever's behind the kidnapping is far more likely in New York.

"I think he simply knew I was bringing her with me today. And that, because of the conference, I wouldn't be with her all the time. Which he figured should make grabbing her...

"I'm even wondering if what happened to Lizzie's mother wasn't part of the plan."

"What *did* happen to her?"

"She was mugged. Injured badly enough to put her in the hospital—and send her only daughter running to her bedside."

"Instead of coming to Boston with you and Amy."

"Exactly. But getting back to where we were, I'm almost positive the legwork will have to be done in

New York. And what the kidnapper has in mind is going to take virtually all my time, so…''

''So I'll go to New York with you,'' Chelsea said.

He exhaled slowly once more. Amy was gone because of Chelsea, and now he'd be relying on her to help.

Man, his feelings about that were too confusing even to begin trying to sort out. So the smartest thing he could do was totally set aside any feelings toward Chelsea.

He'd gotten his anger under control and he'd keep it there. He'd simply work with her toward their common goal and not let himself—

''Are you going to tell me what the kidnapper has in mind?'' she said.

He nodded. If this was the way he was playing things, he might as well get started.

''The guy wants me to throw a case,'' he said. ''Bungle the prosecution so that someone who's guilty gets off.''

She eyed him uncertainly. ''But…you're not a prosecutor anymore.''

''Right. That's the first problem.''

''AND THAT,'' Trent concluded, ''is why I figure my initial assumption was wrong. This probably has nothing at all to do with revenge.''

From the sound of things, Chelsea thought, he was undoubtedly right. ''And you figure the guy who has Amy is just a hired hand because…?''

''Aside from anything else, he didn't sound bright enough to have devised a plan as convoluted as this one. So I'd say he must just be working for the fellow whose case I'm supposed to blow—that *he's* the brains behind things.''

She began mentally fine-tuning her picture of what was going on. She'd been framing it in terms of the kidnapper working alone, motivated by his hatred of an ex–prosecuting attorney. But things were more complicated than that.

There were at least two people involved, and it was somebody wanting to avoid a jail term who'd come up with the plan.

The bizarre plan, an imaginary voice whispered.

Well, she'd certainly second that sentiment. Maybe whoever was behind things *was* intelligent, but the plan was bizarre, nonetheless.

Regardless of that, however, it simply had to work.

Trent had to get himself back into the D.A.'s Office, get assigned the right case and then ensure that the defendant walked.

If he couldn't pull off all those things, they'd never see Amy again.

When that thought made her feel cold and hollow inside once more, she told herself, for the hundredth time, that she shouldn't even consider it as a possibility.

The kidnapper had given them a way of getting Amy back and that was exactly what they were going to do. Then…

Then nothing.

She glanced surreptitiously along the park bench at Trent, trying not to remember that only yesterday she'd decided to come to Boston with him and Amy because she hadn't wanted them to disappear from her life. Because a tantalizing awareness had been drifting around in her head, telling her that Trent was a one-in-a-million man who just conceivably could become part of her future. That she might finally have found her soul mate.

Now, though, there was no conceivable way they'd end up together.

As civil as Trent was managing to act, she could practically hear his anger at her simmering away.

What a difference a day makes, the voice murmured.

Boy, she'd second that sentiment, too.

She and Trent were the same people they'd been yesterday. And her feelings for him...

She snuck another peek at him, this time pushing all the thoughts crowding her mind aside for a moment.

And sure enough. Just glancing at his chiseled jaw, his dark good looks, was enough to start her pulse stuttering. However, his feelings for her...

Well, there wasn't any point in even speculating on exactly how negative they'd become. But on a scale of one to ten, they were probably around minus a thousand.

If the two of them got...*when* they got Amy back, his anger might subside some. But regardless of how this turned out, she'd always be the woman responsible for letting a kidnapper snatch his daughter. And she had no illusions that Trent would ever want to forgive her for that, let alone be able to. He was a man, not a saint.

"So?" he said, dragging her back to the moment. "What do you think?"

"Well, tell me more about the case. Who's the accused and what's he being tried for?"

"I don't know yet. The guy isn't going to give me

the details until they're sure I'm actually in. Basically, all he said was that the trial's coming up soon and it isn't high-profile.''

"Then…'' She paused. With each new bit she learned, this all seemed stranger and stranger.

If the case wasn't high-profile, not a murder trial or something like that, why would anyone have gone to the extreme of having Amy abducted to ensure that Trent cooperated?

Of course, someone whose case didn't make a big media splash could still be looking at a lengthy prison term, which he'd do just about anything to avoid.

And since she didn't have the feeling that Trent was withholding any details from her, there was no point in asking him more questions. She'd simply have to assume things would become clear further down the line.

She only wished she felt completely confident that there'd *be* a further down the line. But no matter how hard she was trying to keep her attitude positive, she couldn't ignore the fact that an awful lot of pieces would have to serendipitously fall into place.

"You know,'' Trent muttered, "this is just too damn ironic. Here I've spent three years worrying about someone harming Amy as a way of getting back at me. Then, when something *does* happen to her, it's not because I sent anyone to prison. It's because I have an in with the D.A.'s Office.''

"Which I guess brings us back to square one,'' she said slowly. "Convincing the district attorney to take you on.''

"Right,'' he said. "That's definitely square one.''

"And is there liable to be any difficulty with it?''

She'd done her best to sound as if she assumed that

was only a remote possibility. But in reality, they might not even get over the initial hurdle.

Trent, however, said, "I don't think there should be a problem. Matthew Blake, my ex-boss, is still the D.A., and he calls me every few months, trying to convince me that I don't belong in Ridley, that I should come back and work for him again.

"Which isn't to say I was God's gift to the office," he added. "But I *was* good at my job."

She nodded. From what he'd told Shawn and her earlier, he'd been a lot more than merely good.

But something about this was bothering her and she wasn't sure exactly what. Then it came to her.

"Do you think whoever's behind this *knows* that the D.A.'s been calling you?" she said. "Realized that your doing what he wants shouldn't be too much of a stretch?"

"The possibility occurred to me. Someone else in the office *could* be involved in the kidnapping."

"That's a scary thought."

"Yeah, but it's only a maybe. And for the moment, the important thing is that Matt is always chronically short-staffed, so getting him to go along with things shouldn't be too much of a stretch. At any rate, I've already phoned him. I'm seeing him later today."

"Ah." Then they weren't going to waste any time before heading to New York.

"Did you get into the reason you wanted to see him?" she asked.

"Not in any detail. I figured face-to-face would be better. But if I tell him I'm starting to think he's right, that I miss the courtroom and know I won't be content with teaching forever…

"Well, I expect I could get him to agree to a short-term stint, say for the rest of the summer—on the theory that I can see myself wanting my old job back in the not-too-distant-future and don't want to get rusty in the meantime.

"Of course, the clincher will be that—as I said—the department's chronically understaffed. And I'll be an experienced prosecutor *volunteering* my services. When Matthew hears the word *gratis,* he should jump at the offer."

"And nobody else will have to approve the idea? I mean, even the D.A. has to answer to someone."

"The mayor," Trent told her.

"Ah. Then when you consider that we're talking government, and that a prosecuting attorney is hardly your standard volunteer position…"

He shrugged. "They might want me to sign a contract for some nominal salary—a dollar a week, or something. But Matthew has a talent for cutting through red tape. He'll figure out a way.

"And how tough is it likely to be when they're drowning in cases and can have me virtually for free?

"Hell, anyone who wouldn't sign off on that would have to be crazy."

"That sounds…reasonable." Still, she wasn't as convinced as he seemed that the leap from square one to square two would be easy, so she said, "I guess that only leaves the question of how you get assigned to the case you're supposed to screw up."

"That's being taken care of."

"Really? How?"

"The prosecutor who's been preparing it will be having an accident tomorrow. Not a serious one, but serious enough to keep him off work for a while."

A chill eased up her spine. The kidnapper might

have said "not serious," but they'd be smart to doubt the truth of every word that came out of his mouth.

"They wouldn't kill him," Trent added as if reading her thoughts. "That would risk drawing attention to the case, which is the last thing they'd want."

Well, okay, that made sense. Someone trying to obstruct justice wouldn't do anything that would make people sit up and take notice.

And regardless of whether it made sense or not, she simply couldn't let herself start worrying about the safety of a prosecuting attorney she'd never even met.

This situation was already into overload when it came to worries, and since Trent hadn't entirely put her mind at ease about the last one they'd been discussing, she said, "Look, I don't want to sound negative. I'm just playing devil's advocate, all right?"

He waited for her to go on.

"I can't see this accident *guaranteeing* that the D.A. will turn that particular case over to you. I mean, won't there have been other people working on it?"

"Not necessarily. It isn't high-profile, remember? So at most there'd have been an underling or two. Nobody qualified to take it before a judge and jury."

"You're sure about that?"

"I'm not positive. But the timing will be perfect. Just as I show up, they'll lose the lawyer prosecuting that particular case. Everyone else will already be carrying a full load, and there I'll be. Ready and able, as they say.

"The logical thing for Matthew to do will be to simply give me the majority of this fellow's cases. At least, as many of them as he figures I can handle, coming in cold."

He paused, shrugged, then added, "And if the right one's not included, I'll come straight out and ask for it. Tell him it's of particular interest to me for some reason or other."

She nodded, wondering if Trent could actually be feeling as confident as he sounded.

It was doubtful, considering he was stressed to the max.

Oh, on the surface he might be the same man she'd come to know. A man who thought straight and acted decisively. But beneath the surface...

Well, in the back of *her* mind, there was a constant buzz of fear. She could only imagine how much worse the buzz must be in his.

Merely contemplating that made her heart start aching once more, for both Amy *and* him.

Having your child kidnapped had to be one of the worst things in the world to cope with. And as hard as he was trying to convince himself he could ensure a happy ending to this, there was a chance he *wouldn't* get assigned that case. And if he didn't...

She stopped the thought without completing it, reminding herself she wasn't even going to consider it a possibility.

He *would* get the case, and then the rest of the pieces *would* fall into place.

"We're going to make this work, Chelsea," he was saying. "The creep who has Amy will keep her safe until the trial's over. If he harmed her, they'd lose their hold over me. And you're going to learn who he is *before* the trial's over."

"Right," she said.

She was almost about to close her eyes and begin praying that everything would go according to Trent's script, when he pushed himself up off the bench and added, "Okay, let's grab a cab back to the hotel. We'll just throw our stuff in the car and head for New York. Whatever else we need, we can buy, because we don't have time to waste going home.

"This guy said he'd call me again tonight, and I'd like to be able to tell him then that the D.A.'s agreed to take me on. I don't want him starting to think this is dragging out too long and panicking on me."

She nodded again, suspecting the thought that he might have a positive answer by tonight was a quantum leap beyond optimistic, but hoping she was wrong.

"I'll have to phone the friend who's looking after our dog," he added, checking along the street for a taxi. "Make sure he doesn't mind keeping him longer. And I should call Lizzie, too. Anyone you need to get hold of?"

"Not immediately."

As he raised his arm to flag down a cab, she fleetingly wondered what it would be like to have someone worry about her when she took off without a word to anybody.

Her parents and friends had long ago learned not to be concerned if she disappeared for a couple of days, and she'd always thought she liked things that way. But right this minute...

She let her gaze linger on Trent for another few seconds, then forced it away.

WHEN CHELSEA stepped into the hotel room where she'd been expecting to spend the night with Amy, her throat grew tight.

After they'd checked in this morning before setting

off to see the sights, the little girl had unpacked her bag and put her things neatly into a drawer. The stuffed animal she'd brought along—a grinning tiger—she'd placed lovingly on a pillow.

"Where he'll be comfortable," she'd said.

While Chelsea repacked Amy's case she was blinking back tears, and telling herself yet again that they *were* going to track the little girl down.

It wasn't enough, though. As she tucked the tiger under her arm some of the tears spilled over.

She took a few seconds to splash cold water on her face before heading down to the car with Trent, and if he suspected she'd been crying he said nothing about it.

In fact, he'd hardly said a word about anything by the time they reached Highway 95 and began heading south toward the Big Apple.

The farther he drove, the more the lack of conversation bothered her.

Boston to New York was roughly two hundred and ten, two hundred and fifteen miles. And she really didn't like the prospect of spending most of the next three hours in this virtual silence.

She could practically feel its heaviness weighing on her, reminding her that even though Trent had forced himself to accept her help he probably could barely stand being with her.

But at least not talking gave her time to regain control over her emotions before he finally glanced across the car and said, "There's something we'd better discuss. We've got a potential problem."

"Oh?" she said as he focused on the road again.

When he didn't immediately elaborate, she simply

sat gazing at his even profile and thinking that they had *a* potential problem? As in *one? Singular?*

Under different circumstances, she'd have laughed. She'd bet it would take her all of sixty seconds to come up with a list of a hundred.

"And the problem is?" she said at last.

"Your friend Shawn." He looked over at her once more.

When she eyed him uncertainly, he added, "What the kidnapper wants me to do is illegal."

"Well…yes."

She *had* realized that, of course, but she wasn't quite sure what Trent's point was. After all, they were talking about his daughter's life. And given that, what was a little illegality?

"I don't see why Shawn should be a problem," she said. "He has no idea what's going on. And even if he did, anyone would understand that your main concern isn't what's legal."

Trent shrugged. "He might understand, but he's a Fed. If he knew what was happening, he'd be obliged to turn me in."

"Trent, I really don't think—"

"He *would*. Trust me, Chelsea. I know the law and so does he.

"If he was aware of what I was doing, didn't report it, and then I got caught, he'd end up in prison right along with me. That's why I couldn't say anything to him about the kidnapper's demand."

She considered that, then said, "Okay, I guess you have a point. But the fact remains that he has no idea what's going on."

"Maybe he hasn't got a handle on the specifics, but he's hardly just going to forget that Amy was abducted. Or that the kidnapper wants me to do something for him.

"And since the last he saw of you, you were hot on my heels, determined to help me whether I liked it or not...

"By the way, what does he figure our relationship is?"

The question was unexpected; she had to give it some thought.

"I'm not really sure," she told him after a minute. "I referred to you as a friend, but when I did he gave me one of those looks."

"One of those looks that said he suspected we were more than that?"

"Yes. Why?"

Trent didn't reply. He merely sat staring through the windshield while she sat watching him ignore her question, an unhappy feeling fluttering in her chest.

Was he thinking the same thing she was? That if she hadn't been so damn irresponsible, hadn't let anything happen to Amy, they would have *become* more than friends? That it would only have been a matter of time, because the chemistry between them had been so strong?

But that was then. This was now. And whatever magical connection there'd been...

She was in the midst of telling herself that was something she'd be better off not thinking about when he said, "The point I was going to make is that Shawn's bound to phone you. To ask what happened when you caught up to me."

"Well, yes, he probably will."

Actually, she had absolutely no doubt he would.

Trent was right. Shawn certainly wouldn't just forget about what had happened.

"My cell phone has caller ID," she said. "I could avoid his calls. Let the voice mail take them."

"Uh-uh. If he left a message and you didn't get back to him, he wouldn't have much doubt why. But if you *did* return his call and gave him some phony story…"

"What?" she asked.

"Chelsea, it's one thing for you to try to track down the kidnapper. But if you start lying to a Fed for me you'll be an accomplice."

"Do you think I care?"

"I think you would if you were sitting in a jail cell."

She shrugged. "Let's just figure out a story Shawn will buy."

When Trent glanced across the car once more, she added, "I told you before, finding Amy is the *only* thing that matters.

"If there's any fallout I'll worry about it later. So let's start thinking."

CHAPTER SIX

FOR THE NEXT FEW MINUTES, Chelsea thought hard enough to make her brain hurt.

"How about this," she eventually suggested. "What if I tell Shawn that when I caught up with you, you just told me to get lost. So I don't know anything more than he does."

Trent shot her a skeptical look. "I doubt he'd let go of it that easily. He was there when Amy disappeared. He helped you search for her. That's got to make him feel involved.

"So if you can't, or won't, tell him what's going on he'll try to find out on his own—by checking into what I'm doing.

"And when he discovers I've suddenly offered my services as a prosecutor, he'll know it's somehow related to the kidnapping. Then he'll get down to learning *exactly* how. And he won't be doing it with a view to helping me."

She nodded slowly. "Right. We need something better."

"Yeah, we do. Because if he starts nosing around, I'm done."

And so is Amy, she knew he was thinking.

"Dammit," he muttered. "There must be *something.*"

Chelsea went back to concentrating on the Shawn problem, until another idea popped into her head.

"What if I tell him you got Amy back?" she said. "That things have miraculously been resolved?"

Trent looked at her again. "Miraculously, how?"

"Maybe she managed to escape and called you to come get her."

For a moment, his expression said he'd give anything in the world if that would actually happen. Then he said, "Okay, that's a possibility. But logic says he wouldn't simply believe the story on your say-so.

"He's been trained to be suspicious, so he'd poke around to see whether the story was really true. Which gets us straight back to his discovering I'm in New York. Helping out in the D.A.'s Office. With no sign at all of Amy.

"Hell, he sure wouldn't have to be Sherlock Holmes to realize we'd only been trying to throw him off."

"I guess," Chelsea murmured. Then she just sat gazing out at the cars they were passing, hoping against hope that something else would come to her.

"Let's see if we can push your idea any further," Trent said at last. "Say Amy *did* escape and called me. It would be only natural for me to worry that the guy would try to grab her a second time.

"So what if I decided to take her to a friend's? Or a relative's? Someplace the creep wouldn't know about, where she'd be safe for a few weeks. Until Lizzie's back and I've had time to work on a way of keeping anything like this from ever happening again. Do you think he'd buy that?"

"Well, I'm not sure. As you said, he's been trained to be suspicious, so I think he'd want to check out *any* story with loose ends. And that one would still leave the question of why you were suddenly working for the D.A.

"I mean, Shawn would have to wonder about your priorities. About why, wherever you'd taken Amy, you hadn't stayed there with her."

"Yeah, that's true. Especially when she'd just been through a traumatic experience. So we need a believable explanation for why I'd let her out of my sight."

Trent drove in silence for a good two or three miles, before saying, "All right, what if this deal with the D.A. was supposedly firmed up months ago?"

"Okay," she said, not sure where he was going with that but glad to know he'd been thinking during the silence.

"We tell Shawn basically the same story about why I volunteered that I'm going to use on Matthew," he continued. "Say that I figure I might want my old job back somewhere down the line. And since I'm concerned about getting stale when it comes to the courtroom, I arranged to spend most of the summer with the D.A.'s Office—ostensibly until the fall term starts at Ridley.

"That would put things in a whole different perspective. Obviously, the D.A. would be counting on me. And if I let him down it would hardly encourage him to rehire me in the future.

"So if we assured Shawn that Amy was with someone she was really close to…"

"I bet he'd ask who."

"Well, the answer to that is we're not telling *any-one* who. But the implication could be it's her grandparents, and that they're taking her someplace no one will be able to find them. You think *that* would be convincing enough?''

She considered the question for a minute, then said, ''Even if it wasn't enough to convince him, I think it might be enough to satisfy him.''

Trent glanced at her. ''I don't get the distinction.''

''Well, he's basically a good guy,'' she said, telling herself, once again, that the shallow side he'd displayed earlier had been nothing more than a reaction to Trent's refusal to confide in him.

''So even if he still had his suspicions,'' she went on, ''we'd have given him a credible enough story that…''

She paused, not wanting to inject even a hint of negativism. But when Trent looked over at her again, clearly waiting for her to finish, she made herself say, ''If by any chance this plan *did* blow up in our faces, he could just claim that he'd believed what I told him. Which would let him off the hook if anyone at the Bureau suggested he should have made an effort to learn what was really going on.''

''Okay, then that's got to be our best plan. So we'll go with it and hope to hell it flies.

''I'll see Matthew as soon as we reach the city. And once I'm absolutely certain there isn't any problem there, I'll phone Shawn and—''

''Wait a minute. I thought *I* was going to call him.''

Trent shrugged. ''I told you. If you lie for me you become an accessory. So I'll talk to him and… But no, phoning him today would be too soon.

''I'd better leave that until tomorrow night or Monday morning. That way, there'd have realistically been enough time to take Amy somewhere and make sure she was feeling safe enough.

"At any rate, I'll give him the story and say that I just wanted to let him know how things had turned out because I figured he'd be wondering."

Before she could say anything in response to that, he added, "Now, the next thing we need is an explanation for why *you* would suddenly end up in New York. Because if Shawn doesn't decide the story's believable enough, if he still figures he should check things out for himself, he'll discover you're there.

"And he'll figure that must be because I took you up on your offer of help. Which would tell him I'd lied. I mean, if I actually had gotten Amy back, why would I need help?"

She looked at him blankly. That wrinkle hadn't even occurred to her.

He shrugged again, saying, "I have an idea, but I don't know how you'll feel about it."

THE MOMENT the words were out, Trent half wished he could call them back. Because regardless of how Chelsea felt about what he was going to suggest, *he* didn't like it. Not even remotely.

Unfortunately, there was nothing else on the horizon—not that he could see, at least—and they didn't have a whole lot of thinking time left.

Besides, as he'd told himself several times already, *his* feelings weren't a consideration in all this. He'd do whatever it took, like it or loathe it, to get Amy back.

Still, he'd a whole lot rather he could have come up with a *whatever* that didn't involve sharing living quarters with Chelsea.

Every time he looked at her, it reminded him of what had happened to his baby.

Of course, he didn't actually need reminding. Amy was pretty much all he could think about, regardless of whether he was looking at Chelsea. Which was hardly surprising when...

Enough, he silently muttered.

How often did he have to tell himself that he had to keep his fears locked tightly away and his emotional dial set on numb?

Functioning at top form for the next while was crucial. And he wouldn't have a prayer of managing it if he spent any time at all imagining the ghastly things that could happen to Amy.

So he couldn't entertain a single thought about the situation not ending up just fine. He had to keep the belief that it would front and center in his mind.

And every time the fear of never seeing his little girl again came creeping out of the dark recesses, he had to shove it back into the shadows once more.

As for his feelings about Chelsea—it was totally counterproductive to dwell on the fact that if she'd just been more careful...

But, dammit, there he went again, when he had to accept that what had happened was over and done with. He couldn't change it.

However, he *could* affect the future. So he should be expending his mental energy solely on the plan to get Amy back.

And since Chelsea was an integral part of that plan, he forced himself to glance across the car once more, right then and there, and say, "You mentioned that you're not scheduled to teach a course next week."

"No, I'm off, but even if I wasn't—"

"I know, you already told me," he interrupted, simply wanting to get this over with. "So let me run my idea by you."

When she looked at him expectantly, he continued. "I've been thinking that if you and I were supposedly...*involved,* you might want to spend your time off in New York. With me.

"So I figure that when I phone Shawn, I should tell him we're in the city together.

"Tell him right up front," he added when she didn't seem to be following. "As kind of a preemptive strike.

"With any luck, it would stop him from even thinking you might be there to help me find Amy."

"Together," she said, eyeing him uncertainly. "You mean...like..."

He nodded. "I doubt Shawn would believe the *involved* part if he checked and learned we had separate rooms."

"Ah. Well...I'm not sure if—"

"For heaven's sake, Chelsea. You don't think I'm talking anything but pretense, do you?"

"No, of course not."

"And have you got a better idea?"

She shook her head.

"Do you have *any* other idea?"

"Well...not yet."

"Fine. If a good one comes to you, we'll go with it. Otherwise I can't see that we have a choice."

As CHELSEA had anticipated, Trent didn't waste a minute when they reached Manhattan.

He drove directly down through SoHo to One Hogan Place, home of the D.A.'s Office, and left her in charge of parking the car, telling her that he'd call her to come pick him up when he was done.

He half turned away, then looked back, saying, "Don't answer your phone while I'm gone. It's too soon to talk to Shawn, and he just might phone."

"But if you're going to call me…?"

"I'll leave a message and you can get back to me."

"Right."

After he turned away again, she watched him walk toward the building, wondering how many times she'd sat gazing at those broad shoulders, eyeing his masculine stride and imagining…

But why was she letting herself do it now?

Pure masochism. That was the only answer when, at this point, it made her feel like the proverbial kid with her nose pressed against the window of a candy store, and no hope of *ever* having any candy-buying money in her pocket.

She dragged her gaze from him, then pulled away from the curb and began looking for an empty parking space.

She found one only a couple of blocks away, then wandered up Broadway until she came to a little café with shaded tables on the sidewalk.

Even though it was past five o'clock the day was still sweltering and the air so smog-laden she could almost hear her lungs groaning in protest.

In Indiana, where she'd grown up, summer skies were a clear, brilliant blue. And people there would never even be able to imagine humidity like this. It made her feel like taking her clothes off and wringing them out.

Normally, on a day when it was too hot to do any-

thing that required effort, she'd have spent the time
people watching.

But she finished one glass of lemonade and started
on a second without feeling any particular interest in
what was happening around her.

A dozen naked men could probably have paraded
by and she wouldn't even have noticed, because just
sitting there by herself had left her prey to her own
guilty thoughts.

About Amy. About Trent. About the fact that if
only…

Taking another sip, she reflected how unlike her it
was to experience "if onlys." Her father had taught
her to learn from her errors without dwelling on them.

Everybody makes mistakes, darling, he used to say.
*And you can never go back and redo something
you've done. That only happens in time-travel movies.*

*So there's no point in beating yourself up over any-
thing you regret doing. Just take care not to do it
again.*

Good advice, she'd always thought. But she'd
never before done anything as incredibly awful as letting a child get kidnapped.

How could she conceivably not beat herself up over
that? And over the way Trent had to be feeling.

When an image of him appeared in her mind's eye,
his handsome face was drawn and there was a brown-
ish-green aura of distress surrounding him.

She blinked hard to make the image disappear, trying, yet again, to assure herself that she and Trent
would ensure there was a happy ending to all this.

Assuming the bizarre plan proved feasible.

She was doing her best to ignore the possibility it
might not, when her cellular began to ring. She

grabbed it from the table, so eager to hear what Trent had to say that she almost forgot he'd told her not to answer.

Almost, but not quite.

She glanced at the call display and saw that the *caller ID blocked* message was on the screen. Most likely someone using a cell phone, then.

Probably Trent, but not necessarily.

Telling herself to just be patient, she let the ringing continue until the call was switched to her voice mail. Then she waited, counting to sixty twice before she checked for messages.

It turned out that not answering had been a good plan.

"Hey, Chelsea, it's Shawn," he said. "I can't stop worrying about that little girl, so I figured I'd phone and see if you know what's going on. Give me a call as soon as you get this message, huh?

"I'd like another shot at convincing Trent he should involve the police. Unless you've already managed to do that.

"Either way, though, phone me back as soon as you can. My cell's always on, but, hey, you already knew that."

"Damn," she muttered, clicking off.

As Trent had said, if she didn't return the call, Shawn would figure out why. It was late enough, though, that she could probably get past tonight without arousing his suspicions.

That gave them a little breathing room, but she'd have to talk to him in the morning. Or Trent would have to. And he'd said he wanted to leave it until tomorrow night or Monday.

But…maybe he could say he was calling from

wherever they'd supposedly taken Amy. Say they were getting her settled in, and *then* the two of them would be going to New York.

She thought about that idea a little more and decided it wasn't bad. Maybe not good enough to keep Shawn from doing some snooping, but it *might* strike him as pretty reasonable.

Setting her concern about him aside for the moment, she checked her watch and saw that she'd been waiting for more than an hour, which had to be a good sign.

This Matthew fellow obviously hadn't thrown Trent out on his ear the minute he'd finished outlining his proposal. And the best-case scenario had them already in the process of doing whatever had to be done to put Trent temporarily on staff. After that…

After that, she'd be sharing a hotel room with him.

She absently lifted her hair up off the back of her neck and hoped for a breeze, trying to convince herself that only the heat was making her uncomfortable, not the prospect of being Trent Harrison's roommate.

They had to play things that way, of course. He'd been right when he'd said they couldn't count on Shawn not nosing around, regardless of *what* they told him. And if they didn't want to risk his ferreting out the truth, they had to cover all the bases.

But as incredibly worried as she was about Amy, and as appalled as she was that she'd been responsible for what had happened…

Well, nothing had changed when it came to how attractive she found Trent. And being alone in a room with him all night long, knowing that every time he looked at her he had to be blaming her…

She didn't *want* to start imagining how that was

going to make her feel, but words like *awkward, unsettled* and *ill at ease* began jockeying for position in her mind.

She shooed them all away, and when she did, a thought that had been shuffling around the perimeter of her brain drifted into focus.

If you lie for me you become an accessory, Trent had said.

That was why *he* wanted to be the one who called Shawn.

But after what she'd done, how could he have even the slightest concern about whether she ended up in trouble?

Because he's a decent man, she silently answered her own question. *A good man. The kind of man a woman was lucky to come across once in a lifetime.*

She'd realized that way back in what seemed like a former life, of course. And the fact that he was such a rarity made it even sadder that she'd lost whatever chance she might have had with him.

As she was trying to force her mind off that track, her cellular rang a second time.

Again, the screen told her that the caller ID was blocked, so she went through the waiting and counting routine once more. But this time the message was from Trent.

"So far so good," he said. "When you phone back I'll tell you where to pick me up. And I need to know if you like Chinese food. And beer."

TRENT HAD WORKED at One Hogan Place for enough years that he was familiar with all the districts south of Houston, not only SoHo, but Little Italy and Chi-

natown, as well. And Wong's Palace had the best
Chinese food for blocks in any direction.

Even if he'd been flying blind, though, he'd have
gotten takeout of some sort. The kidnapper had said
he'd phone again tonight, and he'd rather he and
Chelsea weren't sitting in a restaurant when the call
came.

He paid the cashier, picked up the brown paper bag
and the six-pack he'd bought at the grocery store
down the block, then headed out to the sidewalk to
watch for her, still really not quite able to believe that
his meeting with Matthew had been such a success.

Oh, he knew that getting the D.A. onside was a
long way from ensuring Amy's safe return. But now
that step one was behind him it had to be far more
likely that he *would* get her back, which had him feeling enormously better than he'd been earlier. So much
better, in fact, that when Chelsea arrived and he
climbed into the car, he actually managed a smile.

"Things must have gone really well," she said,
smiling back.

For half a second, he recalled how her smile used
to practically turn him inside out. But that had been
before this morning. Before his world had caved in.

Reminding himself, yet again, that dwelling on her
role in the abduction was totally counterproductive,
he said, "No problem at all with Matthew. He phoned
the mayor right while I was sitting there and got a
green light from the top."

"At dinnertime on a Saturday? He really does have
a talent for cutting through red tape."

"Uh-huh. He didn't get where he is by being ret-
icent."

He stashed the bag and the beer in the back, and

as he was turning forward again Chelsea checked the traffic and pulled away from the curb, saying, "So? Where to?"

"Just over to Tribeca. Do you know the city very well?"

"I'm fine farther north, where the street names are numbers. But I could use directions down here."

"Okay, take a left up ahead at Lafayette, a right onto Centre, then another right onto Chambers. That'll pretty well get us there."

"And *there* is…?"

"An apartment tower near the corner of Greenwich and Harrison. That's where we'll be staying."

When she shot him a puzzled look, he said, "I didn't mention it, but I was worried that Matthew might be suspicious of my offer. That he'd guess there was something I wasn't telling him."

"He didn't, though?"

"Didn't seem that way. But I figured he'd be a lot more likely to if I was volunteering my services *and* expecting to pay for my accommodations.

"I mean, volunteering is one thing. Volunteering and having it cost me a small fortune is another. So I asked about using a safe house as part of the deal."

Chelsea shot him another glance.

"The D.A.'s Office has several," he explained. "They're primarily for witnesses whose lives are at risk—because they're testifying for the prosecution. Matthew was happy to go along with letting me stay in one, though.

"And if Shawn does decide to check up on us, it'll look a lot better. I mean, he wouldn't figure it was realistic that I'd be planning to spend a couple of months in a hotel. Not unless he thinks I'm awfully rich.''

Chelsea nodded, then said, ''Speaking of our favorite special agent, he's already phoned and left a message. So we'll have to decide exactly what we're going to do.''

''He didn't waste any time, did he? But let's leave discussing that until we get to the apartment.''

She nodded again, driving in silence for a minute before saying, ''Did you tell the D.A. I'd be staying with you?''

''No. I couldn't see any reason to.''

He stopped there, but his thoughts forged on ahead. *No reason,* they continued, *to say he'd be sharing a tiny apartment with one of the most beautiful women he'd ever met.*

He told himself to kill those thoughts, that her appearance was completely immaterial to the situation.

Then, for good measure, he told himself not to even look at her again.

He might as well have tried to stop breathing. And when he glanced across the car once more, he felt a twinge of the sexual pull that had started growing between them on day one.

It caught him completely off guard, although after he'd had a moment to reflect, he decided it shouldn't have.

Ever since he'd realized Chelsea's help was going to be essential, he'd been reminding himself that she hadn't intentionally let that creep grab Amy. And telling himself—repeatedly—that dwelling on her mistake was *not* going to help anything. So why should he be surprised that he'd managed to stop?

That he'd more or less managed to, at least.

And regardless of anything else, she was a gorgeous, sexy woman. That hadn't changed. But even so, he felt very…

He couldn't put his finger on the right word. *Peculiar,* maybe? Or *weird?*

Neither seemed exactly right, but if Amy died…

Dammit. No matter how hard he tried to pretend there was absolutely no way that might happen, the possibility kept snaking around in the back of his mind, seizing every chance it could to bite him.

And if Amy…

Well, if the worst *did* happen, he knew he'd never be able to so much as look at Chelsea again. Which led back to the question of how he could be feeling even the slightest twinge when he looked at her now. Especially when he didn't want to be.

He didn't like the idea of his heart being at odds with his brain. And he sure as hell didn't want *anything* distracting him. Especially not something he couldn't make rational sense of, because…

He mentally shook his head, aware that he'd been here before. Several times, already.

His mind was simply unable to integrate the facts that one, Amy was gone at least partly because of Chelsea, and two, he was relying on Chelsea to help get her back. And not only relying on her, but…

Oh, hell, he just wasn't in any shape to sort that one out, so he shouldn't even try. He probably shouldn't let himself think at all. Not about anything that had even a scrap of emotional content.

Emotional dial on numb, he reminded himself as Chelsea said, "Where should I park?"

He looked out of the car and saw they were at

Greenwich and Harrison, even though he hadn't told her where to make the last couple of turns.

"It's that building," he said, pointing toward it. "And there's underground tenant parking. Matthew gave me a pass," he added, taking it from his pocket and setting it on the dash.

CHAPTER SEVEN

CHELSEA STOOD in the doorway of the galley kitchen, watching Trent stick the take-out cartons into the microwave and feeling just the way she'd expected she would.

Those words that had been roaming around in her head earlier were back: *awkward, unsettled, ill at ease.* And a few others had joined them for good measure.

All in all, she desperately wished she didn't have to be alone in this apartment with Trent Harrison, because it was almost too tough to handle.

A hundred years seemed to have passed since they'd been on the road to Boston with Amy. Yet it had only been this morning.

The three of them smiling and laughing. Looking forward to what the day would bring.

But none of them had imagined it would bring disaster. And now just being here and looking at Trent was so hard.

It kept reminding her how awful he had to be feeling. And that he wouldn't want her even trying to comfort him.

As strong as her desire was to wrap her arms around him, to hold him and murmur reassuring words, it was the last thing she could do.

He wanted her help. He didn't want *her*. And that

hurt. Even though she knew she'd have reacted exactly the way he had if she'd been in his shoes.

She also knew that if he didn't need her help he wouldn't be having the slightest thing to do with her.

They *certainly* wouldn't be staying together. Not anywhere, let alone in an apartment where they'd be bumping into each other every time one of them took three steps.

The place was small verging on minute, with one junior-size bedroom and a bathroom so tiny that she'd bang her elbows trying to wash her hair.

The living room had just enough space to house a pullout couch, a coffee table and the little table with its two chairs in the corner by the kitchen.

There wasn't even a good home for the phone book. It simply sat on the floor, mostly hidden beneath the couch.

Her gaze lingered on it for a moment, then drifted to the coffee table, where Trent had put his Beretta.

She'd been a bit surprised when she'd seen him take it from the car's glove compartment.

Even though she'd known he'd completed both of the RCI handgun training courses, she hadn't thought of him as the type of man who'd actually carry a gun.

Of course, until today she'd had no idea that his wife had been murdered and Amy was at risk.

At any rate, when her curiosity had made her ask if he was licensed to carry, he'd said that yes, he had been since shortly after Sheila died.

Apparently, prosecuting attorneys rarely had difficulty getting licenses because they so commonly received death threats.

Trent switched on the microwave, then looked over at her, picking up their conversation where they'd left off by saying, "I think you're right about how we handle Shawn.

"The only thing to do is call him in the morning and tell him we've got Amy back and we've taken her someplace safe. But that we're coming into New York later on—because of this commitment I have to the D.A."

She nodded. She'd been hoping they could work out a better story. Actually, she'd been hoping for brilliant. But her original idea was apparently going to have to do.

"Want a glass for your beer?" he asked, taking two cans from the fridge.

"Please."

After he'd retrieved one from the cupboard, they stood with an uneasy silence between them until the timer dinged and they could busy themselves plating the food.

That done, Trent picked up his cellular from the counter and they moved to the little table to eat.

The silence accompanied them; the chow mein tasted like chalk.

She kept eating anyway. They hadn't had any lunch, and if she skipped two meals in a row she'd end up with a headache.

When they'd finished, they carried the dishes back into the kitchen. Then there was nothing to do but wait for the kidnapper to call, sitting on either end of the couch, Trent's cell phone on the coffee table in front of them.

She took another sip of her beer, and found herself watching the cords in Trent's neck move when he did the same. As he set the can down, her gaze shifted to his broad chest.

That got her back to wishing she could wrap her arms around him, which made her realize she'd better keep her eyes to herself.

"He didn't give you any real idea what time he'd phone?" she asked, more to have something to say than anything else.

"No. He said after dinner. But I don't know whether that meant after five or after six or what."

Glancing at her watch, she saw it was almost seven, which did absolutely nothing to make her happier.

Anyone with even a basic knowledge about abductions knew there was *always* the risk of something going wrong. A prime one, which Trent had alluded to earlier, was that the kidnapper would panic and they'd never hear from him again.

So even though Trent had told the man he'd talk to the D.A. and do all he could to set the plan in motion...

Their guy *was* going to call, though. She just had to be patient and sit here quietly. Clearly, Trent was in no mood for conversation.

Less than a minute later, however, she found herself saying, "*Whenever* he phones, he'll let you talk to Amy again?"

"Uh-huh."

But, of course, she'd known the answer before asking the question. She'd been listening the last time the kidnapper had called, and Trent had made that a condition.

The problem was that whenever the silences began to stretch she couldn't keep her fears for Amy from surfacing—and there were all sorts of horrible possibilities she just didn't want to think about.

She was in the process of trying to make her mind

go completely blank, when Trent's cellular finally rang.

He took a deep breath and answered. A second later, he said, "Yeah, the D.A. went for it. I start Monday morning.

"Wait," he added after another moment. "We're going to make this work, and I want to hear all the details about the case in a minute. But first put my daughter on.

"And don't cut us off this time. You're getting what you want, and there's no reason we can't talk a little. Otherwise, you'll just make her more upset than she already is."

The kidnapper must have had Amy right beside him, because it was only a few beats before Trent was saying, "Hi, baby. Are you hanging in there okay?"

He listened, then said, "I know. But are you still staying in that woman's apartment?"

Chelsea watched him, wishing she had superhuman hearing. Then he nodded—to tell her Amy hadn't been moved—and said, "Just the two of you, huh? And she's still being nice to you?"

She held her breath until he said, "Good. Then—"

A brief pause before, "It'll be as soon as I can possibly make it, darling. I've just got to take care of something for that man. And once I've done it you'll be home again."

He listened for a little longer this time.

"No, I'm not there," he said at last. "I'm in New York. That's where the thing that needs taking care of is.

"But Pete's going to be okay. I talked to my friend,

and he doesn't mind looking after him a little longer—says walking him is good exercise.

"As for Chelsea, she's right here. We—"

When his gaze met Chelsea's there was so much raw emotion in his eyes that she almost looked away.

Before she could, he said, "I don't see why not."

Then he held the cellular out to her, saying, "Amy wants to talk to you."

Chelsea swallowed hard, took the phone and said, "Hi, Amy. I've been listening to your dad's side of the conversation, and it sounds as if you're being really brave."

"I'm trying to, but I'm scared."

"I know, honey," she murmured. "I'd be scared, too." She closed her eyes then, unable to bear looking at Trent for an instant longer.

"Really?" Amy said.

"Of course. Anyone would be. But we'll get you back just as fast as we can. Once your dad's finished talking to that man, we'll start working on what he wants. Right away."

"You're gonna help?"

"Oh, Amy, I'm going to do everything I can to help. Because the sooner we get it done the sooner you'll be home."

"I wish I was there now."

Amy was clearly close to tears, which made Chelsea feel completely empty inside.

"It won't be long, honey," she managed to say.

"But *how* long?"

"Not a second longer than it has to be."

"Not even half a second?"

"Right. Not even half a second. I promise."

Amy went quiet briefly, then said, "Chelsea?"

"What?"

"I bet you *never* break your promises, do you?"

"Oh, Amy, I *never ever* do."

WHEN THE KIDNAPPER hung up, Trent was left with the sense that even though the man had spent a good ten minutes rambling on about the case there were things he hadn't mentioned.

But that shouldn't matter a whole lot. Now that they had a starting point, he and Chelsea could fill in whatever blanks existed. Hopefully, at least.

Telling himself they *would,* that there was no "hopefully" involved, he set down his cellular, fully expecting Chelsea's first question to be about what the man had told him.

Instead, she backtracked to near the start of the call, saying, "I'm glad you thought to ask Amy if she was still in the same apartment."

He nodded. "I was worried it might have just been a stopping-off place. And if it was, we wouldn't have her location narrowed down even as far as somewhere in the central Boston area."

"Well, I've got a feeling they're going to keep her right where she is. And…I thought she seemed to be holding up really well."

"I did, too," he said. And that was a major relief, because despite what they'd told her, it could be a while before they actually got her home.

Doing his best to ignore the imaginary whisper of "*If* you actually get her home," he said, "Something else she told me was that the kidnapper went out right after he phoned earlier. And he only showed up again a few minutes ago. It was just the woman with her all day."

"Oh? I'm surprised he'd let her talk about something like that. About how they're handling the details, I mean."

"Uh-huh, I was, too. But maybe he has a heart. Listened when I said she'd be less upset if we got to chat more.

"And it's not as if she told me anything significant—although it did make me realize how well they've got things organized.

"Everyone involved has a specific role. He was responsible for the abduction and he's the one contacting me. But whoever this woman is, her job is looking after Amy."

"And whoever she is, I gather Amy said she's still being nice?"

"Yeah, she did."

"Thank goodness for that," Chelsea murmured.

Then she eyed him expectantly, but only for a few seconds, not really giving him long enough to organize his thoughts before she *did* move on to his conversation with the kidnapper.

"I'm dying to know what the guy told you," she said. "I want to hear every word."

He slowly rubbed his jaw, unsure whether he should start by giving her a blow-by-blow or by telling her he'd been wrong. That their perp probably wasn't the brains behind this any more than the guy he'd just been talking to was.

But since she'd realize that for herself once she heard the facts, he began with, "Well, the prosecutor who's been preparing the case is going to have his 'accident' tomorrow."

She grimaced.

"So either Matthew will get a phone call then, or

he'll hear the news when he arrives at the office Monday morning. Whichever it is, he'll have to make a quick decision about what to do with everything the fellow's been working on.''

"And he should turn most of his cases over to you.''

He nodded, thinking they were both obsessing about the aspects of this that might blow up in their faces.

She knew that Matthew had to turn those cases over to him. Had to turn over the one they needed, at least. Otherwise they'd be dead in the water.

Yet she was still thinking in terms of "should," not "would"—hadn't managed to completely convince herself this was going to go smoothly any more than he had.

Of course, that wasn't exactly surprising when they had absolutely no guarantees.

Rather than saying anything to that effect, though, he said, "The one we care about is scheduled for court on Wednesday.''

"Wednesday. Oh, Trent, that's so soon. You don't think the D.A. will decide to have it rescheduled, do you?''

"Not if I say I can get up to speed fast enough. With the backlog the way it is, every continuance they ask for only puts them further behind.

"And its coming up that soon is actually good news. It'll mean Matthew will be *expecting* me to devote most of my time to it. I won't have to be secretive about it.''

"But…''

"But what?''

"I have no idea how long it'll take me to learn the

kidnapper's identity, let alone exactly where Amy is.''

Exhaling slowly, he wondered if she could hear that imaginary voice whispering, ''Assuming you can *really* do either.''

Man, he hated that voice. And hated the fact it was speaking the truth.

They couldn't be certain Chelsea would learn a damn thing that would help them.

Reminding himself they both had to stay positive, he said, ''Well, I'll have to make sure the trial drags on until you've had enough time, won't I.''

He could see she was trying to smile at that, but she ended up just gnawing on her bottom lip.

Once again, a sexual tug caught him off guard and gave him the sense that his body and his brain were into serious disconnect.

He didn't like that. Not at all. But letting himself worry about it wasn't going to help. And, hell, if he wanted something to worry about he had six million other things he could choose.

As he was managing to force his gaze from Chelsea's mouth, she said, ''And what's the trial about? What's the fellow charged with?''

''Break and enter,'' he told her.

Sure enough, the uncertain expression he'd been expecting to see appeared.

''Just a garden-variety crime of opportunity on the Upper West Side,'' he elaborated.

''The perp, whose name is John Brown—''

''You've got to be kidding.''

He shook his head. ''A lot of people have common names. That's what makes them common.

''In any event, a while back *our* John Brown spotted a couple leaving town, loading suitcases into their car. And they'd barely driven down the block before he'd bypassed the alarm system and was in their house.''

''He's an experienced perp, then.''

''Uh-huh. Unfortunately for him, though, they'd forgotten something and came back. They opened the door, realized someone was inside and called 911.

''Also unfortunately for him, he was carrying a gun, which let the police charge him with attempted armed robbery.''

''Way more serious than unarmed?'' Chelsea said.

''Yeah. *Way* more. Burglars normally don't carry—for that precise reason. But, as I said, this was a crime of opportunity.

''Anyhow, after they'd arrested him, they checked his apartment and found stolen goods.''

She nodded. ''I heard you asking where he'd been living.''

''Right. Talking to his ex-neighbors might give us something useful.

''Getting back to what happened, though, the stolen goods meant the police threw in a charge of possession. Plus, he's already done a couple of stretches. And when you add everything together, you end up with a guy who'll be in prison till he's ninety if he's found guilty this time around.''

''And that explains why he desperately doesn't want to be found guilty.''

''Exactly. And the judge realized just how desperate he'd be. Denied him bail, which means he figured that if Brown could come up with the money they'd never see him again.''

''You know,'' Chelsea said slowly, ''after you told

me we weren't talking a high-profile trial, I started assuming our guy would turn out to be a white-collar criminal. Charged with embezzlement or a computer crime—something along those lines.''

''That's how I had it figured, too.''

''Really? Why?''

''Because most other types of criminals aren't very smart. If they were, the police wouldn't catch nearly as many as they do.

''Aside from that, someone facing white-collar charges is more likely to be out on bail, which would have given him the opportunity to set this all up.

''So I was figuring our perp was walking around loose, not stuck on Rikers Island.''

''Which is…like Alcatraz?''

''Only to the extent that Alcatraz was on an island, too. It was maximum security, whereas Rikers is primarily for detainees—people awaiting trial who've been denied bail. Or who can't post it.

''But the point I was going to make is that learning John Brown has been locked up all along changes the picture entirely. It means it's virtually impossible that he's the brains behind things.''

''Because it would have been too hard to orchestrate everything from a prison cell,'' Chelsea said.

''Right. Kidnapping Amy to force me to help someone beat a rap isn't exactly a simple plan. And the more I think about it, the more complicated I realize it is.

''Just for starters, whoever dreamed up the idea had to know I existed. And that I'm a former prosecutor.''

''And that you have a daughter. Maybe even that Matthew's been talking about you coming back.''

He nodded. ''Maybe. Plus our 'whoever' even

knew I was speaking at the conference. And that I was taking Amy to Boston with me.

"Then there's Lizzie's mother—the possibility that she was mugged to keep Lizzie from coming with us."

"Which you said happened in Philadelphia."

He nodded. "So if it *was* part of an overall scheme, then we'd be getting beyond the definition of even a complex plan. We'd be into the realm of a conspiracy.

"But whether the mugging was related or not, we're still talking an incredible amount of detail. And until Brown found himself in trouble, he had no need of me."

"So he wouldn't have done any planning before he was arrested," Chelsea said thoughtfully. "Then, after he was, it would have been too late."

"Exactly. And if Brown can't be the brains, and the kidnapper isn't smart enough to be, then we're left with either the woman or someone else entirely. Somebody we don't even know about yet."

"Could the kidnapper be faking? Just pretending he's not too bright?"

He considered that, then shook his head. "I guess it's possible, but I doubt it.

"Aside from anything else, remember what Shawn said? He told me to try asking Amy questions, but that the kidnapper would probably cut me off—unless he was a screwup.

"So, when we know that he wasn't even smart enough to be listening in…"

"Maybe he's never kidnapped anyone before. Or maybe the woman *is* the one behind it."

"Or maybe there's somebody else involved," he

said, aware that they were beginning to go round in circles.

"Hell, maybe there are half a dozen other some-bodies. But if it *is* the woman, who would she be?"

He eyed Chelsea while she considered that.

She was trying so damn hard to help. And he couldn't keep from thinking that if she just hadn't had anything to do with the fact that Amy was gone...

But she had. And regardless of how hard she was trying now, regardless of how much he needed her help...

He looked away, warning himself, once again, that he just didn't have any spare mental energy. Certainly not enough to start reflecting that before this had happened he'd suspected he was at risk of falling in love with her.

Yet merely watching her was forcing him to remember, whether he liked it or not.

"You said earlier that you figured she could be the kidnapper's girlfriend," Chelsea said, drawing his gaze back to her.

"Uh-huh."

"Well, she could as easily be John Brown's girl-friend. Or maybe his wife. That would explain why she'd get involved."

His pulse quickened. If that was it, they should be able to ID her. Then from there...

Chelsea was only guessing, though, so he shouldn't get too excited about the possibility.

"You could be onto something," he said. "It's certainly an avenue worth exploring.

"In fact, we should give priority to checking out Brown's old apartment. If there *is* a woman in his life, maybe she'll be there.

"Of course, at the moment she could be in Boston, looking after Amy."

"Even if she is, there'd still be the neighbors to talk to," Chelsea pointed out.

"Right, so we should definitely see what's what. And tomorrow's the only time I'll be free to go with you. After that, I'll be in the D.A.'s Office and you'll be on your own."

"Sunday's probably a good day to ask around, anyway. More people are home."

He nodded, glad to have a concrete plan for the morning. Then he said, "Look, I'd like to do some more thinking, but why don't we try coming at things from a different angle.

"I mean, whoever's behind this has put an awful lot of effort into trying to keep Mr. Brown from spending the rest of his life in Sing Sing. And the obvious question is why?"

"Motivation," Chelsea murmured. "Love, if it's a woman. Aside from that, we'd only be guessing."

"Well, let's see what we can learn about our boy. On Monday, when I get the case file, we should be able to pull some leads from it. But I'd like to know more before then."

He retrieved his laptop from where he'd stashed it in the corner and set it on the little table.

"Will you be able to find much?" Chelsea asked as he took the computer out of its carrying case.

"There should be a fair bit. The man's got a criminal record. And there are so many legal and law enforcement databases that a lawyer with good access can do just about all his case prep online."

"I take it you have good access."

"I'm a law prof," he reminded her, plugging the computer into a phone jack.

"I can use every law-related database that Ridley University subscribes to—which is pretty well all of them."

CHAPTER EIGHT

INITIALLY, Chelsea hovered behind Trent's chair, skimming the data he was bringing up on the computer screen and telling herself that he'd been right. Something in it might at least point them in the right direction.

However, she wasn't a lawyer. And he was searching through various records and articles so quickly she couldn't make much sense of them.

Once she realized that all she'd get if she kept trying was eyestrain, she gave up. Which left her simply standing there, far too close to him for comfort but reluctant to move away. Very aware that sexual attraction was an extremely powerful, elemental force, so strong that it was even managing to sneak around her concern for Amy in order to make her aware of its existence.

That fact made her feel more than a little guilty. As if she was a failure at keeping her priorities straight.

Yet she simply couldn't be this near Trent without those broad shoulders of his whispering that she should trail her fingers across them.

And the way his dark hair curled—just a little—onto the back of his neck made her lips dry and her palms wet.

It was his scent, though, that *really...*

Oh, not "scent" as in aftershave, but as in phero-mones. That was the scientific term for the chemicals she knew were at fault, the reason the air between Trent and her was so often electric. Or at least had been before this morning.

She'd read an article about pheromones, and they were what caused…

Well, regardless of whether you called it instanta-neous attraction or love at first sight, they were re-sponsible for the way her heart raced and her body temperature soared whenever she got too near Trent Harrison.

They'd been causing the reactions all week long. From the very beginning.

Because they weren't even remotely related to tak-ing the time to get to know a man, or growing fond of him gradually.

Uh-uh. They were part of nature's design to ensure procreation. Virtual sex magnets, which in most spe-cies attracted just about every member of the opposite sex.

But in humans they only affected people whose pheromone receptors were tuned to the right band. And hers were obviously finely tuned to Trent's. *Very* finely tuned.

Which meant that standing this close to him was really dumb. It had only started her body reminding her brain about what might have been. But now would never be.

Rather than torturing herself any longer, she retired to the couch and waited while he continued search-ing—watching him make the occasional note as he went along.

Finally, he closed the laptop and turned his chair around so he was facing her across the room.

There wasn't very much room to face her across, but the fact that he hadn't come over to sit beside her made her wonder if he was intentionally avoiding *her* pheromones.

Or would they still have any effect on him after what she'd done?

She was just deciding that was highly unlikely, when he said, "Well, I think we can safely rule out the possibility that John Brown is any sort of genius."

"Oh?" she said, turning her full attention to the subject at hand.

"I came up with some excerpts from a court-ordered evaluation, and they don't indicate he's terribly bright.

"He was expelled from school in the eighth grade—that was the end of his formal education—and he has sealed juvie records, which means he's been in and out of pretty serious trouble ever since he was a kid."

"Not exactly one of the world's shining lights."

"No. He's the kind of guy I used to run across every day when I was a prosecutor. Late twenties or early thirties. Never married—they tend to avoid any sort of responsibility."

"That's the end of the wife possibility, then."

"Yeah, but the woman could still be his girlfriend. At any rate, men like Brown just live from one crime to the next. Sometimes can make their rent, sometimes can't.

"Which means he'd never have had the money it would take to *pay* somebody to come up with a way of getting him off. Especially not when the plan's as complex as this one.

"And here's another interesting little fact. He's got a high-priced defense lawyer."

"Really?"

"Uh-huh. Where did the money for that come from?"

When Chelsea didn't offer any ideas, he said, "It never even occurred to me that we'd be looking at anything other than court-assigned representation. But according to the preliminary-hearing record, he's represented by an associate from a big enough law firm that I'm familiar with the name."

"So where *did* the money for that come from?"

"I wish to hell I knew," he muttered. "But it looks as if somebody with brains *and* money is determined to see our guy walk."

"A rich relative?"

"Not likely. His family was on welfare while he was growing up, so unless one of them won a lottery…"

"Then let's get back to this lawyer," she suggested. "Will you be able to find out who hired him?"

"Maybe, maybe not. The defense isn't always prepared to divulge something like that. Or if the somebody wants to keep his name out of it, the defense might not even know who's actually footing the bill."

She thought about that, then said, "Well, whoever it is, I'd say he's incredibly determined."

"Because…?"

"Well, I might be missing something, but he really seems to be into overkill. I mean, hiring a pricey lawyer *as well as* kidnapping Amy to make you cooperate? Don't you think that's excessive?''

''Not necessarily,'' he said thoughtfully. ''They hired the lawyer before they could be certain they'd get me onside.''

She shook her head. ''How many fathers wouldn't do *anything* to get a kidnapped child back?''

''Yeah, but if they *hadn't* managed to kidnap Amy...''

He stopped there and broke eye contact, while a fresh wave of guilt flooded her.

They *had* managed to kidnap Amy. Because of her.

After a minute, Trent met her gaze again, his eyes not revealing any emotion. But she had little trouble imagining what he was feeling, which made her feel even worse.

''Even if they *did* have Amy,'' he said, ''and even if I *did* agree to cooperate, they couldn't have been certain that I'd be able to get myself back into the D.A.'s Office. Let alone appointed prosecutor for one particular trial.''

''Ah, right. I wasn't thinking about that part. So they were figuring that with a good defense lawyer, even if you couldn't or wouldn't help, they'd still have a shot at getting Brown off.''

''Not much of a shot, but...''

''What?'' she said when he paused again.

He wearily shook his head. ''I'm just back to thinking about all the planning that's gone into this. And when it comes to crimes, people who plan carefully also tend to cover their tracks—try not to leave any clues or loose ends.

''That's got me worried about how tough it could be for you to learn much.''

"Well, as you said, we can get going tomorrow on finding out if the woman is Brown's girlfriend. And even if she isn't, I should be able to come up with some things about his personal life. Ones that aren't in any of your databases.

"Then there's the lawyer angle. If either of us can learn who hired him, that might be the key. There'll be *something* that will tell us what we need to know."

She tried to give Trent an encouraging smile, but it felt completely wrong.

And she doubted it had looked right, either, because when he said, "Yeah," he sounded nowhere near convinced.

Then he squared his shoulders and added, "You're right. There *will* be something. There *has* to be."

She nodded, but her throat was suddenly tight. Deep down, they both knew there didn't *have* to be anything at all.

Another uneasy silence settled in over them, until Trent said, "Look, let's work our way through what we already know one more time. Maybe there's something that should have leaped out at us but didn't."

TRENT FINISHED summarizing what facts they had, then sat waiting while Chelsea considered them again.

Waiting and watching. Unable to stop himself from gazing at her as she absently wound a strand of golden hair around her finger.

Absently. Sexily. Silky hair.

He forced his thoughts in a different direction; seconds later they'd returned.

He'd never so much as touched her hair, but just looking at it made him certain it was silky. The kind of hair a man would plow his fingers through while kissing a woman. While making love to her.

He uncomfortably cleared his throat, once again cognizant of the implausibility of what was going on here.

With his daughter's life at risk, how could there be room in his brain for even a vague awareness of what a sensual woman Chelsea was? Especially when she was the one who'd...

He didn't know. And he'd asked himself those questions so many times since this morning that it was getting totally ridiculous.

Yet he couldn't make any more sense of his feelings now than he'd been able to earlier—in part, at least, because they'd been bouncing all over the map.

He'd started the day half-crazy about her. Then, when he'd first learned that Amy was gone, he'd felt ice-cold hatred. Now...

Hell, at this point he was too exhausted to know *what* he was feeling. But he couldn't deny that, regardless of anything else, there was still a sexual attraction.

Whether there should be or not, it hadn't vanished. Hell, it hadn't even diminished in strength.

When she'd been standing behind him, focusing over his shoulder on the computer screen, her body heat had been seeping through his skin, making him almost too hot to breathe.

And when he *had* breathed, her night-blooming flowers scent had been distracting enough that he'd felt as much relief as disappointment when she'd sat down.

"I'm not the legal expert here," she said, interrupting his thoughts. "So let's make sure I'm perfectly clear on this. Under normal circumstances, there's absolutely no doubt the case would be open-and-shut.''

"Right. Open-and-shut." Good. Back to business. Back to the only reason they were together in this depressing little safe house.

"When the cops catch a perp at the scene of the crime," he continued, "the defense rarely has a prayer. And when you add in Mr. Brown's priors and the additional charges...

"Well, it's practically a textbook-perfect example of a case that should be a gimme for the prosecution."

"But with your involvement, it won't be."

"Well, yeah, we know that's what they're counting on."

She eyed him quizzically, then said, "Trent, is there something you aren't telling me? You almost sound as if you don't really intend to do what they want."

He shrugged. "Actually, I'm hoping I won't have to."

"But...I don't understand. As long as Amy's—"

"I know, I know."

He pushed himself up from the chair and paced the small room, then turned to face Chelsea again, saying, "As long as the bastards have her, I can't possibly double-cross them. But if this all works out the way it could, if we can not only get Amy back but also ID the kidnapper and the woman...

"*And* figure out who the brains behind this is..."

"Then?"

"Then I'd make sure the whole damn bunch of them ended up with long-term accommodations. Courtesy of the state."

Chelsea simply gazed at him for a minute.

"And get yourself killed for your trouble?" she finally said.

HER WORDS HUNG in the air for so long that Chelsea had almost decided Trent wasn't going to respond to them.

Then he slowly shook his head and said, "I wouldn't get myself killed if we nailed everyone involved."

Everyone. The kidnapper. The woman. The mastermind. Assuming the woman wasn't the brains, he was talking three people. Minimum.

As he'd said earlier, for all they knew, that could be half a dozen others. And given how much thinking had gone into this plan, whoever was behind it would have considered the possibility that Trent might try to double-cross them.

There'd be a plan in place for dealing with him if he did, and he undoubtedly *would* end up dead.

After all, she was an amateur at sleuthing. Which meant there probably wasn't the slightest chance she could actually ID *everyone.*

For that matter, she didn't want to try. She simply wanted to find Amy.

"Look, I shouldn't even have mentioned that," Trent said. "I'm getting miles ahead of myself, just contemplating it. Only…"

"Only what?"

He shrugged again. "This is going to make me sound like the most unexciting man on earth, but the last time I willingly did anything against the law— aside from occasionally driving too fast—I was about seventeen years old. And the idea of helping John Brown walk, of cooperating with that crew…''

''You're doing it to get Amy back,'' she said quietly.

''Yeah, I know. I keep reminding myself of that. And telling myself that the only way we can play this is one step at a time, which means there's really no sense in trying to strategize beyond the next one. So, well, just forget I said anything, okay?''

Sure. Piece of cake. Just forget that both Amy and Trent could end up dead if she didn't come up with the necessary information.

No pressure there. None at all.

''It's not late,'' he said, checking his watch. ''But I'm beat. You must be, too.''

''I am.''

The dusky shadows of evening had only begun to close in outside their windows, so it couldn't be more than something after nine. Still, she felt exhausted.

But that was only to be expected. They'd gotten off to an awfully early start this morning, and the stress of the day had made it seem a thousand hours long.

''There's really nothing else we can do tonight,'' Trent was saying, ''so it makes sense to turn in, doesn't it?''

When she nodded, he added, ''You take the bedroom.''

''I wouldn't mind the pullout.''

''Just take the bedroom, all right?''

''Well…fine.''

She rose from the sofa bed and helped him move the coffee table over to the wall. When he pulled the couch open, it covered almost every inch of available floor space.

"At least the bed's made," he said, turning down the blanket. "I'm so tired I doubt I could have faced making it."

They'd left both of their overnight cases sitting at the end of the couch, and he reached for hers, adding, "Do you want the bathroom first?"

"No, I'll wait," she said, taking the case from him. "I'll probably be longer than you. I'm kind of obsessive about brushing my teeth. Then there's moisturizer and stuff. I spend so much time in the sun, out on the track, that…

"Well, you know." She stopped there and told herself to quit babbling.

She never babbled. Except when she was feeling like the proverbial fish out of water. And that rarely happened.

It was happening now, though. She did *not* belong in this apartment. With this man. Yet…

Oh, Lord. There were so many different vibes in the air she'd never be able to count them if she tried. But this was where she had to be, so there was nothing to do but deal with it as best she could.

She took a couple of backward steps, which put her in the bedroom doorway.

"'Night," she said, pausing there.

"'Night," Trent repeated, glancing in her direction.

His gaze lingered long enough to make every last one of those vibes begin to quiver before he looked away and started to open his case.

She took one more backward step, then closed the door, sank onto the bed and sat listening to the faint rustles from the living room. A minute later, she heard him going into the bathroom.

When the shower began to run, she opened her case and stared unhappily at its contents.

She always traveled light. And since she'd been expecting to share a room with Amy—not an apartment with Trent—she hadn't bothered bringing a robe. All she had to put on was her Boston Red Sox nightshirt.

Wishing it were ankle-length, rather than mid thigh, she changed into it.

After hanging up the clothes she'd been wearing, as well as the one dress she'd packed and the jeans and T-shirt she'd intended to wear to the baseball game, she flicked off the light and sat in the gathering twilight until Trent was done in the bathroom.

As soon as she'd heard him make his way to bed, she opened her door and slipped across the hall, not allowing herself even to glance toward the living room.

However, on her return trip to the bedroom her willpower deserted her. She paused and gazed along the short hallway.

Trent was lying on his side, facing in her direction. There was enough light left for her to see that his eyes were open. And his chest was bare.

She swallowed hard. He looked more like Antonio Banderas than ever.

Resisting the urge to tug down the bottom of her nightshirt, she quietly said, "'Night, again."

"Right. See you in the morning. Sleep tight."

Sleep tight. That was what her father had always said to her when she'd lived at home. And it must be what Trent always said to Amy.

But not tonight.

A lump forming in her throat, she continued into the bedroom and closed the door once more. Then she crawled into bed, feeling so bone-weary that she assumed she'd be asleep in two minutes. She was wrong, though.

Her thoughts wouldn't stop swirling, forcing her to relive what had been—hands down—the worst day of her life.

Finally, she tried a little visualization, pretending she was on a fluffy white cloud and would fall asleep before she could count to a hundred.

It didn't work. One hundred found her staring into the darkness, her mind still racing.

Tomorrow, either Trent or she would have to call Shawn Madders. And if he didn't buy their story…

But he had to. Or at least had to pretend he did. Because if he got in the way of what they were trying to do the kidnapper would kill Amy.

Her eyes were suddenly stinging with tears and she began desperately wishing she were psychic. If only she could magically figure out where the little girl was.

That wasn't going to happen, however. It would take time, not magic. And the longer it took, the harder this would be on Amy.

Just as Chelsea was—yet again—trying to force away the fear that they'd never manage to find Amy, she heard Trent moan.

She sat bolt upright in bed and listened for another sound.

She didn't have to wait long, and the second one put her in mind of an animal in pain.

He was having a nightmare. Hardly surprising. But what should she do?

She thought rapidly, trying to decide.

The last few years before her father had retired from racing, he'd been plagued by nightmares about dying in a fiery crash. That had been one of the reasons he'd finally quit.

Before he'd done that, though, he'd sought professional help. So nightmares weren't foreign territory to her.

She knew they were often brought on by an intensely frightening or highly emotional experience. Like a near miss on the track. Or your daughter being kidnapped.

She also knew how bad the raw terror that lingered after them could be. And she remembered her mother would always waken her father, then hold him and comfort him, reassuring him that things in nightmares weren't portents of what would happen in real life.

According to his therapist, that was really all anyone could do to help.

But when it came to Trent…

He might not be the least bit grateful if she tried to comfort him. And if she—

The next noise he made sounded as if someone was extracting his teeth without anesthetic. It sent her scrambling out of bed and into the living room.

The glow from the city made it less dark in there than in the bedroom, and she could see that he looked, as well as sounded, in pain.

Not giving herself even a second to think about what she was doing, she rested her hands firmly on his bare shoulders and said, "Trent, wake up."

When he merely groaned, she repeated her words, shaking him this time.

He came awake with a start and flailed at her, knocking her hands away from him.

"Trent, it's all right! You were just having a nightmare."

For a long moment, he simply stared up at her from his pillow, then he covered his mouth with the back of his hand and whispered, "Oh, God, I thought she was dead."

"No, she isn't," Chelsea said, her heart aching. "You talked to her only a couple of hours ago, remember? And she's going to come out of this just fine. We'll make sure of that."

Tentatively, she sank onto the edge of the bed and brushed his hair back from his forehead. His skin was damp with sweat and he was breathing so hard the rasping sound of it filled the room.

"Here, you're going to catch cold," she murmured, pulling the blanket up a little.

That done, she didn't know whether to stay or go.

"Would you like something?" she said at last. "I noticed there's tea in the kitchen. I could make some."

"No. No, thanks. I just want to get completely awake." He eased himself into a sitting position, then simply sat gazing into the grayness of the room.

"Would it help to talk?" she finally asked.

"I don't know," he said wearily. "Maybe."

She waited.

Eventually, he said, "Amy was lost in a fog. And I could hear her calling me. She was afraid and calling for me. But every time I started in the direction of her voice, the direction changed.

"All I could see was this damn cold fog. And I was getting more and more afraid that I'd never find her in it. I…

"Hell, I guess we don't need Freud to figure that one out, do we? A two-year-old would get it."

"Trent," she murmured, "we *are* going to find her."

"Yeah," he said. "That's the plan."

She had no idea what else to say, so she said nothing—just sat beside him feeling downright ill.

"I used to have nightmares after Sheila… About her dying," he said at last.

"They weren't exactly true to the way it happened. I mean, in reality I didn't see her car explode. Only heard it. But in the nightmares, Amy and I were always standing at the front window, watching her leave. She'd open the car door and wave. And we'd wave back. Then she'd climb in and turn the key and…"

When he slowly shook his head, Chelsea rested her hand on his, knowing she couldn't have stopped herself if she'd tried.

She wasn't sure he even noticed. There was no apparent reaction.

"I haven't had a nightmare for at least a year," he continued. "Not until tonight."

"I'm sorry," she whispered. Sorry that she hadn't been more careful. Sorry for what it had led to. "Sorrier than I can ever tell you."

"I know you are," he said quietly.

He sounded as if he really *did* know; it made her even more uncertain whether to stay or go.

"Would you like me to sit here for a while?" she

asked at last. "In case the nightmare comes back when you fall asleep again."

She didn't breathe while she waited for his answer.

He hesitated, then shook his head once more. "Thanks, but I've never had two in the same night. And you need your sleep."

"Right, I do," she said, removing her hand from his as casually as she could.

"See you in the morning," she added, telling herself that the pain in her heart was *not* the sting of disappointment—but aware she was lying to herself.

CHAPTER NINE

HIS HEAD ON THE PILLOW, Trent watched Chelsea walk away, almost desperately wanting to call her back, yet warning himself that it was probably the most dangerous desire he'd ever known.

If this morning hadn't happened, things would be entirely different. He'd have pulled her into bed with him and kept her there for a week. Maybe longer.

But this morning *had* happened. And even though he realized that what she'd told him was true, that she was sorrier than she could say...

Even though he believed she wanted to find Amy almost as badly as he did...

He mentally shook his head. Once again, his body had been saying one thing and his brain another.

His body had been telling him to just go ahead and reach for Chelsea, telling him how comforting it would be to have someone to hold.

Someone? Oh, who did he think he was fooling? He'd wanted to hold *her*.

Hell, merely her hand resting on his had felt better than he could ever have imagined.

His brain, however, had been asking whether he wanted to risk ending up on a guilt trip from hell. Because if he let himself...

Dammit, now he was back to having trouble coming up with the right words.

But Amy was heaven only knew where. With strangers. With no one to comfort *her*. And as long as that was true, nothing on earth would really comfort him. *Especially* not Chelsea.

He closed his eyes tightly once she'd shut the bedroom door. He could still see her in his mind's eye, though. As vividly as if an image of her had been etched there.

Her pale hair was tousled. Sexier looking than he'd ever seen it. And that nightshirt she had on left little to the imagination. Its fabric clung to her breasts, and it was short enough to reveal exactly how shapely her legs were. Even more gorgeous than he'd guessed. And...

Just go to sleep, he told himself.

He tried, but couldn't manage it. Couldn't stop wishing it were possible to turn back time. Wishing he'd left Amy at home with Martha Wilson, where she'd have been safe.

But...would she have?

The question began slithering around inside his head, starting him thinking, once again, how carefully this whole exercise had been planned. Thinking of all those details that whoever was behind it had learned about him.

And there had been that contingency plan in place, as well—a good lawyer for John Brown, so that even if the prosecuting attorney had refused to come onside there'd still have been a chance of a not-guilty verdict.

The more he thought, the more convinced he grew that whoever the mastermind was, he'd have a contingency plan for kidnapping Amy, too. And maybe...

The possibility that the mugging had been part of things began nagging at him once more.

If putting Lizzie's mother in the hospital had been a step in the master scheme, one designed to get Lizzie out of the picture, then grabbing Amy in Faneuil Hall wouldn't have been the original strategy.

Logic said that if Lizzie took off for Philadelphia he'd leave Amy at home while he went to Boston.

And hell, given all that research, there was no doubt their whoever would have known that Martha Wilson was his usual backup. And so would have figured he'd do the obvious and ask *her* to take care of Amy. Which meant that plan A had likely been to kidnap her from Martha's.

Someone would have been watching the house this morning, to see for sure that he *did* take Amy next door. And when he didn't, the someone would have followed them to Chelsea's, then trailed them to the hotel in Boston. And from that point he'd have just played it by ear.

Pushing himself up in bed, Trent tried to decide if that was really what had happened. Was he adding things together right?

He reviewed his reasoning and concluded he must be. Amy's abductor had been determined to grab her. From wherever she was. Regardless of who she was with.

She might have been at Martha's. Or with Lizzie. Or even with him. So how much was Chelsea really to blame?

He slowly rubbed his jaw, suspecting the honest answer was *not as much as he'd been thinking*.

The kidnapper had had his orders, and would have done whatever it took to get Amy—which undoubtedly would have included shooting Chelsea if it had come down to that.

He looked through the darkness toward the bedroom door, a chill inching up his spine.

Obviously, the people involved in this were prepared to go to whatever lengths necessary to get the required results.

So, were he and Chelsea being crazy? Were they going to end up dead if they went ahead with trying to learn where Amy was?

Instead of that, should he just do as he'd been ordered? Ensure that John Brown walked and hope to blazes…

Suddenly, he found himself remembering that, until Monday, he wouldn't be *completely* certain he'd be in a position to ensure that Brown *could* walk. Wouldn't be *completely* certain Matthew would assign the case to him.

Oh, man, how had that thought managed to sneak up into his consciousness and sting him?

He'd been doing a good job of keeping it repressed, and having it resurface was enough to start a second chill crawling after the first one.

He *was* going to get the case, though. There just wouldn't be a problem with that. Most likely, Matthew would hand it to him without a second thought. And even if that didn't happen…

Well, one way or another, he'd end up with it.

Now, where had he been before that unsettling little interruption?

He needed a moment, but he remembered. He'd been wondering if he maybe shouldn't…

But that had been a really stupid thought. Simply going along with making certain Brown got a verdict of not guilty, and hoping for the best, wasn't a viable option. No more than it had been earlier.

He could practically hear the incredulous tone in Chelsea's voice when she'd said, *Are you just going to do*…whatever *the kidnapper wants and trust that he'll give Amy back?*

He'd replied, *Of course not,* and nothing had changed since then.

There was absolutely no way he could trust that guy. Or any of his coconspirators—whoever they were.

The *only* person he could trust was Chelsea.

And wasn't that ironic.

CHELSEA CAUGHT herself chewing on a fingernail and stopped.

She hadn't bitten her nails since she was seven, when her father had bribed her to quit with the promise of a dirt bike—overriding her mother's objections that she was too young. But her nerves were so on edge right now it seemed that…

Of course, this waiting was a major part of the problem.

She and Trent had turned in early enough last night that, despite his nightmare, they'd both been awake first thing this morning. So even though they were ready to get going, it was still too early to phone Shawn. Or pay a visit to John Brown's old neighborhood.

That was why they were perched on either end of the folded-up sofa bed like a couple of human bookends, gazing at the dust motes drifting through the sunlight and glancing at their watches every ten seconds.

Absently, she picked at a tiny nub in the denim of her jeans—the order of dress for the day.

According to Trent, Brown hadn't lived in one of Manhattan's better areas. And even in jeans they were going to look out of place among the locals.

"What time does Madders usually get up?" he said, checking his watch yet again.

"I don't know. I told you—we aren't that close."

He met her gaze then. Just for a moment. But it was enough to cause a whomping sensation in the pit of her stomach.

She looked at the floor, wishing her body would stop reacting to him at all, let alone so strongly. But at least she had her mental set halfway to where it should be. Her brain had definitely accepted the reality of the situation.

Regardless of what Trent might have felt for her a mere twenty-four hours ago, at this point those feelings were stone-cold dead. If she'd had any lingering doubts about the truth of that—which she hadn't—they'd have been totally shredded last night.

Even remembering how she'd been sitting on the side of his bed, half-naked and shamelessly wanting him to reach for her—only to have him send her away—was painful.

"We can't waste any more time," he muttered, picking up his phone. "If I wake Madders up, I wake him up."

She watch him hit the numbers for Shawn's cellular, thinking it was probably just as well that he'd played his "I don't want you lying for me and making yourself an accessory" card again.

After all, Shawn knew her a lot better than he knew Trent. And that made it more likely something in her voice would tell him he was being fed a crock. Although FBI agents were trained to recognize lies regardless of who was telling them. So how well would Trent make out?

"It's ringing," he told her, which meant they'd soon have an answer to the question.

She only hoped it was one they liked.

"Shawn, it's Trent Harrison," he said.

"Yeah, there's news. And it's great. Hell, it's fantastic. Amy managed to escape and I've got her back with me."

Chelsea could feel herself relaxing a little. So far, so good. He sounded deliriously happy.

"Well, after the kidnapper called yesterday," Trent elaborated, "he and the woman locked her in the bathroom and went out somewhere.

"The window was small and nailed shut. They obviously figured it was secure enough. But Amy broke the glass and managed to wriggle through.

"Fortunately, that put her on a fire escape. So she made it down to the street and just ran to beat hell. Eventually, she got some woman with a cell phone to call me."

Trent caught Chelsea's eye while he listened to whatever Shawn was saying.

She gave him a thumbs-up.

"No, I didn't involve the police," he said.

She held her breath, knowing only too well how Shawn would react to that.

"Well, partly because Amy got totally lost while she was running. When I picked her up she had no idea where the apartment was. And partly because she was so damn upset…

"Hell, she was safe, physically unharmed, but still

terribly frightened. And I just couldn't see putting her through the trauma of a police interview. Especially when, as soon as the kidnapper discovered she was gone, both he and the woman would have taken off.

"All I wanted to do was get Amy out of Boston. Take her someplace where I could be sure she'd *stay* safe."

Chelsea anxiously waited as he listened again, wondering what the odds were that Shawn was going to buy the explanation.

Even to her and Trent, the idea of not calling the cops had seemed pretty implausible. But they hadn't been able to come up with a better reason than the one he'd gone with.

"No, I'm not surprised you think it was a mistake," he said at last. "And yeah, I *am* a lawyer. But what I cared about most was Amy's best interests, so that's the way I played it.

"At any rate, I just wanted to let you know she's all right. And she's going to be staying…

"Well, I don't want to go into the details of where she is with *anyone*. I have to be in New York for the next little while and—"

He frowned, clearly not liking what Shawn was telling him, then pushed himself up and paced into the kitchen and back.

"Yeah, I know," he said, stopping in front of the window. "But I made a commitment to the D.A. there. And as bad as the timing has turned out to be, it's just not something I can renege on. So I'm leaving Amy with, well, people I trust implicitly."

She waited again, this time wondering how many questions Shawn was going to ask.

When they'd rethought their story over breakfast,

they'd agreed he should cut it substantially, fearing that the more details Trent volunteered, the more likely he'd trip up on one of them.

So he was going to say as little as he could get away with. And nothing at all about Chelsea's being in New York with him.

Of course, he wasn't letting on that he was actually already here. But he didn't plan on saying she *would* be with him when he came.

They'd decided that just making some allusion to their "relationship" should be enough. Then, if Shawn did nose around, he wouldn't think it strange to find they were together.

"Yeah, I realize that," Trent was saying. "And I agree with you. It's far from the ideal conclusion. But as I said, my main concern was doing what was best for Amy. Whether that left a criminal walking around loose or not.

"Oh, and there's one other thing. Something Chelsea asked me to mention."

She held her breath once more.

"Actually, she's with me right now. Here with Amy and me," he added, sinking back onto the couch beside her—close enough that she could feel the warmth of his body.

She told herself not to take any notice, but there wasn't a chance in a million of managing not to.

"I...well, I know you and Chelsea were kind of seeing each other," he continued.

"But the two of us... She wasn't in Boston with me *just* to help look after Amy. And she thought it was only right to let you know that we're..."

There was a pause before he said, "Yeah, she told me it was nothing serious. Even so, she said she'd feel better if she was up front about it with you. Or, I guess, as it's turned out, if *I* was up front.''

He glanced at her, his expression saying he thought they just might be getting away with this.

She started praying that was the case.

''Yeah, sure I'll tell her hi for you. And thanks again for your help yesterday. And for your advice. I might not have followed all of it, but I appreciated it a lot.''

''Well?'' she asked as he clicked the phone off. ''What do you think?''

''I'm not sure. He was so damn mad when I said I hadn't called the police that he focused more on that than anything else. But now he'll be busy adding up everything I said, and if he doesn't like the total…''

''There was nothing that would have made *me* very suspicious,'' she assured him. ''I mean, I think you did extremely well.''

''I just wish I could be certain I convinced him.''

She hesitated, then said, ''We're doing okay, Trent. No, we're doing way better than okay.

''You had no trouble getting Matthew to go along with what you wanted. We already have a couple of starting places for learning what we need to know. And with any luck, Shawn will just forget about us. Even if he doesn't…well, I really think we're going to make this happen.''

''I sure as hell hope so,'' he said, raking his fingers through his hair.

''What's wrong?'' she said quietly. He *had* done well, yet he looked terribly discouraged.

He shook his head. ''I just wish so badly that Amy really had escaped. Because if we can't make it happen…''

"Oh, Trent," she murmured. "I know."

This time, she didn't let herself say they *would* find Amy. Even though they'd been playing the reassurance game almost from the beginning, they both knew the reality of the situation. And more empty words weren't really going to help.

Then he caught her gaze, and his dark eyes were so troubled it made her wish she hadn't given up the game.

"Chelsea…I…"

"What?"

He shrugged. "It's just so… She's only nine. And she sounded so damn scared last night."

She tried to think of the right words, then gently said, "But she *did* tell you the woman's being nice to her. And kids can get through a lot. They're tougher than we realize."

For a long moment, he merely continued to look at her.

Then, ever so tentatively, he wrapped his arms around her and pulled her close.

It almost made her cry.

She pressed her cheek against his chest, afraid he'd push her away again any second. And when it felt so wonderful to have him hold her…

Even though they'd met only a week ago, she'd come to know him so well. To know him and—

She stopped herself right there. Thinking about how much she'd come to care for him was *not* a good idea.

He needed a human touch and she was the only other human within reach. She'd be very foolish to read anything more into this than that.

"Sometimes, when I'm working at home," he said against her hair, "Amy will crawl onto my lap and say she needs a hug. I guess…well, I guess that's where I'd gotten to by this point."

"Me, too," she whispered.

She snuggled closer still, then just sat breathing in his scent and listening to the beating of his heart. It brought that whomping sensation back in spades.

When he began to stroke her hair, she could almost believe there was a chance he might forgive her.

Then an imaginary voice with a truly nasty edge said, *If you don't get Amy back, he'll never forgive you in a million years.*

She swallowed hard, knowing that was true.

It made her feel like such an impostor, here in his arms, that she hardly cared at all when he said, "I guess we'd better head out."

ON THEIR WAY down to the safe house's parking garage, Trent gave himself a stern lecture about what had just happened—and shouldn't have.

One minute he'd merely been talking with Chelsea and the next she'd been in his arms.

He wasn't entirely sure how he'd let that come about. Somehow, though, he simply hadn't been able to resist holding her. Or stroking her hair.

It had felt exactly the way he'd known it would— as soft as silk. And whatever she'd washed it with smelled so good that he'd wanted to keep breathing in the scent forever.

As for the sensation of her warm body cuddled against him, well, nothing in the world—other than his love for Amy—would have made him suggest they do anything except stay right where they were.

But it was a damn good thing he'd said it was time to leave. Until he could…

Uh-uh, he wasn't going there again. Wasn't going to try, even one more time, to figure out exactly where his head was at as far as Chelsea was concerned.

It was just too confusing, so any figuring would have to wait until after Amy was safe.

In the meantime, he'd be smart not to let himself feel the need of any more hugs. Because if he couldn't understand why he was doing something, he shouldn't do it.

That was true at the best of times, when he was thinking straight—never mind at the moment, when he was into total overload.

So he just had to ensure that his relationship with Chelsea remained…

Remained *wherever* the hell it was right now.

As they reached the car, he told himself to keep all of that firmly in mind. Then he forced his thoughts from Chelsea to John Brown.

Before Brown had ended up awaiting trial in jail, his residence had been an apartment in Little Italy—which would take no time at all to get to from Tribeca.

He drove up to street level, and when he stopped at the exit to wait for a break in the traffic, Chelsea said, "I assume we don't tell any of Mr. Brown's former neighbors that you're a prosecuting attorney who wants to put him away for life."

"Good assumption."

"Then who do we say we are?"

"Depends on who we end up talking to. It's the sort of thing you usually have to make up as you go along. Are you good at that?"

"Not bad. When I was a kid I was always inventing stories to amuse myself. Only children often do that—which supposedly explains why a disproportionate number of writers are onlys."

He got his break and pulled out onto the street, wondering if Amy invented stories. She'd never said anything about it to him, but maybe she did.

She remained on his mind as he drove across Lower Manhattan. Once he'd found a parking space down the block from Brown's tenement, however, he told himself he had to focus his full attention on what he and Chelsea were doing.

The two of them began walking back toward Brown's building—him trying not to think that this was exactly the kind of place he hated leaving his car. A street where car alarms went off so regularly that nobody paid them the slightest attention.

But he'd locked both his gun and his laptop in the trunk, so they should be safe. And he had a disabler on his ignition, which meant the car would still be there when they got back. Although he *did* suspect that the tires might be missing.

"Not exactly a Martha Stewart sort of neighborhood," Chelsea murmured after a drunk lurched out of a doorway and practically stumbled into them.

"Not exactly," he agreed, now thinking it was a damn good thing he was with her.

Even on a Sunday morning the dealers were out in force. There were a few pimps thrown in for variety, and he'd bet every one of the half-dozen teenagers who were lounging against parked cars, watching the world go by from behind slits of eyes, had a concealed knife or handgun. Some were probably carrying a couple of each.

Of course, Chelsea *had* taken all the RCI courses, so maybe he should be thinking it was a damn good thing *she* was with *him.*

But whichever way he chose to view it, he was glad she hadn't come here on her own. Because even though she'd gone along with his advice to dress down... Hell, given the way her jeans fit, every guy who saw her had to be taking a second look. Probably a third one, as well.

She was just the sort of woman who grabbed male attention. Beautiful face, great body and hair that practically sparkled in the sunlight.

But, dammit, he didn't want to be thinking those sorts of thoughts. So he just wouldn't let himself.

He silently repeated that resolution a couple of times, then they reached the tenement's entrance and started up the crumbling stairs.

Inside, the floor was littered with butts, the walls were covered with graffiti and the air was heavy with the unpleasant kind of cooking smells that leach into old plaster over the decades.

"Which apartment?" Chelsea said.

"Three-fifteen. But let's check the name on its mailbox before we go up. See who we're getting."

He walked over to the row of battered metal doors and had a look, then said, "Three-fifteen is a Frank Sheen."

"So if there *was* a woman living with John Brown, she's not there any longer."

"Wouldn't seem so.

"We don't want to use Sheen's name up front," he added as they headed over to the worn staircase. "If we do, he'll figure we're cops or bill collectors or something."

She nodded, and when they reached the third floor she simply waited in silence while he knocked on the door.

"Yeah?" a man called from inside.

"Just like to talk to you for a minute," Trent called back.

"I'm busy."

"Really won't take long."

That didn't garner a reply.

"Let me try," Chelsea murmured.

"Go ahead," he told her. She could hardly do worse than him.

She tapped and said, "Hello?"

There wasn't a sound from inside.

"I'm really sorry to bother you," she persisted, "but I'm trying to locate my brother and I was hoping you'd be able to help me."

When Trent glanced at her, silently asking where the breathless voice had come from, she shrugged and whispered, "Whatever works."

A few moments later, the door opened.

Only an inch at first. Then the guy inside got a look at Chelsea and opened it farther.

Frank Sheen was sporting a scraggly ponytail, hadn't shaved in days and was dressed in a dirty undershirt and ripped cutoffs.

Chelsea smiled as if mistaking him for Brad Pitt.

"Mr. Brown?" she said. "John Brown?"

For a second, Trent thought this character was going to claim he *was* Brown.

Then he shook his head and said, "Nah. He usta live here, but not anymore."

"Oh." Chelsea's expression melted into one of distress. "Do you know where he moved to?"

"Uh-uh. He's not a friend of mine or nothin'. All I know's his name was on the mailbox when I moved in."

Trent doubted that was really *all* Sheen knew. Unless he never spoke to any of the other tenants, he'd have heard that Brown was in jail. It was the sort of thing people talked about, even in neighborhoods like this.

But the Frank Sheens of the world tended not to volunteer information—except when there was something in it for them.

"Well, maybe you could still help me," Chelsea said.

Sheen glanced from her to Trent, looking unfriendly.

He also looked ready to shut the door on them, so Trent quickly said, "I'm her cousin. Her brother's cousin, too, of course. I'm just helping her try to track him down."

He didn't risk uttering another word, because he had no idea where Chelsea was going with this. But at least Mr. Dirty Undershirt stayed where he was, in the doorway.

"My family lives in Hartford," Chelsea said.

"Connecticut," she added when the fellow appeared to be drawing a blank.

"And my brother—his name is Rob—came to New York a few months ago. Actually, it was more than a few. He'd lost his job in Hartford and…well, the thing is that my parents only heard from him once after he got here. He phoned and told them he'd met someone with an apartment to share and…

"The someone was named John Brown and this was the address."

A dubious look appeared on Sheen's face. Clearly, he wasn't buying that Chelsea would have a brother who'd even consider living in a dump like this.

"My brother... Part of the reason I'm worried about him is that he has a lot of...*problems.*

"He's just not like the rest of the family. He's been in and out of trouble for years and, well, I'm sure you understand what I'm saying. Losing his job was only one of a whole bunch of...*things.*"

Sheen nodded; Trent felt relieved. She'd recovered nicely.

"At any rate," she continued, "it isn't unusual not to hear from Rob for long stretches at a time. And he doesn't like it when he thinks we're checking up on him. That's how he always refers to it.

"So my parents waited quite a while, hoping he'd phone again. But he didn't. And when we finally tried calling him, we got that *this number is not in service* message. You know the one I mean?"

"Uh-huh."

"So...well, then we waited again, thinking that sooner or later he'd call. But it's been so long now that my cousin and I decided we'd better come to New York. Find Rob so we're sure he's okay. Only..."

She stopped speaking and shook her head, then said, "Look, I'm sorry. I shouldn't be rambling on at you just because I'm worried."

"S'okay," Sheen said with a shrug.

"No, it's not. If you never even met John Brown, then you can't have a clue where Rob might be and I'm simply wasting your time.

"But some of the other tenants must know John. And know where I could find him. So if you'd just tell us which of your neighbors you figure could still be in touch with him..."

Chelsea blinked hard, then wiped her eyes, which made Trent nervous. To him, it smacked of overacting.

But darn if Sheen didn't say, "Well, I think the guy across the hall has lived here a long time. Want me to see if I can get him to talk to you?"

She rewarded Frank Sheen with a killer smile and said, "I'd appreciate that *very* much."

CHAPTER TEN

THE ''GUY ACROSS THE HALL,'' who Frank Sheen introduced only as Mike, was initially no friendlier than Frank had been.

He clearly wasn't pleased about being railroaded into talking to Chelsea and Trent and he didn't invite them in. But he *did* listen to Chelsea's story.

By the time she was nearing the end of it, he'd begun nodding sympathetically—which made her optimistic that they might get something useful from him.

''Wish I could help you,'' he said when she was done. ''But I never seen anyone around here that fits your brother's description. And if he *did* stay with John, it wouldn't 'a been for long.''

''Oh? Why not?''

''In a one-room apartment? Maybe John's girl-friend wouldn't 'a minded someone crashing for a night or two...''

Chelsea's pulse jumped. So Brown *did* have a girl-friend. Now they just needed to know who she was.

''But she's the kind that speaks her mind,'' the man continued.

''Nice enough, but not someone who'd put up with a stranger there for more'n a few days. So if your brother said he was gonna be sharin' the place with

John…'' Mike shook his head. "I don't think so."

"The girlfriend lived there, too, then?" Trent said.

The suspicious glance that Mike shot in his direction reminded Chelsea of the hostile look Frank Sheen had given him. And it made her think she'd have been better off without Trent along.

She'd never tell him that, though.

"Yeah," Mike said at last. "The two of 'em lived there."

"Do you know where they are now?" she asked.

"John Brown's the only lead we have," she added when he seemed reluctant to answer.

He scratched his belly, then said, "I don't know for sure where Darlene's at, but Brown's in jail."

"Oh. Really." She gnawed on her lower lip and waited to see what else he'd say.

"Been there for ages," he elaborated. "But you could probably get in to see him."

"You think so?" she said, trying to look as though she didn't relish the prospect of that—which wasn't tough to do.

He shrugged. "Can't keep a guy locked up forever without visitors."

"I guess. But…what about his girlfriend? Would it be hard to find her?"

"Dunno. After John got arrested she went to stay with her sister. Maybe she's still there, maybe not."

"Do you know the sister's name? Where I could find her?"

"Uh-huh. Her name's Brenda, and she waits tables in a bar near the corner of Hester and Mott. That's only a few blocks from here.

"She might be working today. But if not, she rents

the apartment over the bar. So you could just take the stairs at the back and see if she's home.''

"Thanks. And her last name is…?''

Mike shook his head. "Darlene's name's Clinton. She's always tellin' people she's related to Bill and Hillary. But I think Brenda mighta been married, so I don't know about her.''

"Ah. Well, thanks again. We really appreciate your help.''

"No problem. Hope you find your brother,'' he added, then turned toward his door without even a glance at Trent.

"I feel like the invisible man,'' he muttered as they started for the staircase.

"Never mind. We're making real progress.''

"You're right. We are. So I shouldn't complain.''

She followed him down the staircase, feeling seriously encouraged. If they continued the way they were going… Then a fresh concern began nagging at her.

When they reached the street, she said, "You don't suppose Mike will show up at Brown's trial, do you? Recognize you and…''

"No. I didn't get the sense they were anything more than two guys who lived across the hall from each other. And even if they were…well, a guy like Brown wouldn't want any of his buddies sitting in the courtroom. Wouldn't want them to see him get convicted. And they'd know that.

"But the girlfriend's a different story. He'll expect her to be there—unless she *is* in Boston, looking after Amy.''

"So I'll have to do the next bit on my own,'' Chelsea said. "If Darlene *is* still at her sister's, we don't want her seeing you."

"Yeah," he agreed reluctantly. "And even if she isn't, the sister might go to the trial with her. The moral-support thing."

"So I'll just drive you down to the bar, then wait for you.

"If you *do* connect with this Brenda," he added, "you'll have to stick to the same story."

"I know. Next time Mike sees her, he'll ask if I caught up with her."

They walked in silence for a minute before Trent said, "You did well."

When she looked at him, he actually smiled. "The brother story. It was really believable."

"Thanks," she said, a warm glow igniting inside her.

She'd made him feel a little better about things, and that made *her* feel better, as well.

The glow lasted until he found a place to park, not far from the corner of Hester and Mott. However, it faded rapidly once she got out of the car.

She had no idea how she'd make out with Brenda. Or Brenda and Darlene, if that proved the case. But this was definitely going to be harder than Frank Sheen and Mike had been.

Somehow, she had to find out everything she possibly could about John Brown. And hope the *everything* included a clue. One that would help Trent and her determine who was working so darn hard to keep the man from being convicted.

But she had to get the information without it seeming as if Brown was the actual reason for her visit. And that might not prove even remotely easy.

When she reached the bar, there was no waitress in sight and the bartender was on the phone, so she simply headed up the stairs to the second floor.

The stale-beer smell was only slightly less strong than it had been downstairs. And when she took a deep breath before knocking, she decided she was at risk of getting drunk on the fumes.

"Who's there?" a woman responded to the knock.

Good. She had at least one of them.

"Brenda?" she said.

"Who wants to know?"

"My name's Chelsea Everett. John Brown's neighbor, Mike, suggested I talk to you. He's the one who told me where you lived."

She heard whispering inside the apartment and warned herself not to start counting her chickens. Virtually anybody could be in there with Brenda.

"This is about John, then?" she said.

"No, not really. I'm trying to locate my brother and John knows him. So I'm hoping your sister knows him, too.

"I guess that sounds kind of roundabout, but Mike thought she might. And that she might still be staying with you."

There was more whispering, then she heard a bolt being slid and the door opened on a chain.

The woman who peered out was somewhere in her twenties and attractive in a washed-out sort of way.

"You're not a cop, are you?"

She shook her head.

"A caseworker?"

"No. I'm a teacher. And I live in Connecticut. I'm only in New York to look for my brother. Would you like to see some ID?"

While she was taking her wallet out of her purse, from behind the door another woman said, "What's your brother's name?"

"Rob. Rob Everett."

"I don't know him."

Bingo. She had Darlene.

"Well," she said slowly, "he might not have used his real name with John. He's…he has some problems and…"

She paused and shook her head, very aware of Brenda's suspicious gaze on her.

"I'm sorry to be bothering you like this," she murmured at last. "It's just that I don't have much to go on and Rob *did* give my parents John Brown's name and address. I…"

This time, she punctuated the pause with a weary shrug. "It's hard when you love someone who's in trouble and you can't seem to do anything to help him."

While Brenda glanced toward where Darlene had to be standing, Chelsea willed the two of them to let her in. If she could only get them talking…

"We don't have long," Brenda said, glancing into the hall again. "We're going out in a few minutes."

"I'd appreciate any time at all."

Brenda hesitated, then finally removed the chain and opened the door.

WHEN CHELSEA turned the corner, Trent was standing on the sidewalk next to his car.

He started rapidly down the street toward her, his expectant expression making her feel even more like a failure.

She'd been hoping to leave Brenda's with something that would *really* point them in the right direction. Something good enough to make Trent tell her she'd done well again. But that wasn't going to happen.

"So?" he said as they reached each other.

"I didn't learn much," she said, figuring she'd get the bad news out of the way immediately.

He merely nodded, which made her feel even worse. He was probably thinking that if *he'd* been able to go with her, to ask some of the questions…

And he might well have done better. She imagined a lot of women would fall all over themselves trying to please a man who looked as good as he did.

"They were both there," she said as they began walking. "Brenda *and* Darlene."

"Then Darlene *isn't* the woman looking after Amy."

"No, she can't be. And…I *did* get her talking about John a little. I told her that my brother had said they were going to be working together.

"So that when Mike mentioned that John was in jail, it made me even more concerned about what might have happened to Rob.

"And she felt sorry enough for me that she said she was absolutely certain John had been working alone when he was arrested. And that she'd never even heard him mention Rob's name."

"No surprise there, huh?"

She glanced at him, thinking it was a wonder he still had even a shred of his sense of humor left.

"No. No surprise there is right. But Darlene was…she made such an effort to be kind to me that she had me feeling guilty. She said that even if John and Rob *were* planning a job together she was sure it

hadn't happened. So that was at least one thing I
shouldn't let myself worry about.''

"And what did she tell you about John?''

"Nothing that's going to help much. Basically, just
that he's a really nice guy who's had some bad breaks
in his life.''

"You know how many times I heard that song
while I was a prosecutor?''

"Six million?''

"Yeah, that's a pretty good guess. But did you get
her talking about the trial?''

"Some. As far as the charges go, she basically said
that he's a victim of circumstance. Was simply in the
wrong place at the wrong time.''

"And had the wrong stolen goods in his apartment,'' Trent muttered.

"That's exactly what popped into my head. But
saying anything would hardly have furthered the
cause, so I just acted sympathetic and asked whether
she figured he has much chance of getting off.''

"And?''

"She said she really doesn't know. That he's been
telling her he's going to walk because he has a friend
with connections who's helping out behind the
scenes.''

"No surprise there, either, huh?''

"Well, not to us. But she isn't sure whether she
should believe him.

"She's never heard anything about this friend before, so she can't figure out who it could be. Yet she
realizes somebody has to be paying the pricey lawyer.''

"You don't think she knows who and just isn't
telling?''

"That might be it, but my instincts were saying no. I had the feeling she's praying this friend is for real because she wants John to get off.

"On the other hand, if he does exist, then John obviously doesn't trust her enough to tell her who he is. Which has her feeling hurt because John's keeping secrets from her. Hurt and angry and insulted. But only if this friend *does* exist.

"So, since she isn't sure about that, she's basically a bundle of mixed emotions and...well, by the time Brenda eased me out of there I was feeling as sorry for Darlene as she was feeling for me."

They'd reached the car, and just as Trent was pressing the remote to unlock it, his cellular began ringing.

He answered, then said, "Matthew, hi. What's up?"

FOR THE SECOND TIME in the same day, Chelsea caught herself gnawing on a fingernail.

She stopped and silently delivered a short lecture on the subject of bad habits. Then she went back to gazing out of Trent's car at the door of One Hogan Place and waiting for him to reappear.

While the kidnapper had told him that a member of the D.A.'s Office was scheduled to meet with an "accident" today, they hadn't been expecting Matthew Blake to phone Trent as soon as he heard about it. However, they'd taken the fact that he had as a good sign.

And an even better sign was that he'd asked if Trent would mind giving up the rest of his Sunday—which would let him get a head start on some of the stack of cases that suddenly had to be reassigned.

Needless to say, Trent had minded so little that they

hadn't even wasted time going back to the apartment to change.

Not that it mattered if *she* was still in jeans and sneakers, but...

Of course, given how desperately Matthew needed help, he probably wouldn't have cared if Trent had arrived in ripped cutoffs and a dirty undershirt, à la Frank Sheen.

Pushing the image of Sheen from her mind, she began visualizing that stack of files. John Brown's would be in it, and the all-important question was whether his would be one of those that Matthew gave to Trent.

It would be, though. Because otherwise, their hopes for getting Amy back safely would...

Uh-uh. She'd already told herself ten thousand times not to entertain those sorts of thoughts. So she turned her full attention back to her current "assignment" and checked the street again—making sure that no one from the city's parking control was sneaking up behind her.

Even though being parked directly outside the D.A.'s Office shouldn't cause problems for anyone on a Sunday, a No Stopping zone *was* a No Stopping zone, which was why Trent had suggested she move over to the driver's seat while she waited.

She patted the steering wheel, imagining herself doing zero to sixty in less time than it would take a parking enforcement officer to write the date on a ticket.

Then she looked back at the building's door again, just as it opened and Trent appeared.

His grin said it all. One of that pile of files tucked under his arm was John Brown's.

She felt weak with relief.

He got into the passenger's side, saying, "You drive. I've got a case to read through."

"That's it? I don't get any details?" she said as he stuck all but one of the folders onto the back seat.

"Well, the 'accident' was a mugging."

"Oh? Just like Lizzie's mother."

"Uh-huh. That thought crossed my mind, too. At any rate, the fellow is someone I know.

His name's Les Masson, and he's been with the D.A.'s Office for years."

"And he's not seriously hurt."

"I expect *he* figures it's pretty serious, but he should be out of the hospital in a couple of days."

"And did you have any trouble getting Brown's case?"

"Nope. Didn't have to resort to even a little arm-twisting.

"Matthew had made a list of the cases he was assigning me, so that he could give me a brief overview of each of them, and there was the City of New York *versus* John Raymond Brown staring off the page at me."

"Then it's clear sailing from here."

He looked across the car at her and said, "I sure hope you're right."

She forced a smile, as aware as he was that being given the case was only one more step down the road to getting Amy back. And there were still a lot of steps ahead.

As he opened the file on John Brown, she pulled away from the curb and said, "Where are we going? The apartment?"

"No. Let's grab a fast lunch someplace, then we'll head for Rikers Island.

"Now that I'm official, I'll be able to have a look at the records of who's been to see Brown. And that'll let you get started checking out his visitors."

DURING HIS CAREER as a prosecuting attorney, Trent had visited Rikers Island numerous times. Closing in on it now was making the fact that he was back in the D.A.'s Office seem more real.

Located in the East River, near the entrance of Bowery Bay, Rikers was accessible only by water or the bridge that connected the island to Queens.

The prison had been developed as a correctional facility in the 1930s—then had grown over the years, until at this point the island actually housed ten separate jails.

"This bridge wasn't built until the late seventies," he told Chelsea as they neared the guard station. "Before that, the only way over was by boat."

He stopped at the barrier and produced his newly acquired D.A.'s Office ID.

The guard punched something into his computer, then turned back toward the car with a suspicious expression and said, "Your name's not in the system."

"No, I guess it wouldn't be. I haven't had any reason to come here for a few years, but the D.A. gave me a special assignment just an hour or so ago—and I need some information from one of your detainees.

"I assume my name will go into the computer on Monday," he added when the man didn't look convinced. "But for the moment you could call Matthew

Blake. Confirm that I'm legit. As far as I know, he's in his office.''

"I'll do that. And what about her?'' He nodded toward Chelsea.

"She's assisting me.''

"See some photo ID?'' the guard said.

As she took her wallet from her purse, Trent started hoping Matthew wouldn't say he knew nothing about any "assistant.'' But there probably wasn't much risk of that.

Matt trusted him. And with Les Masson out of the picture, the D.A. was so desperate for help that he wouldn't likely worry about where an assistant had suddenly come from.

Chelsea handed over her driver's license and her RCI staff ID card; the guard studied them for a few seconds, then looked at her.

"What's this Risk Control International do?''

"Security,'' she told him.

He nodded, obviously satisfied. "Just take me a minute to call the D.A.''

Once the man had established they were kosher and they'd signed in, Trent drove the rest of the way across the bridge and headed for the main administration building.

"This place is enormous,'' Chelsea said.

"Uh-huh. The inmate pop runs around twelve thousand.''

"It's scary that there are that many criminals just in New York City.''

"What's really scary is the number still wandering around loose.''

She gazed out of the car again, then shook her head. "It's so depressing-looking.''

"Yeah, most prisons are."

He doubted Rikers was any more depressing-looking than the majority of the others, but there was absolutely *nothing* welcoming about it.

Not even the newest buildings—the two square monster structures of the punitive-segregation unit—would be described as anything other than formidable.

Their design was modern, but they afforded a perfect example of the architectural maxim "Form follows function."

Obviously, *their* function was to prevent anyone locked inside them from getting out.

"I assume I just wait here," Chelsea said once he'd parked in the admin building's lot.

"Yeah, we might have gotten you over the bridge, but they're pretty strict about who they let inside.

"And I'll probably be a while," he added, handing her Brown's file. "At least you'll have something to read while you wait, though."

As he climbed out of the car and started up the steps, he began wondering how Matthew would react if he knew what was really going on. It didn't take much effort to come up with a scenario. If Matthew had any inkling...

Telling himself the D.A. was too busy juggling cases to be thinking about much else, he opened the front door.

It was every bit as heavy as he remembered, and stepping from the bright sunshine into the gloom of the old brick building was just as he recalled it, too—like stepping from the real world into an Edvard Munch painting.

His first breath of the stale air brought back a hundred more memories, none of them pleasant.

He'd never found it hard to understand why so many of his classmates had gone into corporate law and worked in modern office towers.

He showed the guard at the desk his ID, signed in at this second checkpoint and walked through the weapons detector.

Then he approached the counter, provided his ID for inspection yet again and told this guard that he needed a list of all visits that had been made to John Raymond Brown. Prisoner number 03–713411.

EVEN WITH THE WINDOWS rolled down, the car was so hot that Chelsea finally decided enough was enough.

She stuck Trent's stack of case files—including John Brown's—into the trunk, then locked up and set off on a stroll around the parking lot.

Not that walking on hot asphalt with the sun blazing down was much of an improvement, but she'd always had trouble sitting still for too long and she'd definitely reached "too long."

Trent had been gone for well over an hour, which she assumed said something about how slowly the wheels of this particular bureaucracy turned.

But at least that had given her enough time to read through everything in the file on Brown's case. And then read through it again, even though that hadn't really been necessary.

Between what the kidnapper had told Trent and the additional bits she'd gleaned from Darlene, they'd already had a pretty clear picture of what had happened.

As for where things were going from here, the data in that file basically just confirmed what Trent had told her. Under normal circumstances, this would be an open-and-shut case, with a guilty verdict.

And that had her wondering how he was going to bungle it without raising suspicions about what he was up to.

There'd been so many other things to think about she hadn't spent any serious amount of time considering the question. But maybe it was one she could safely ignore.

Taking care of what happened in the courtroom was Trent's part of the job, not hers. He was the expert on trials, and if he knew how to win cases, then he had to know how to lose them, as well.

She glanced toward the admin building's entrance, not wanting to miss seeing him when he was through, and as she did, her peripheral vision caught a flash of light at the corner of the building.

It was just a little burst of brightness against the dirty brick. Head level. There and gone in the blink of an eye.

But she was certain she hadn't hallucinated it. So what was it?

Curiosity killed the cat. That was one of her mother's favorite sayings—but not one Chelsea had ever paid any attention to. And she wanted to know what that light had been.

Bending, she pretended to tighten the lace on her sneaker, assuming enough hair was falling across her face that nobody would be able to tell where she was looking, which was directly toward where the flash had been.

She saw nothing except the building, so she started in on sneaker number two.

Just as she was beginning to think she *had* been

hallucinating, there was a second flash. The same place as the first one. And this time she realized what it was.

Sunlight. Momentarily dancing on glass.

Glass. As in binoculars. Or a camera lens. A telephoto lens that brought objects up close and personal.

Could someone be watching her?

There was no one in sight, so if someone was hiding beside that building…

She could feel her adrenaline beginning to pump and her brain kicking into high.

She was on Rikers Island. People didn't freely come and go here, which meant it couldn't be just anyone in the world over there. It had to be someone with access. But who?

The possibility of a guard flitted through her mind.

That didn't seem likely, though. Why would a guard be hiding? Guards were like cops. They made a point of being highly visible—of being right there in someone's face, an obvious deterrent to whatever.

Yet if it wasn't a guard, then what the hell was going on?

For half a second she wished her Glock was clipped to her waistband instead of sitting in her apartment, back in Hartford. Then she told herself that the middle of a prison compound wasn't a good place even to *think* about drawing a gun.

But she'd be damned if she was simply going to pretend she hadn't noticed whoever that was.

After brushing some imaginary dirt off the toe of her sneaker, she stood up and casually began walking toward the corner of the building.

CHAPTER ELEVEN

TRENT HAD BEEN waiting for what felt like forever—more than long enough to decide that the prison's computer system had to be working at half the speed it used to. And it had always been slow.

Finally, however, the guard waved him over to the counter and handed him a printout, saying, "There you go. Visitors to prisoner 03–713411.

"Names, addresses, phone numbers and time of visit, up to and including yesterday."

"Thanks, I really appreciate this."

He folded the page and stuck it into the safety of his back pocket before turning and heading toward the door.

When he opened it, the brilliant sunshine blinded him for a moment. Then his vision returned and he spotted Chelsea.

She was walking along the edge of the parking lot, so he started after her, wondering why she'd be wandering around in the heat.

And then she was suddenly running.

He broke into a run himself and turned on the afterburners, now wondering what the hell was happening. But he'd barely gotten going before she disappeared around the corner of the building, still tearing along like a track star.

She yelled, "Wait!"

A second later, he heard the quiet *Spit! Spit! Spit!* of a gun with a silencer.

His heart began racing faster than his legs were, and he rounded the corner to discover Chelsea plastered against the building.

That sent his heart from top speed to dead stop. Her face was the color of ash.

She was standing, though. And he couldn't see any blood.

His heart started again. She hadn't been hit.

"Are you all right?" he demanded, moving closer and resting his hands solidly on her shoulders.

Just the warmth of her made him feel a little better.

She nodded and took a deep breath, finally saying, "Yes, I'm fine. But someone was shooting at me."

"I know. I heard." And he had to find out *who*.

He stepped back a foot—wanting another look to assure himself that she really was okay—then said, "Which way did he go?"

"Around the back of the building."

When he started to turn in that direction, Chelsea grabbed his arm, saying, "Trent, don't be insane. He's gone by now. And if he isn't, he's got a gun. And you haven't."

He thought about that for a second, then said, "Yeah, you're right."

His Beretta was in the trunk of the car, and there was a difference between playing cop and being a fool. But who the hell had been shooting at her?

When he asked that aloud, she said, "I have no idea. I noticed a couple of light flashes and started thinking someone might be watching me—through binoculars or a telephoto or something. So I started walking, wanting to get as close as I could before whoever it was realized I knew he was there.

"Then, the instant he did, he took off. And so did I. But he'd practically reached the back of the building by the time I turned the corner."

"So you didn't get a good look at him?"

"Are you kidding? He was shooting and I was trying to make myself an inch wide."

"Well, come on. We've got to report this."

She hesitated before saying, "Are you sure? They'd call the police, wouldn't they? And the police would start asking questions about why we're here. Trent, we don't want them poking around and finding out…"

He weighed her concern, then said, "I'm working for the D.A. That explains me. And we just stick with the 'assistant' story to explain you."

"I don't know…" she said uncertainly. "What one guard bought and what a bunch of cops would buy might be two different things. What if one of them called the D.A. and it started him thinking you've got a hidden agenda?"

"Well…" That was a possibility, but…

"Look," he continued at last. "I know the fellow in charge here. He's been chief warden longer than I've been a lawyer, and I don't expect he *will* bring in the police. At least, not until his men have had a shot at finding our guy. This is his domain and he's territorial."

Chelsea slowly rubbed her hands down her jeans, making him very aware of her hips.

He asked himself whether he was going crazy. He was thinking *those* sorts of thoughts about a woman who was probably in shock from being shot at?

This simply wasn't the time or place. Or the woman, for that matter.

Hadn't he resolved, mere hours ago, that he was simply not going to think about her that way?

Of course he had. Yet here he was, doing it again, and—

"It could easily waste hours," she said. "So I think maybe we should just—"

"Chelsea, whoever that was could have killed you."

Merely saying the words sent a chill down his spine—and her expression said that hearing them had sent one down hers, too. Because they were true. He might have come around that corner and found her dead.

Man, oh, man. Back when he'd accepted her offer of help, he'd realized there could be danger involved. Still, he hadn't thought she'd practically be taking bullets.

And if that had been this guy's objective…

He tried not to let his mind go any further along that line, yet it kept right on chugging ahead.

If that had been this guy's objective, he'd try again, unless they could stop him. And to do that, they had to learn his identity.

Was he someone on John Brown's "team"—for lack of a better way of putting it? Was the team onto the fact that he was trying to locate Amy?

Considering all the thought they'd put into their planning, it would certainly have occurred to them that he might do exactly that. So had they been keeping an eye on him?

Did they know where he was staying? That Chelsea was there with him?

Hell, maybe they were aware of every move the two of them had made. And had decided it would be a good idea to remove Chelsea from the picture.

Damn, if that was it…

"We can't just let this go," he said firmly. "If they find the guy, tell us who he is, turn him over to the police…"

She nodded. "I guess you're right."

He led the way to the entrance of the admin building, and by the time they were ushered into the chief warden's office Chelsea seemed pretty much back to normal.

In addition to all her other attributes, she was obviously resilient.

Trent rapidly explained to Andrew Platt that he was temporarily back in the D.A.'s Office and that he'd come to Rikers to get records of a detainee's visitors.

Then, not wanting to tell Andy any lies that might trip them up, he simply said that Chelsea was a friend, who'd come along because they'd been intending to head someplace else after leaving here.

If Andy didn't like the idea of Trent bringing his girlfriend to Rikers Island, he had the good grace not to say so. But the chief warden had always been a man of few words.

While Chelsea told him her story, Trent kept one eye on her and one on Andy, doing his best to read the man's reaction. However, his face revealed nothing other than interest in what Chelsea was saying.

Likely, after all the years he'd been here, not much was going to surprise him. Although Trent doubted there could have been *many* incidents of someone shooting at a civilian on Rikers.

When Chelsea finished, Andy said, "Can you describe the man?"

She shook her head. "Not very well. He had some sort of camouflage on his face and a black watch cap hiding his hair. Actually, he was dressed entirely in black."

"How does a guy with camouflage on his face go walking around Rikers?" Trent said.

The warden shook his head. "He doesn't. He must have slapped it on when he was already in hiding, and wiped it off the first moment he could. Same with the clothes. Could have had the black stuff in a backpack or something.

"Did you notice anything else about him?" Andy continued, looking at Chelsea once more.

"Well, he was about six feet tall. And from the way he moved I'd guess he was in his thirties. Definitely in good shape. But that's about all I had time to register.

"It was over so fast that I seriously doubt I could pick him out of a lineup."

The warden reached for his phone, connected with one of the guards on the bridge, and told him to triple-check the IDs of every male in his thirties who was leaving the island. And that if they saw anyone with traces of camouflage to detain him.

Enough time had passed that Trent figured the guy was already off Rikers. But there had to be a chance he was still here, lying low. Not wanting to make a move for a while. Fearing that someone else might have been close enough to hear the shots and was still watching for him. Or that Chelsea had a gun of her own and was searching for him.

After all, she'd probably surprised the hell out of him by chasing after him in the first place.

The warden finished talking to the bridge guard, then punched in another extension.

Five minutes later there were half a dozen other guards in his office. Uniformed but not carrying, of course. In prisons, weapons were kept in strategic locations for emergency situations. But guards working with inmates were never armed with guns. They had stun guns or Tasers and Mace-pepper spray. Nothing that would be lethal if it got turned on them.

Andy quickly briefed his men about what had happened, then said, "Go down and check out the area. I want those bullets. And if there's anything else that looks like it might be evidence, bag it.

"Kramer and Stott, you two follow the route the shooter took around the back of the building. See if there's a sign of where he went after he disappeared. And check that none of the doors in the vicinity is unlocked.

"Then have a good look around the grounds. If you come across anyone you think could be our guy, I want him in here."

Andy waited until the guards had left before saying, "Nobody gets on or off the island without an ID check at the bridge, so even if this jerk's long gone we've got a record of him.

"The only problem is, given the volume of traffic through here on a Sunday…"

"Roughly twelve thousand prisoners," Trent said, half to himself.

"Uh-huh," the warden agreed. "Which translates into a whole lot of weekend visitors."

"Any chance he could have gotten here by boat?" Chelsea asked.

"No. Rikers has its own harbor patrol."

Andy paused for a moment, and Trent thought he knew why. The Rikers harbor patrol had been one of the first units to respond to the September 11th tragedy.

Most of the men had died and, not surprisingly, the warden had taken that hard.

"Plus," he went on, "the guards walking the tower would spot a boat. So the guy definitely had to come across the bridge."

"Carrying a semiautomatic pistol," Chelsea said.

"Right. And that gets us straight to the heart of this. Because it seriously limits who he could be."

"It lets us rule out…?" Trent said.

"Everyone who signed into one of the buildings. Even our own people go through detectors, so nobody who entered a building was carrying. Which means that if my men don't find this guy we can do a computer search—one that will ID anyone who signed in at the bridge but didn't sign into a building."

"Sounds like a good idea," Trent said. There was a problem with it, though.

Andy didn't have the entire picture of what was going on here. Didn't know anything about John Brown's people, let alone how thorough they were.

So the warden wasn't thinking that their shooter could have actually gone in to visit a prisoner, leaving his gun in his car, and then come back out and targeted Chelsea.

He rapidly tried to gauge just how real a possibility that was.

First off, he hadn't decided to come to Rikers until after the D.A. had given him John Brown's file. That meant the shooter could only have known they were here if he'd been following them all morning.

There wasn't any question that he might have been doing that, but when they got to the bridge…

He wouldn't have been permitted to cross it unless he'd given the guard the name of a prisoner he was supposedly coming to visit.

Trent thought about that for a moment, imagining the shooter sitting in his car, near the entrance to the bridge, talking on a cell phone.

Considering the sort of people they were dealing with, if he hadn't happened to know someone currently on Rikers, there was little doubt that one of the boys in the 'hood could have supplied him with a name.

So far, the theory was holding. And all that was left was the issue of time frame.

It had taken ages to get that printout he'd wanted. Easily long enough for the shooter to have followed along to the parking lot, paid one of the prisoners or detainees a quick visit, then come back out to his car.

He'd have gotten his gun and the binoculars, or whatever he'd used to spy on Chelsea, from it. Then he'd have positioned himself and watched her. Waiting for an opportune moment, when she was alone in the lot, to close in on her.

But then she'd decided to take a walk, so he'd just hung in beside the building, still waiting for his chance.

When she'd spotted him, though…

Yeah, all those pieces *could* conceivably fit together. The scenario was a definite possibility.

As he turned his attention back to the moment, Chelsea was saying to Andy, "What about the guards who walk the towers? Do they have handguns as well as semiautomatic rifles?"

Trent cleared his throat and tried—unsuccessfully—to catch her eye.

He didn't want her making Andy suspect that she was anything other than his girlfriend. And he doubted the words *semiautomatic rifles* came rolling smoothly off the tongues of most women.

Or that most women knew exactly what standard-issue weapons were for perimeter guards.

Of course, most women hadn't completed each and every one of the RCI courses.

When he glanced at Andy, he felt even more uneasy. The warden definitely looked suspicious.

"Chelsea has no brothers," he said before she had a chance to ask something that would definitely give her away.

Like whether the Rikers guards were armed with Ruger Mini 14s or Colt Carbine AR–15s.

"So her father taught her a lot about guy things," he continued. "Guns. Sports."

Chelsea was eyeing him, clearly wondering why he was suddenly rambling on about her. Then her expression changed and he knew she'd clued in.

"I was a serious tomboy," she told Andy.

"And you wouldn't believe how much she knows about cars," Trent added. "Her father is Slick Everett."

"Really?" the warden said. "I used to be a big fan of his. Was sorry when he retired."

"It was time," Chelsea told him, while Trent congratulated himself on doing a good job of changing the subject.

But the next thing he knew, Andy was saying, "Getting back to business, were you suggesting it might have been one of my guards shooting at you?"

Chelsea gave him a smile that assured him she wouldn't dream of suggesting such a thing, and said, "No. As I told you, he was dressed in black, not a guard's uniform. I was just wondering if there were normally *some* handguns on the island."

Andy nodded. "The tower guards carry 9 mm Glocks. But they sure wouldn't lend one out to anyone."

Was that undeniably true? Or could John Brown's people have a Rikers guard on their payroll?

If so, he might have changed into black civvies, slapped on his camouflage and tried to kill Chelsea during his meal break.

Hell, at this point it seemed conceivable that Brown's team could have come up with just about any plan.

"'Course, if the guy's already left the island he's out of my jurisdiction," the warden was saying. "But we'd still have the computer search.

"And if it doesn't give us someone who came across the bridge but didn't actually visit anyone, then we can run a list of everyone who was here today. Staff on duty and all the visitors. The police can take it from there."

"Right," Trent said, but he knew just how much effort the police would put into finding the perp.

Chelsea hadn't been hurt and the trail would be ice-cold. They'd know that trying to identify the shooter would be like looking for the proverbial needle in the haystack. And they'd proceed accordingly.

"Do something for me right now?" he said to Andy.

"What?"

He took the printout from his pocket and handed it over. "This is the defendant I was checking on, but it only lists his visitors through yesterday... Could you find out if he had any today?"

"Sure."

Andy picked up his phone and barely ten minutes later a guard delivered the information he'd requested.

Obviously, Trent thought, watching Andy read this most recent data, the system worked a whole lot faster for the chief warden than for an attorney from the D.A.'s Office.

After he'd finished skimming the information, Andy slid the two sheets of paper across the desk to Trent, saying, "David Christopher Brown. John Raymond Brown's brother... Was here right at the start of visiting hours. Stayed fifteen minutes."

Trent focused on the first page, which contained the standard visitor info—name, address, et cetera.

The second page was headed *Criminal Record: David Christopher Brown,* and at the top were full-color mug shots.

He stared at them, wondering if he was looking at the face of a man who was part of John Brown's team. Then he began reading and barely stopped himself from saying *holy shit* right out loud.

Unless fate was playing a cruel hoax, the odds on finding Amy had just skyrocketed!

When he looked at the mug shots again, icy hatred began roiling inside him. Never mind part of John Brown's team. David Christopher had to be the guy who'd grabbed Amy.

"Sounds like he's as upstanding a character as John Raymond, huh?" Andy said.

Trent exhaled slowly, trying to calm down. Then, as casually as he could, he said, "Yeah, he sounds like a real winner."

"What?" Chelsea demanded, her tone telling him he'd completely failed at "casual."

Andy glanced at her curiously.

Trent shot her a look. This time, given the sheepish expression that flickered across her face, he knew she'd gotten the message immediately.

She was supposed to be his girlfriend, not someone interested in either John Raymond Brown *or* his brother.

TRENT WAS WALKING so fast that Chelsea could hardly keep up with him.

She wasn't exactly sure why he was in such a hurry, but there was little doubt it had something to do with that information the warden had given him about John Brown's brother, and she was dying to know precisely what the something was.

However, asking him would have to wait until there was no risk of being overheard. Which meant she had to be patient until they were out of the admin building.

As she followed him into the still-bright light of late afternoon, she glanced nervously to either side, not seriously expecting to see the man in black but aware she wouldn't be entirely surprised if she did. And the mere possibility sent a chill through her.

He'd provided her with her first-ever experience of being shot at—aside from RCI exercises that used dummy bullets—and she'd never been so terrified.

On the other hand, she wasn't dead. And as her father used to tell her, smart people learned from bad experiences.

From this one, she'd learned that sneaking up on someone who could well have a gun was incredibly stupid.

Filing that away in her mental book of *Life Lessons,* she took a couple of rapid steps to catch up with Trent and said, "Okay, tell me about David Christopher Brown."

Rather than doing that, he dug the pages from his pocket and let her see for herself.

She skimmed the first one, then turned to the second and focused on the mug shots. They bore enough similarity to the pictures in John Brown's file that nobody would doubt the two men were brothers.

Then she began reading David Christopher's record and her pulse was suddenly doing the mambo.

"Kidnapping!" she said as the word leaped off the paper at her. "He was once arrested for kidnapping!"

Which *surely* had to mean he was their man. The brains—whoever that was—had recruited David Christopher Brown to help his brother's cause by abducting Amy. Anything else would be simply too much of a coincidence.

And now that they knew who he was, they practically had him. Then he'd lead them to Amy.

A little choir stood up in her head and began singing the Hallelujah chorus.

"Strange how you ignored the string of auto thefts, the crimes he actually did his time for," Trent said. "Just zeroed right in on the charge that didn't stick. I did exactly the same thing."

She glanced at him, checking that he was intentionally trying to be droll, then said, "Gee, I wonder why we'd do that?

"Charges dropped," she added, gazing at the print-out again. "Lack of evidence?"

"I'd say the odds are about ninety-nine percent. I can check the details on my laptop when we get back to the car. See if he might have just turned out to be the wrong guy. But it's doubtful."

"So then he's the one who took Amy. The one who's been calling you," she said, keeping her gaze on Trent and hoping he wouldn't say he thought there was even a chance it had been anyone else.

She began to breathe more easily when he said, "It sure looks that way."

Glancing at his watch, he added, "It's a little past five, but I told him he had till nine to phone me. And since he doesn't have to be where Amy is until then, he might not leave for Boston for another hour or so.

"There has to be at least a chance of catching up with him at his apartment."

"You don't think he's *staying* in Boston then? Don't think he just drove down this morning to give his brother an update?"

"Could be. But... Hell, for all we know they've moved Amy and she's right here in New York now. And if she is, we've got an even better chance of catching up with him. I..."

She waited a couple of beats, then said, "What?"

"I guess..." He paused again and shook his head.

"I don't know," he went on at last. "I want to get to him so badly that... Well, I guess I'm just afraid that if I let my hopes rise they're only going to be dashed."

She wasn't sure what to say.

Although she'd been doing her best to think positively, in the back of her mind she was afraid, too. Regardless of what they did, there was still no guarantee they'd get Amy back. And the doubts and fears had to be so much worse for Trent.

"We're making real progress," she finally said.

"Yeah," he agreed, not sounding convinced.

"I know it seems as if Amy's been gone for an eternity," she pressed on. "But this only happened yesterday. And we've already learned who took her."

He nodded. "It *has* to be him, doesn't it? Yet I keep wondering if we could be jumping to the wrong conclusion. It just seems so damn obvious, though."

"That's because it *is* him. Trent, how could it not be? Everything adds up. So if we get to his place and find he *is* home—" She stopped there, not entirely sure what they'd do at that point.

"Either he'll agree to take me to her or I'll kill him," Trent said, so quietly she almost couldn't make out his words.

She managed to, though, and something in his tone made her believe he actually might make good on that threat. Which meant it would be better if she was the one with the gun.

"Well, let's get going," he said, starting off again.

Once they reached the parking lot, they took enough time for him to get his laptop from the trunk so he could run a search on David Brown's kidnapping charge.

"Just to be sure we're not adding things up wrong," he said, setting the computer on the hood of the car.

"I can hardly see for the sun," he muttered once he'd gotten started.

She anxiously waited while he typed some commands, doing his best to shade the computer screen with his hand.

Then her heart gave a crazy little jump when he said, "I was right. Charges dropped for lack of evidence."

"So he probably *was* guilty? And they just couldn't prove it?"

"I'd say that's got to be what happened. The police obviously figured he was their man or they wouldn't have charged him. Then they decided—or the D.A. decided—they didn't have enough to get a conviction.

"Happens all the time. Not as often with kidnappings as other crimes, but in this case the child was unharmed and the abductor was wearing a mask, so there was no positive ID."

"*Unharmed.* That's good news, isn't it?" she said softly.

Trent nodded again. Then he stashed his laptop away, took his gun from the trunk and put it in the glove compartment.

"You feel up to driving?" he said, glancing at her.

"Sure. But why?"

"Because I think someone was following us this morning."

"Oh?"

Her throat suddenly felt dry, even though, earlier, she'd been adding things up that way herself. How else would anyone have known they were here?

And whoever it had been, it was probably the same man who'd tried to kill her.

That thought almost made her shiver. But she was safe at the moment.

Still, she'd like to hear Trent's read, so she said,

"You figure it was whoever followed us that shot at me?"

When he met her gaze, she saw what looked like concern in his eyes. Or was that merely wishful thinking?

He was so worried about Amy that she doubted he'd have any concern to spare. And even if he did…

"It could have been," he said. "But regardless of that, you'd do a better job of losing a tail than me. So in case we spot one, you drive."

She took the keys and they climbed into the car.

The air inside it was practically sizzling, but by the time they'd crossed the bridge and were back in Queens the air conditioner had it feeling downright chilly.

"I haven't seen anyone," Trent said at last.

"Me, neither."

And she'd been checking the rearview mirror every ten seconds. If somebody *was* following them, he might be planning on shooting at her again. And if there was a next time she definitely wanted advance warning.

"So exactly where am I going?" she asked as they headed toward Manhattan.

The address they had for David Brown was on Elizabeth Street, but she didn't know where that was.

"Back to Little Italy," Trent said. "Elizabeth isn't far from where we were this morning."

She drove in silence for a few blocks before Trent said, "Maybe you should wait in the car while I see if Brown is home."

"What?" There was no way she intended to do that.

When she glanced over, Trent didn't look at her, just said, "You don't have a gun."

"It would make sense for *me* to carry yours."

"Oh?" This time, he *did* look.

"You're wearing a tucked-in shirt," she pointed out. "I'm wearing a loose T-shirt. Which of us can more easily conceal a gun?"

"I can untuck my shirt."

"I'm a better shot."

He looked at her a second time.

She shrugged and said, "A *lot* better. I've seen your course records."

CHAPTER TWELVE

THE CAR'S WINDOWS were closed and the air conditioner was blowing full blast.

Even so, the minute Chelsea turned onto Elizabeth Street, Trent could hear music booming out over the pavement.

"You think David Brown's the music lover?" she said when they realized the sound was emanating from his building.

"If he is, he sure won't hear us coming."

They drove slowly past the tenement, which looked much like the one they'd visited this morning. The one in which John Brown had resided prior to his arrest.

This morning, Trent reflected as they continued down the block in search of a place to park.

As Chelsea had said, Amy seemed to have been gone for an eternity, while in reality, this nightmare had only begun yesterday.

But it had been before noon yesterday. And if a kidnapped child wasn't recovered during the first twenty-four hours, the odds that she'd be returned safely began dropping fast.

He'd been trying not to think about that, but he knew it was a fact.

However, this wasn't a standard sort of kidnapping, so surely the standards didn't apply. Besides, they were getting so close to finding Amy that he could almost feel her in his arms.

"There's a space," Chelsea said, gesturing toward a very small one between two cars.

He couldn't have squeezed into it if he'd had three hours, but she deftly maneuvered the Mustang in.

Then, having won the argument about who should carry the gun, she reached past him and took his Beretta from the glove compartment, saying, "Just let me tuck this away before we get going."

He told himself not to watch as she leaned forward and pulled up the bottom of her T-shirt so she could stick the gun out of sight.

Himself didn't listen, though, and his gaze lingered on her back. Her skin was pale and creamy smooth. The kind of skin that begged to be caressed.

That, however, was exactly the sort of thought he kept trying not to entertain, so he forced it from his mind.

While she was pulling her T-shirt back down, he began to consider having another shot at convincing her she should wait in the car.

Before he'd decided one way or the other, though, she said, "Okay, let's go see if David Christopher is home."

She opened her door, the volume of the music jumped and she climbed out into the street—making it too late for discussion.

But he had to assume the effort would have been wasted, anyway. Once Chelsea Everett made up her mind about something, there didn't seem to be any changing it.

As she closed her door he got out from the passenger's side, thinking it was probably just as well that there were two of them. For all he knew, her help would prove invaluable.

If David Christopher Brown hadn't always been a tough customer, the stint he'd served in prison would undoubtedly have made him one. So having Chelsea with him...

He just wished he could stop picturing her with an ashen look of fear on her face. The one he'd seen when he'd come racing around the corner of that building and found her plastered against the bricks.

If anything awful happened to her, it would be because she *was* helping him.

If anything awful happened to her...

Keep the emotional dial set on numb, he reminded himself one more time.

Nothing awful was going to happen to her. Or to Amy. He had to believe that or he'd make himself crazy.

He focused his mind on the task at hand, aware that he'd be a lot happier if he had a better handle on how this upcoming scene was going to unfold.

Oh, they'd arrived at a plan for what they'd do if David Brown wasn't home. But if he answered the door they'd have to play things by ear.

There was no predicting how he'd react when he learned who they were—although trying to kill them would likely be high on his list of choices.

He wouldn't succeed, though. Not when they had the element of surprise on their side. And one way or another he was going to take them to Amy.

If convincing him required more than words...

Well, Trent might have been a lawyer before he became a father, but he cared more about his daughter than about all the laws in the country added together.

When they reached the foyer, they pulled the standard ploy of pressing random buzzers until somebody simply buzzed the door unlocked without asking who was there.

He'd never been sure whether the trick worked because there was always someone expecting a visitor or because the occasional person was just too bone lazy to bother asking.

In this instance, however, he didn't really care *why* it worked. Only that it did.

The inside of the apartment building—graffiti on the walls and stuffy, hot air—was as much like John Brown's as the exterior.

They climbed the stairs to the second floor, the temperature rising with each step they took, then walked along the hall and stopped outside the door of 217.

The music turned out to be coming from the end unit next door—an oversided apartment stretching from the front to the back of the building.

That made the layout unusual. Most tenements were basically the same, with a row of apartments down each side of the hallway and a window opening onto a fire escape at the end.

For a moment, he wondered whether this design had caused anyone a problem with the fire marshal's office. He didn't wonder for long, though. That music was too intrusive to let him keep a thought in his head for any length of time.

He could feel the beat vibrating through the soles of his sneakers—the volume so damn high that he doubted the neighbors would hear a gun firing over it.

While he was wishing that thought hadn't popped into his head, Chelsea shot him a nervous smile.

He gave her a thumbs-up, doing his best to look calm despite the way his heart was hammering.

Without stepping in front of the door, she reached over and pounded on it.

He held his breath.

There was no response.

She knocked even harder, this time shouting, "Mr. Brown? A mutual friend gave me your name."

Still nothing.

I don't think he's home, she mouthed into the noise.

Trent nodded, trying to ignore his disappointment.

But he'd desperately wanted the creep to be there. Wanted to get the confrontation over with. To get his daughter back.

Unfortunately, sooner-rather-than-later apparently wasn't going to happen.

He watched Chelsea try the door. Then, having established it was locked, she glanced either way down the deserted hall.

When she looked at him he nodded again, telling her to go for it.

She dug a set of picks from her purse and went to work on the lock—while he kept a watchful eye on the stairway.

Picking locks was one of the skills taught in an RCI course he hadn't taken. It was called Basic Technics, and ostensibly focused on methods for getting yourself out of sticky situations. But he remembered that the first time he'd read the course description he'd figured it would be more aptly named Basic Crime.

In addition to lock picking, it covered the how-tos

of hot-wiring vehicles and several other procedures that struck him as having a lot of potentially illegal applications.

As for why Chelsea would have a set of professional burglary tools in her purse, when he'd asked her she'd said it was because she was always locking herself out of her apartment.

He'd decided not to worry about whether he should buy that explanation. He had more than enough other things to worry about right now.

She caught his eye again, then turned the door handle. Three seconds later they were inside the apartment with the door locked behind them.

The place was a one-bedroom, and even hotter than the hallway had been. It was also a complete mess.

Every surface in the living room was covered with junk. Old tabloids, fast-food cartons and enough miscellaneous clutter that they could be looking through it for a long time.

He almost started to say that, but since the music from next door had the adjoining wall shaking, there was no point trying to talk.

In the bedroom, the bed was unmade and there seemed to be as many clothes—both a man's and a woman's—on the floor as in the closet.

The window was propped wide open with a stick and the "view" was the brick wall of the building on the far side of the alley. Beneath the window…

He touched Chelsea's arm to get her attention, then pointed at the blue plastic rope.

One end of it was securely tied to the legs of the room's old cast-iron radiator. The rest lay in a coil on the floor beneath it.

What's that for? he mouthed.

She eyed it for a moment. *Escape route?*
You mean out the window?
She nodded.
He looked at the rope again.

The apartment was only on the second floor, but he could understand someone not wanting to make even that much of a free fall. He sure wouldn't.

And the rope was long enough that it would probably get anyone using it to within a couple of feet of the pavement before the final drop. So if David Brown was worried about having to get out of there fast…

While Trent was wondering what sort of people Brown was prepared to escape from—whether his concern was other criminals or the police—Chelsea walked over to the bedside table and picked up a picture in a metal frame.

She flashed it at him so he could see that it was a five-by-eight snapshot of a woman with long dark hair, then she slid the picture out of the frame.

After turning it over, she motioned excitedly for him to come look.

To David. Love, Gloria was written on the back.

She tapped on the name Gloria and mouthed, *This could be the woman looking after Amy.*

But he hadn't needed her words. His heart had begun beating rapidly as soon as he'd read the inscription.

He'd hypothesized from the start that the woman might be the kidnapper's girlfriend. And maybe his hypothesis was right.

He stared at the photo, wishing he were psychic, wishing that merely gazing at the snapshot would tell

him whether this Gloria *was* the woman with Amy.
And if so, *exactly* where they were.

He was a long way from being psychic, however.
And for all he knew, Gloria was simply at the corner
store.

Logic said that *somebody* hadn't gone far. Not
leaving the window open the way it was.

Of course, they didn't know these folks. Maybe
that wasn't the sort of thing that concerned them. But
to be on the safe side, he and Chelsea had better not
waste any time. They needed to learn what they could
fast.

Because if Gloria *wasn't* the woman taking care of
Amy, she might arrive home any minute.

For that matter, they really didn't know whether
David Brown was en route to Boston or where he
was. And the last thing they wanted was him suddenly
appearing—the element of surprise on his side.

Chelsea stuck the picture back in its frame and
stuffed that into her purse.

Then she grabbed the tattered little phone-numbers
book sitting beside the phone and stashed it away,
too.

He didn't think taking things was a good idea—
they might as well leave a note announcing they'd
been in here. But he was hardly going to try debating
the issue via sign language, so he simply began rum-
maging through the dresser drawers while Chelsea
started in on the closet.

There was nothing of interest, and apparently she
hadn't turned anything up in the closet. She shot him
a disappointed glance, then gestured that she was going to check out the bathroom.

He headed into the living room, his frustration

growing as he looked through the junk on the end tables without uncovering anything even resembling a clue.

And then he hit pay dirt.

On the coffee table was a little pile of stuff—just a few scraps of paper and a single snapshot, but when he glanced at them his heart froze.

They were more than enough to tell him they'd come to the right conclusion.

David Christopher Brown was their man. Was *definitely* the one who'd grabbed Amy.

He was just about to go fetch Chelsea when the music abruptly quit.

The unexpected noiselessness was startling, and it gave him an edgy feeling that they should be getting out of there right now.

A minute later Chelsea walked into the living room and quietly asked, ''Find anything?''

''The mother lode.'' He handed her the bits and pieces, adding, ''Put these in your purse and let's hit the road.''

She must have developed the same sense of urgency he had, because she didn't even look to see what he'd given her, just stuck it all away and started across the room with him.

They were halfway to the door, when someone pounded on it and yelled, ''Police! Open up!''

''Oh, shit,'' he muttered.

''If we just keep quiet they might go away,'' Chelsea whispered.

''Yeah. Maybe.'' Or maybe not.

As he mentally began adding up how many laws he and Chelsea had broken in the past twenty minutes, the trickle of perspiration running down his back turned to ice water.

He might be prepared to do anything it took to get Amy back, but if he ended up in jail, it would be game over. And she'd would be dead.

He was in the midst of telling himself the worst possible thing he could do was panic, when a second man yelled, "Come on, Brown. We know you're in there. And we just want to ask some questions. About a couple of friends of yours. Cooperate and you can avoid a trip to the precinct."

They waited, barely breathing, for what seemed like an eternity—Trent desperately wishing the apartment looked out onto the street so they could see whether the cops had actually left.

Then, just when he'd started to think they'd dodged that particular bullet, the officers were back at the door, one of them saying, "Okay, Brown, the landlord gave us a pass key and we've got a warrant to search this place, so we're coming in."

"Oh, shit," he muttered again.

"What do we do?" Chelsea whispered.

"Well, we *don't* get ourselves arrested."

He grabbed her hand and they raced into the bedroom.

After checking that there were no cops lurking in the alley beneath the open window, he tossed the free end of the rope through it and said, "Go! Fast!"

She didn't hesitate a second, just grabbed the rope and climbed out.

When she was almost down to the pavement, he could hear someone inserting a key in the lock. As he scrambled over the windowsill, he heard the door opening.

He swore to himself, then began praying the cops didn't head straight into the bedroom.

The rope burned his hands some, and he hit the pavement hard enough to cause a bone-rattling jolt.

But he was still mobile. And they had to get clear away before one of those guys looked out and saw them.

They tore along the alley, skidding to a stop as they reached the street.

The car double-parked outside Brown's building might as well have had Unmarked Police Car written on it. But it was empty. The officers were still inside.

And thank heavens there was just one car. If there'd been more, it would have meant cops in the alley for sure. But since there were only two of them they'd stuck together—undoubtedly figuring that Brown could give them trouble.

"We're okay now," Chelsea said. "We just have to walk nonchalantly back to your car."

He started walking—as nonchalantly as he could, given that his heart was still pounding like crazy. For all he knew, one of those officers *had* looked out and seen them.

And if that had happened, both of them would come bursting onto the street any second and drag Chelsea and him away. Charge them with B and E.

Not to mention theft. He wasn't forgetting that she had some of David Brown's possessions in her purse. Along with those burglary tools. And there wouldn't be a chance that a couple of cops would believe she carried them because she kept locking herself out of her apartment.

"Don't look back," she murmured. "If they come out, we don't want to draw attention to ourselves."

"Right," he said. Then he concentrated on simply putting one foot in front of the other.

WHEN TRENT CLOSED the door of the safe house behind them, he had to resist the impulse to sag against the wall.

He'd never have believed that he'd be downright overjoyed to find himself back in this crummy little apartment. But the few minutes it had taken to drive from David Brown's place hadn't been nearly long enough to let his nerves recover.

And right this moment, "safe house" seemed like the perfect phrase. He felt as though he was in a veritable sanctuary.

"That bad, huh?" Chelsea said.

"I've had *better* days," he admitted. "And being a lawyer...well, I was just thinking we've been breaking a lot of laws."

He didn't add that it wasn't the first time the thought had lodged in his mind.

"I guess the total's getting to be pretty impressive."

It was a veritable record setter for him. But he didn't say that, either. And when he merely nodded, she eyed him with an expression of...

The right word wasn't coming, but he had the distinct feeling he must look as if he'd just worked a thousand hours straight in a sweatshop.

Deciding he'd better say something, he went with, "I never realized quite how stressful running from the cops is."

"The first time's the worst."

"Meaning?"

She shrugged. "I must have mentioned racing on

dirt ovals in Indiana? Before I had a driver's license? It's part of my standard opening for the driving course."

He nodded that he remembered.

"Well, the state troopers took a dim view of kids doing that. So I had to outrun them a few times."

"Ah," he said, wondering how he'd cope if his daughter turned into the sort of teenager Chelsea had apparently been.

Then he swallowed hard, trying not to contemplate the possibility that Amy might never see her teenage years.

He unclipped his cellular from his belt and set it down, reminding himself that he'd be talking to her soon. Then he'd be certain that she was still all right.

David Brown would phone before nine and...

Pausing mid thought, he reflected on how strange it seemed that he and Chelsea had been right there inside the kidnapper's apartment. Strange that they knew who he was and what he looked like.

If only they knew *where* he was. Where *Amy* was.

"Trent?" Chelsea said softly. "Are you sure you're okay?"

"Yeah, I just...I could use a beer. Want one?"

"Sure. And should I phone for a pizza or something?"

"Good idea." Not that he felt like eating, but missing meals wasn't smart at the best of times, let alone when your stress level was in the stratosphere.

As Chelsea pulled the phone book from its hiding place beneath the couch, he started for the kitchen, his mind back on what had happened at David Brown's.

Man, he'd just about gone into cardiac arrest when those cops had come banging on the door.

But it was hardly surprising that they'd scared the hell out of him. If they'd nailed him, he'd have been out of the D.A.'s Office and no earthly use to John Brown's people.

They hadn't nailed him, though. Which meant nothing had changed.

Even if he didn't have Amy safely back before Wednesday—which he was praying he would—he'd still be prosecuting Brown's case. And as long as he was, as long as he remained critical to the man's avoiding a prison term, Amy would be safe.

They just had to find her before he became uncritical. And surely they could do that. Then…

Well, he hadn't thought much about what would happen if they did. *When* they did, he corrected himself.

He hadn't decided whether he'd make sure John Brown got a nice long sentence and then go after the rest of them, or confess the whole story to Matthew and hope to hell he didn't end up disbarred or worse.

But there wasn't a lot of point in worrying about that just yet. He had to keep taking this one step at a time and see where each of them led.

He grabbed a couple of beers from the fridge and poured one into a glass for Chelsea, gradually starting to feel in control again.

Considering how far they'd come since yesterday, they were actually doing great. All they had to do was keep it up. And those things he'd found in Brown's place would give them some new leads.

If they needed them. If they didn't get dead lucky and David Brown led them to Amy.

Telling himself not to hope for too much, he headed back into the living room and said to Chelsea, "I really wish I had one more day. That I didn't have to report to the D.A.'s Office in the morning."

"Because?"

"Because now that we're sure David Brown's our guy and we know where he lives, the obvious thing to do is go back to his place and stake it out."

He sat down on the couch beside her and handed her the glass of beer, adding, "Then, if he *isn't* staying in Boston, if he comes home, all we'd have to do is tail him tomorrow. Eventually, he'll end up at that apartment again. Or wherever they have Amy now."

"Well, you *do* have to report in," Chelsea said. "But I can handle a stakeout. And tailing him.

"Only, if he *does* come home, I'll probably have to start following him tonight."

When he gave her a quizzical look, she said, "If he comes home I doubt he'll stay long. He'd notice his rope's hanging out the window—realize someone was in there and made a fast getaway. Which would make him pretty nervous."

"Yeah. It would." That had occurred to him, but there wasn't anything they could do about it.

"Besides," she continued, "the next-door neighbor must have known it was the cops who were there.

"I mean, don't you think that's why he turned off the music? Because he was looking out his front window when they arrived, and assumed they were coming to talk to him? Thought that someone had phoned in a noise complaint?"

He nodded. He'd figured it that way, too.

"And I'll bet," she added, "the neighbor was standing in the hall watching while they were knocking on Brown's door. So he'll tell Brown they were there looking for him—tell him about the passkey and warrant and all. And Brown won't stick around in case they come back.''

''Yeah, I suppose you're right.''

''I think I have to be. At any rate, I'll go back over there after he's phoned. Then, if he *does* show, I'll follow him when he leaves.''

''I'll go back with you.''

''Trent, there's no point in both of us spending hours in your car.''

''Well…we'll see,'' he said.

But he sure didn't intend to let her sit on a street in Little Italy by herself. Not when it might be for all night.

He didn't even like the idea of her tailing Brown on her own tomorrow, yet unless he could think of another option…

''Just in case he *doesn't* show,'' Chelsea said, reaching for her purse, ''we'd better establish what else we've got to go on.''

CHAPTER THIRTEEN

TRENT WATCHED CHELSEA spread the things they'd taken from the apartment out on the coffee table in front of them.

She put the picture of Gloria and the little telephone book to one side, the scraps of paper and the loose snapshot he'd found to the other.

The phone book, she'd told him, might prove to be a gold mine, given that it was full of names and numbers of people who knew David Brown.

Trent had a feeling, though, that trying to "mine" it would be slow and discouraging work.

"Trent?" Chelsea said, drawing his attention back to the moment.

"Do you know who this woman is?" she added, gesturing toward the snapshot.

"Uh-huh. It's Lizzie's mother."

He waited while she processed that.

"And David Brown has a picture of her because…*he's* the one who mugged her? To keep Lizzie from going to Boston with you?"

"Uh-huh. That's got to be the explanation. They live in two different worlds. The only conceivable reason he'd have that picture would be to ensure he'd recognize her."

"And Philly's only about eighty miles from here,"

Chelsea said slowly. "So he could have driven there, done the job and been back in no time."

She gazed at the photograph for another couple of seconds, then picked up the smaller of the bits of paper.

He held his breath while she read the two words scrawled on it.

When she glanced at him again, he could see she was feeling the same sort of excitement he had when he'd first seen them.

"Franklin. Boston," she said. "Do you think Franklin is somebody's name? Or a street name? Could it be where they have Amy?"

"That's almost too much to hope for, isn't it?" Even so, he hadn't been able to stop himself from hoping that *was* it.

"But…" She gazed at the scrap of paper once more. "It looks as if somebody tore this in half. And if there *had been* a first name or a street number in front of "Franklin," it would have been on the other part. So…?"

"I don't know," he said. "I couldn't find the other part. But the "Franklin" is certainly something to follow up on."

He set his beer on the coffee table, then headed over to the hall closet, where his suit was hanging. "I picked up a map of Boston before I headed to the conference yesterday," he told her.

After taking it from the pocket of his jacket, he spread it out on the little table by the kitchen and looked at the index.

"Holy guacamole," he muttered. "Ben Franklin must have been a popular guy in Bean Town.

"There are two listings for just plain Franklin and

three Franklin Streets. Plus a Franklin Place, a Franklin Hill, a Franklin Park and Franklin Field.''

''If he was just supposed to meet someone at a park or someplace, that's not going to help us,'' Chelsea said. ''But what about the streets and that Franklin Place? How many of them would be within a half hour of Faneuil Hall? Can you tell?''

He spent a minute checking coordinates, then said, ''Probably all but one.''

''Well, I'll knock on every door on every one of them if that's what it takes.''

He nodded, not wanting to think about how time-consuming knocking on every door would be. Or how many of the knocks would go unanswered.

As he wandered back to the couch, Chelsea picked up the other piece of paper and stared at it for a moment before she looked at him again.

''This address in Ridley. It's your address, isn't it? I recognize the street name from your file.''

He nodded.

'' 'Saturday morning,' '' she said, reading what was written beneath the address. '' 'Meet him outside at five.'

''So David Brown would most likely have gotten these instructions over the phone and jotted them down. And the way he's underlined the *five* a couple of times probably means he was warned not to be late.

''And the *him*... Do you think he was meeting whoever's behind all this?''

''I'm not sure, but it seems like a good guess. Getting their hands on Amy was crucial to their plan, so he'd have wanted to make sure that Brown didn't blow it.''

He took a swig of beer, then quickly filled her in on how he'd put a few other things together, explaining that even before he'd found David Brown's note he'd figured someone—which, given this, would actually have been two people—had been watching his house yesterday morning, wanting to be sure he did what they expected and walked Amy next door to Martha Wilson's.

"When I didn't," he concluded, "they followed me to your apartment building and, well, we both know the rest."

"Yes, we do." She slowly shook her head. "If only I hadn't decided to go with you."

Clearly, she still felt incredibly guilty, which started him wondering whether, deep down, he was still blaming her.

At the conscious, rational level, he'd worked his way through that, but subconsciously... Damn, he just didn't know how he *truly* felt.

Regardless of that, though, she looked so miserable he finally said, "Chelsea, if you hadn't decided to come along I'd have left Amy with Martha."

He took a deep breath, then made himself add, "And they'd have grabbed her from there. That was their original plan."

She met his gaze and held it for a long minute. Then she shook her head again.

"I shouldn't have taken my eyes off her for a second. You warned me, Trent. You—"

"I didn't tell you the real reason I was concerned, though. And there's a big difference between thinking you had to be careful she didn't wander off and...

"Well, obviously, there's no way of knowing what would have happened if I'd told you the whole story.

But they were determined to get her. One way or another.''

''And *I* let them,'' she whispered, staring at the coffee table.

He hesitated, warning himself he was treading on dangerous ground.

But he was sitting close enough to her that he could smell that enticing scent she wore.

Close enough that he could almost feel her emotions as if they were his own.

Or maybe they were just both hurting the same way. Both wanting so badly to make this end well but knowing it might not. And if it didn't...

That might be his *real* problem. Despite where he'd gotten to, consciously and rationally, if Amy died...

''Trent?'' Chelsea murmured.

''What?'' he said quietly.

''If I could take Amy's place, I would.''

''Yeah. I know.''

He told himself to move away from her. To at least look away. But he couldn't manage either.

And almost before he realized what was happening, he was doing the very same thing he'd done this morning. Wrapping his arms around her and pulling her close. Feeling her body heat seeping through his skin and into his bloodstream. Stroking her silky hair.

''I've never been involved in anything even remotely as awful as this before,'' she whispered. ''Let alone been responsible for it. And I just can't...''

He didn't need to hear the rest. He knew exactly how she felt. How could he not?

And it made him think that maybe the most intimate bond people could share wasn't love, but pain.

''It's going to turn out all right,'' he said against

the top of her head. "With even a little luck, by this time tomorrow…"

He couldn't make himself go on, was too afraid he'd jinx things if he did.

Normally, he didn't believe in jinxes, but right now he wasn't about to take any chances.

He began stroking her hair again, even though he was telling himself he shouldn't.

And then his cellular rang.

"That'll be David Brown," he said, his heart racing as he reached for the phone.

"Trent Harrison," he answered.

"What the hell do you think you're playing at?" the man virtually growled.

His blood froze. The last thing he wanted was Amy's kidnapper pissed off at him.

"You were in my apartment!"

"What?" he said, his heart thudding against his ribs now.

"Oh, Lord, what's wrong?" Chelsea whispered.

He couldn't do anything more than shake his head at her as he said, "Where on earth did you get an idea like—"

"Save the bull," Brown snapped. "I know you were there. Saw you with my own two eyes. You and that blond bitch.

"You gotta hell of a nerve. And if you ever wanna see your kid again, cut the crap and play by the rules. You show up at the D.A.'s tomorrow and stay right there. Don't be doing nothin' else.

"I told you how this is gonna work. My brother walks and you get the kid back. He doesn't and you never see her again. That's simple enough for even a lawyer to understand, ain't it?"

"Yes," he said as evenly as he could.

"Good. And don't think somebody won't be watching every move you make. Blondie, too."

"Okay." He waited, desperately wanting to talk to Amy but knowing he'd better be certain Brown had finished before he said a word about that.

"You sure you got it?" the man demanded.

"Yeah. I've got it."

He let a few beats go by, then said, "Is there anything else or are you putting my daughter on now?"

"Maybe I'm not gonna. Maybe you don't get to talk to her tonight."

His chest so tight he could barely breathe, he told himself he had no choice about where he went from there. He just couldn't let David Brown call the shots in this department.

Unless he talked to Amy, he had absolutely no way of knowing that she was still alive.

"I told you yesterday," he said. "If I don't talk to her I'll assume the worst. And act accordingly.

"If you don't put her on, your brother isn't walking anywhere but into Sing Sing. And I'll blow the whistle on you so fast you won't even hear it before the cops are at your door.

"And you're clear about how long people serve for kidnapping in this state, are you? Even if they haven't harmed their victims?"

He nervously waited through the long silence before Brown muttered, "I said *maybe* you didn't get to talk to her. But we made a deal, so I guess as long as you stop with the crap…"

"Consider it stopped."

"And everything else… Everything else stays the

same, right? You're still gonna keep your mouth shut after this is done.''

He exhaled slowly. He'd hoped playing that card would yank Brown's chain. David Christopher didn't want to spend the rest of his life in prison any more than his brother did.

''That was part of the deal,'' he said. ''I get Amy back and I keep quiet.''

'''And you 'member what I said's gonna happen if you don't.''

''Yes. I open my mouth and both Amy and I end up dead.''

''I got friends.''

''I know.''

''So even if I was in prison…''

''I know. Look, David, I only want my daughter. That's why I agreed to go along with this. And right now I just want to talk to her so I'm sure she's doing okay.''

There was another silence, then Brown said, ''Yeah, well, she's in the other room. Wait a sec.''

He covered the speaker holes in the phone with his hand and whispered to Chelsea, ''He knows we were in his apartment.''

''How could he know it was *us?*''

''He said he saw us.''

''But…'' She glanced at her watch. ''Then Amy's not in Boston anymore. They've moved her to Manhattan or someplace near by.

''He couldn't possibly have been anywhere near his place when we were and driven over two hundred miles by now.''

''Daddy?'' Amy said.

The sound of her voice sent relief rushing through him.

"Darling, I've been thinking about you all day," he said. "Every minute. And wondering if you're still in that same apartment," he added, praying she'd figure out a way to tell him where they'd taken her.

But she said, "Uh-huh, I am."

"You're sure?"

"Of course."

Of course. Stupid question. She'd have known if they'd moved her.

Hell, even if they'd drugged her, she'd have realized it was a different place when she woke up.

Dammit, nothing was making sense here.

"Daddy, I wanna come home. I really, really, wanna come home."

He could hear the tears in her voice; it made him feel like crying himself.

"I know, baby. And Chelsea and I are working our hardest to make that happen fast."

"How fast?"

The same question as last night, and he couldn't give her any better answer than he'd been able to then.

"Just as fast as we can," he said. "I miss you so much."

"I miss you, too. And I—"

"Tell him you're fine," he heard Brown interrupt.

"I'm fine," she said, her tone sullen.

"Now, give me the phone," Brown ordered.

BY THE TIME Chelsea had listened to Trent's replay of his entire conversation with David Brown, the pizza had arrived. And even though they ate quickly, it was almost nine-thirty when they finished.

Even so, that worried look she'd come to know so well was still in Trent's dark eyes.

She had no doubt about why.

Given that they'd decided whoever had shot at her must have followed them to Rikers Island, Brown probably hadn't been bluffing when he'd said someone would be watching them.

So they'd have to keep a careful lookout and make sure they ditched anyone who was.

Fortunately, one of the RCI courses covered spotting-and-losing surveillance. And she was pretty good at it. So now that they'd realized what they were up against in *that* area they should be okay.

Except…

She *had* been watching on the trip from Rikers to David Brown's apartment. And considering that both she and Trent were certain nobody had followed them…

Surely the *two* of them wouldn't have missed a tail. They simply weren't that hard to spot. Yet somehow, someone had known what they were up to.

And it hadn't been Brown. What he'd said about seeing them with his own eyes was a lie.

Unless he could fly like a superhero, he'd either been en route to Boston or already there while they were at his place. He only knew about it because he'd been told. So who? And how?

She gave the questions a little more thought, then said, "Trent?"

"Uh-huh?" He focused on her expectantly.

"I keep coming back to the theory that David

Brown's neighbor must have known we were in there. Because if he'd *only* known about the cops...

"Well, that rope hanging out the window wouldn't *have* to mean there was anyone else. Conceivably, they could have tossed it out the window while they were looking around. Just to say they'd noticed it.

"So I think the neighbor's *got* to have seen us. And either he has Brown's cellular number and phoned him, or Gloria came home and he told her the story. About the cops *and* a couple of civilians poking around. In which case, *she* called David.

"Of course, that would mean she *isn't* the woman looking after Amy."

When she didn't say anything more, Trent said, "I don't have any problem buying the neighbor theory. And I like it a whole lot more than the thought of an invisible man following us.

"But unless we can figure out how he could possibly have seen us breaking in..."

"Those apartment doors didn't have peepholes," she said unhappily. "And I don't suppose he can see through walls."

"Not likely. And if anyone had stuck his head out while you were picking that lock, I'd have seen him. I was keeping a very close eye on things."

She shook her head, saying, "My intuition's telling me the explanation is staring us straight in the face and we're just not seeing it. Maybe we've been thinking so hard for so long that our brains have run out of gas."

"I wouldn't be surprised."

They lapsed into a brief silence, then she said, "Maybe the neighbor was looking out his front window when we came into the building and... But how would he have known we were heading for Brown's apartment?''

When Trent merely shrugged, she said, ''There's got to be *something* we're missing. Maybe we should try putting ourselves in the guy's place and talking our way through what happened.''

''Okay. He has his music blasting, sees the cops pull up and shuts down the noise. Then he waits for them to come knocking on his door, but they don't. So he's curious about where they *did* go, and when he looks out into the hall he sees them at Brown's door.''

''Uh-huh,'' she said slowly. ''But you know what? I'll bet I was wrong earlier—when I said he was probably standing in the hall, watching while they banged on Brown's door.

''When I think about it again, that's just not realistic. If he'd as much as stuck his head out, they'd have told him to mind his own business and get back into his apartment. Wouldn't they?''

''Yeah, I'd say so.''

Good. Maybe their brains were back on track.

''And if that's where he was,'' she continued, ''he could easily have been looking out the back and seen us go down the rope.

''I mean, maybe he had no idea whether Brown was home or not. And if they're on even remotely friendly terms, he might have known about the escape route and been checking to see if Brown took off. Or he could simply have happened to look out.

''Either way, it's a plausible explanation, isn't it?''

Trent nodded. ''Yeah, it certainly could have happened that way. Then, as you said, either he phoned

Brown, or Gloria arrived home and he told *her* the story. Then *she* called our boy.

"If she lives with him and she's *not* the woman in that Boston apartment, I'll bet she's in contact with him all the time.

"And can easily get hold of him," he added thoughtfully.

Chelsea could feel her adrenaline starting to pump. "She might know the details of what's going on," she said. "Might know exactly where that apartment is."

"Maybe. Of course, we're talking a lot of *mights*. And even if we're guessing right, we don't know which of them phoned Brown. So, since it could have been the neighbor, we really can't rule Gloria out as the woman in Boston."

"I know, but we still have to go over to that apartment. Because we can't really rule her *in,* either.

"She could be at home right now. And even if she's not, all we need is one of them to show up.

"If it's Brown, then we've got him. End of story."

"Well, he won't be too fast about going back there. Not when he knows the cops are looking for him."

"But all we need is *one* of them," she said again. "If it's Gloria, we make her take us to him. And if she *doesn't* know exactly where he is, then she calls and says there's an emergency. Tells him he has to meet her someplace.

"Trent, if we can get to him, we'll force him to take us to Amy. And whether we get to him directly or through Gloria doesn't matter."

As her glance strayed to the Beretta, sitting on the coffee table, Trent said, "Man, if you'd told me a couple of days ago that I'd be planning to threaten some woman at gunpoint…''

She shrugged. ''We won't have to shoot her. We'll only have to convince her that we're willing to.''

''Yeah, right,'' was all he said—but his expression told her that he was back to contemplating how many laws they'd broken. And how many more they'd likely be breaking in the near future.

It made her think that a conscience wasn't always a good thing.

''If we're going to stake out the place,'' he said, raking his fingers through his hair, ''we have to get from here to there without being followed.''

''Piece of cake.''

He shot her a skeptical glance. ''And we can't be sitting outside the building in my Mustang. Whoever was following us this morning might decide to drive by.''

''No problem.''

She slid the phone book out from under the couch again, then glanced at her watch and said, ''If Brown has a heavy foot, he could easily do Boston to New York in less than three hours, so we'd better not waste any more time.

''Oh, and dig out one of your credit cards,'' she added.

TRENT CLIMBED INTO the passenger side of his car, wondering whether he'd have come up with a plan as simple yet as good as Chelsea's on his own.

That didn't really matter, though. The important thing was they had one that would allow them to observe David Brown's apartment without anyone knowing.

Hopefully, he thought as Chelsea backed out of the parking space, their surveillance would enable them to catch up with either David Brown or his girlfriend.

If it did, he should have Amy back before the night was through. If it didn't…

If it didn't, come tomorrow he'd be sitting in the D.A.'s Office, still worried sick. And Chelsea would be in Boston. Wandering up and down Franklin streets. Knocking on doors. Alone.

He reminded himself that she was competence personified. But even so…

He glanced over at her as she stopped the Mustang on the exit ramp of the safe-house parking garage— several yards before reaching the spot where the car would trigger the door's opening device.

"See you later," she said, giving him a smile.

It made him wish he could stay with her, in case someone *did* follow her. Someone who, no doubt, had a serious gun.

But this plan required two people doing two different things, so he had to get on with his.

Besides, she wasn't going to be in the slightest danger. Not that she'd intimated to him, at least.

He'd rather that final thought hadn't occurred to him. And he didn't like the fact that his definition of danger and hers were undoubtedly far apart. But hell, there wasn't anything about all this that he *did* like.

"Drive carefully," he said, climbing out of the car.

"I always do," she told him.

"And be careful when you get back, too. Underground parking garages and all."

He stopped himself before adding that they were hazardous places for women alone. She *knew* that.

"Trent, I'm still the one with the gun."

"Right."

He turned away and headed up the ramp toward the pedestrian-exit door.

There was no window in it, but if he partially opened it as Chelsea left the garage he'd be able to see whether anyone pulled out from the curb to follow her. If so, with any luck he'd get a good look at the guy. Or be able to read the license plate.

Once he was in position, Chelsea started forward again.

The overhead door began creaking open as the Mustang neared it, slowly revealing the night beyond.

When she stopped at street level, he pushed the metal door a bit, just enough so he could watch what was happening without being seen from the street.

She sat at the exit longer than necessary, ignoring a couple of breaks in the traffic that he knew she'd normally have taken advantage of.

But if there was someone waiting out there, they didn't want him to miss spotting her.

Finally, she pulled into the street and started slowly away. Fifty feet down the block, a car came to life, its headlights flicking on like two bright eyes opening.

He took a deep breath and focused every ounce of his attention on that car. A dark Ford Taurus. Late-model. Thousands and thousands of them in Manhattan.

But if he could just see the driver. And the plate.

"Bright lights, big city," he muttered in annoyance as the car drew closer.

There was so much glare on the windshield that the driver was nothing but a shadowy form behind the wheel.

The plate, though. Surely he could catch the number.

Of course, it might not do them any good. But on the other hand, it might.

Just when the car was passing him, a motorcycle zoomed up behind it and cut to the right, obscuring his view of the plate.

Dammit to hell.

He waited in utter frustration until the Taurus turned up the side street after Chelsea.

Then, telling himself the night wasn't over yet, he stepped out onto the sidewalk and hailed a cab.

CHAPTER FOURTEEN

"THERE YOU ARE, Mr. Harrison."

The kid in the car rental place handed Trent his paperwork and the keys.

"It's exactly what you asked for when you phoned. Dodge Caravan with tinted windows. Parked down toward the end of the lot—the only green van out there.

"If you bring it back after hours," he added, "just leave it locked and put the keys through that slot over there."

"Right. Thanks." He turned, then headed out and across the small lot to the van.

Compared with his Mustang, it was enormous. But that was okay. Since he and Chelsea could end up sitting in it for hours, they might as well be comfortable.

He peered through one of the side windows—or tried to, at least—and mentally awarded Chelsea points for knowing that a Caravan's rear windows were very darkly tinted. Telling whether anyone was sitting in back would be hard during the day, let alone at night.

After climbing into the driver's seat, he located the switch to turn off the overhead lights. He could do without them coming on the instant Chelsea opened the door.

Not that he really figured someone would be watching when she did, but they'd learned better than to take *any* chances.

As he started the engine and flicked on the headlights, he found himself imagining her saying, *Hands at three and nine o'clock.*

The first day of the course, part of what she'd worked on was correcting the bad driving habits her students had acquired over the years. And she hadn't liked his tendency to drive with only one hand on the wheel.

He pulled out onto West Houston, then headed down Varick, repeatedly checking the rearview mirror, even though he doubted it was a necessary precaution.

He was sure nobody had followed the cab he'd taken to the rental place. Whoever was watching them had been too busy following Chelsea.

Still, the nearer he got to the safe house, the higher his anxiety level rose.

But that was nothing more than a function of the entire damn situation, because there was little cause for concern when it came to this part of the plan.

She'd only driven to a nearby deli to pick up a few things in case they got the munchies, then had returned.

So by now, whoever was in that dark Taurus would be back at his post—parked near the exit from the garage and watching for the Mustang to reappear. Which meant he was nowhere near the side door, where Chelsea should already be waiting.

He'd put her cellular number into his phone's memory, and as he reached Moore Street he brought it up on the screen and pressed the call button.

She answered after half a ring.

"I'm almost there," he said.

"I'm ready."

He made one final visual check, then turned down the delivery lane beside the building.

There wasn't a soul in sight, and Chelsea was out the door and into the van in three seconds flat. She was still wearing her jeans but had changed into a black T-shirt he hadn't seen before, and had a black scarf wrapped around her head, completely hiding her pale hair.

He started off again. Then, as she set the brown paper bag down between the seats, he said, "You picked up some clothes at the deli?"

She ignored his attempt at humor. Or maybe it had been so weak that she hadn't realized he was joking.

Whichever, she merely said, "There was a little shop right next door still open. And it was either grab a few things or do a laundry. But did you have any trouble?"

"No. You?"

"Well, I assume you spotted the guy following me."

"Uh-huh. Unfortunately, I could hardly see him. And I didn't get the plate number."

"Me, neither. He stayed too far back."

When he glanced over, she was frowning.

"It probably wouldn't have helped us," he said. "The way they seem to have thought of everything, if we'd had the plates run, either they wouldn't have belonged to that car or it would have been stolen."

"I guess," she said. "I just hate missing out on *anything* that could conceivably give us an edge."

They drove the rest of the way to Elizabeth Street

in silence, then cruised slowly down it, checking that the cars lining the curb were unoccupied.

Even this late, the street was far from deserted. Two or three people minimum were sitting on just about every set of stairs.

The heat of the day had only faded, not disappeared, and the interiors of some of those apartments would still be too hot to tolerate.

At least the safe house, for all it wasn't much, had air-conditioning.

Trent found a place to park that would let them keep an eye on the entrance to Brown's building, then slid the power windows down a little before he cut the ignition.

The car was going to get stuffy, but if the windows were down *too* far, people would be able to see in.

He eyed the street again, thinking that none of the neighbors seemed at all interested in them.

So far so good.

As for the next step, they'd discussed their options earlier but hadn't reached a final decision.

Looking over at Chelsea, he said, ''What do you think? Should we phone Brown's apartment and see if anyone answers, or play it the other way?''

She glanced at her watch, saying, ''I'm leaning toward the other way.

''David can't have made it back from Boston yet, but we don't have a *whole* lot of time before he could conceivably show up. And if we phone and Gloria answers...

''Well, after the cops were here today—not to mention us—a hang-up would make her suspicious.

''Besides, there was an answering machine. So

even if she's home she might let the machine pick up. Then we'd still be left not knowing what's what.''

''Yeah, I guess you're right,'' he said.

And that meant they'd be going with option two, which involved a little trip down the alley that had been their escape route earlier. To check whether any lights were visible in Brown's apartment.

It there were, if it seemed that Gloria *was* home, then they'd have another decision to make. Whether they should try to get to her or wait and see if Brown showed.

''All right,'' Chelsea said. ''I'll be back in a couple of minutes.''

''What?''

He turned toward her. She'd taken him by surprise, although it was hardly the first time.

''I'm in disguise,'' she said, patting the scarf concealing her hair. ''You're not.''

''You call that a disguise?''

''It's better than nothing. At least I'm not wearing what I had on earlier.

''Besides, you haven't done the surveillance course. And I know how to fade into the darkness without anyone noticing me.''

A woman who looked like her? Alone at night in Little Italy and going unnoticed. Ha!

''*And* I've still got the gun,'' she added. ''So just in case there *is* any trouble—''

''Just in case there is, I should be with you.''

''Trent, if there's a problem you can't be involved. What if Gloria spotted you and knew who you were?''

''How would *that* be possible?''

She shrugged. ''Brown had a picture of Lizzie's

mother. So just because you didn't find any others it doesn't mean he didn't have one of you.

"Whereas we *know* they wouldn't have had one of me, because they probably weren't aware I even existed until you picked me up on Saturday morning."

"But—"

"Look, Gloria lives with a convicted felon. She's not going to be any Goody Two-shoes. But she *is* going to be ticked off that we were in her apartment.

"So for all we know, if she spotted you she'd take a shot at you. And people *do* call the cops when they hear gunfire. Even in Manhattan, right?"

"Well...yeah. Usually," he admitted.

"And if you had a run-in with the police it would mean the end of your stint in the D.A.'s Office. At which point you'd be no more use to John Brown's people."

And Amy would be no more use to them as a hostage.

Chelsea didn't say the words aloud, but they were like little ghosts hovering in the air between them.

He swore under his breath.

She was right. Whether he liked it or not.

"So I'll look after this," she added. "And if there's any trouble you take off and I'll phone you as soon as I can."

Oh, sure. There was a likely scenario. Take off and leave her there on her own. In the midst of *trouble.*

'You should probably get into the back seat," she said. "In case someone curious wanders by."

He nodded, thinking that the last time a woman had suggested he get into the back seat of a car...

Hell, it had been so many years ago that he couldn't even remember the details.

"I won't be long," she said, opening the door.

CHELSEA WALKED TOWARD the alley, consciously making both her long strides and the rest of her body language say she was *not* to be messed with.

That was a lesson she'd learned years before she'd become involved with RCI.

Her mother might wish she'd try harder not to "intimidate" men, as she put it, but she'd never suggested the way to go about it was by pretending she was fragile.

Quite possibly, that was only because it would have been so out of character. But whatever the reason, she always used to say, "If you don't look like a victim, the odds go way down that you'll be one."

Of course, her mother probably hadn't been thinking in terms of the sidewalks of New York—let alone at eleven-something on a steamy summer night, with eyes following her as she walked, strange shadows lurking and a faint buzz of menace in the air.

But regardless of what the circumstances were, it was always better to give the impression that someone who chose to tangle with her would regret it.

As she neared the corner of David Brown's building she glanced around. Nobody seemed to be watching her at this particular moment, so she quickly stepped into the alley and began counting her way along the second-story windows.

Some of them had light spilling from them; others didn't. Apartment 217 was in darkness.

Rats.

She could make out that the bedroom window was still propped open with its stick, although the rope had been pulled back inside.

That might mean Gloria had come home, but not necessarily. The cops could have hauled it up.

On the other hand, the lack of lights didn't say *for sure* that Gloria wasn't in there. Maybe she'd already gone to bed.

If so, did that mean she wasn't expecting David Brown to show? Knew he'd be staying in Boston tonight?

Answers to those questions would be nothing more than guesses, so she tried gazing at the window and willing Gloria to appear.

When that didn't work, she swallowed her disappointment about the dearth of answers and walked the rest of the way down the alley.

It dead-ended forty feet or so beyond the back of the building, as well as on the other side of it, forming a mostly enclosed quadrangle where several cars were parked.

Her eyes completely adjusted to the night now, she surveyed the entire space.

A sign informed her it was for tenants only, that cars parked illegally would be tagged and towed.

In the far corner, where the alley met the back wall of another building, stood a ragtag collection of trash cans. Stuffed to overflowing, with half their lids askew, they were obviously ready to be wheeled out to the street on the next collection day.

She headed along to the apartment building's metal rear door and tried it.

Locked. No keyhole on the outside. And she knew it would be securely barred on the inside. This *was* New York, after all.

Even though some of the tenants might be too lazy to check who was buzzing at the front door during the day, none of them would want anyone coming in the back way under cover of night.

Taking a final look around the area, she decided she was basically pleased with what she saw.

The only way Brown could get into his apartment through the back would be if someone inside opened this door for him, which didn't strike her as likely.

Besides, since the alley entrance was visible from where she and Trent were parked, the man couldn't go down it without their knowing.

Assured that there was no way they could miss him if he came home, she turned and started toward the alley again.

When she was about halfway along the back of the building, one of the trash can lids clattered to the pavement ahead of her.

She stopped dead and grabbed the Beretta from the waistband of her jeans.

Then, the gun heavy and solid in her hand, she stared at that small army of cans, her heart pounding and fear warning her there could be someone standing in those dark shadows with a gun of his own. Pointed at her.

She told herself that David Brown couldn't *possibly* have made it back from Boston this fast.

She could have, but not many people drove the way she did when she was in a hurry. So it was still too soon for him to be there.

Wasn't it?

THE TINTED GLASS might prevent people from seeing into the Caravan, but seeing out was no problem.

While Trent waited, he alternated between watching the street for anything suspicious and checking the corner of Brown's building.

Each time he did, he was hoping to see Chelsea coming out of that alley. And each time she wasn't there, he felt more uneasy.

No matter how many times he reminded himself she was an expert at self-defense, he kept coming back to the plain-and-simple fact that women were the physically weaker sex.

Well…all right, he had to admit there were exceptions to most rules. And that Chelsea was an exception to just about *every* rule. But even his awareness of that…

It simply didn't offset a lifetime of being taught there were situations…

Situations like this one. Where some guy with a gun could suddenly come at a woman alone in a dark alley. Or another *woman* with a gun, for that matter. As Chelsea had pointed out, Gloria wouldn't be any Goody Two-shoes.

He sat drumming his fingers on his thigh, resisting the urge to go see what was taking so long.

Aside from anything else, it was getting late enough that if he went searching for Chelsea he might miss seeing Brown. Which was the whole point of the exercise.

He made himself slowly scan the block once more. This time, when he looked in the direction of the alley again, Chelsea was in sight, walking rapidly toward him.

Seeing her sent a rush of relief through him.

As she neared the van, he slid the door open.

She glanced in either direction, then quickly climbed in.

He wanted to hug her.

Instead, he merely said, "Any trouble?"

"Only a cat knocking the lid off a garbage can. It just about scared me to death."

He smiled. "I didn't think *anything* could scare you."

"Oh, every now and then there's something."

There were a few beats of silence before she said, "It was black. Do you believe black cats are bad luck?"

"Uh-uh."

She looked as if she liked that answer.

"Hasn't been any sign of Brown," he told her.

"Well, there might not be. There aren't any lights on in the apartment, so Gloria probably isn't home. But I couldn't tell for sure."

"Either way, we don't have any choice except to wait, do we?"

She shook her head, then took his gun from her waistband and set it on the floor.

That done, she removed her scarf and combed her hair with her fingers.

Surreptitiously watching her, he could almost feel its silkiness. And that was enough to start him thinking about holding her soft body against his and combing his fingers slowly through her hair. About...

Neither the time nor the place.

Of course, that was something he'd told himself before. More than once. But this time he didn't add, *Nor the woman.*

Regardless of everything else, the longer they were together...

"Trent?" she said.

He focused on her, trying to banish those kind of

thoughts about her from his mind, which would be a hell of a lot easier to do if she wasn't so damn gorgeous.

"If Brown doesn't show, if I have to go to Boston in the morning, I should probably stay there, right? I mean, it doesn't make sense to waste time driving back and forth, does it? Not when it would be time I could spend looking for Amy."

He didn't reply for a moment, because he didn't know what to say.

She was right. They couldn't afford to waste a single minute that they could be looking for Amy. And yet...

He didn't want Chelsea off in Boston on her own. He wanted her with him, so he'd know she was safe. He wanted her with him because...

Heaven help him. With the horror of what had happened, how could he be feeling...

But he was.

"I *should* just stay there," she said again.

"Yes," he made himself say.

CHELSEA WAS HALF-ASLEEP and half-awake, trying to hold fast to a dream that was starting to slip away.

She didn't want to let that happen, because it was the best dream she'd ever had.

Someone was holding her, making her feel cozy and safe.

She lazily smoothed her hand across the bed. Only, she wasn't in a bed.

Curious. Waking up but not in a bed.

For half a second more, she lingered midway between sleeping and waking. Then reality pulled her over the line and she realized she was in the van.

Curled up against Trent and using his chest as a pillow.

Oh, Lord, how had that happened?

When she tried to sit up, he said, "It's okay. You're still tired. Just stay where you are."

Then he cuddled her back against him. Back against his solid, reassuring warmth, back to where she was breathing in his scent with every breath she took. To where she felt so hot and liquid that she must be practically melting.

This is dangerous, whispered a voice that she assumed belonged to her conscience.

She already *knew* it was dangerous, though.

Maybe she wasn't one of the world's most perceptive people when it came to the male-female thing, but she wasn't *entirely* clueless. And she had no doubt that with even the slightest encouragement, Trent would be doing a whole lot more than simply holding her.

Which meant she should sit up right this minute and not give him the impression that she was ready to ease on into something more.

Unfortunately, however, her willpower was at its weakest when she wasn't fully awake. And being in his arms was so incredibly nice that she really didn't want to move.

Not when he was making her feel…

She searched for the precise words to describe the "how," and when she found them it was downright frightening. Because he was making her feel as if he was the only man in the world for her. As if total bliss would be staying right where she was for the next hundred years.

Chemistry. Pheromones. She tried to tell herself that explained everything, but she knew it wasn't true.

Oh, the physical attraction was part of it. Absolutely. No denying that at all.

But what she felt for him was much more than mere animal lust. He was the kind of man...

The kind of man she'd never truly thought she'd find. But now she had.

So maybe there was really nothing wrong with being snuggled up here with him. Maybe nothing even remotely wrong.

Except for the complications.

Taking a long, slow breath, she did her best to chase the last of sleep's cobwebs from her mind.

Not only did she tend to wake up with her will-power in a weakened state, it always took her a while to start thinking clearly. And she had to think *very* clearly at the moment.

Because no matter how perfect it felt to have Trent's arms around her, no matter that he *seemed* to have forgiven her...

Well, considering the circumstances, their relationship—for lack of a better word—was a chimera that might well change shape at any second. And that meant the only smart thing to do just now, relationship-wise, was nothing.

This situation was already so convoluted that adding another complication would be downright foolish.

Regardless of how she felt about Trent.

Regardless of how he might be believing he felt about her.

Until everything had been fully resolved, until either they had Amy back or...

Uh-uh. She wasn't going there.

But trying to avoid thinking the thoughts didn't prevent them from lurking in the back of her mind. And one of them simply wouldn't stop pushing its way forward.

If she and Trent *didn't* get Amy back...

Well, she'd been through it ten dozen times before. This could all blow up in their faces at any second. And if they didn't get Amy back there'd be no Chelsea and Trent. Not ever. Wouldn't be the slightest possibility of it.

That put her in mind of a song from back before she was born—one her mother had on an old vinyl record.

There was a line in it about a taste of honey being worse than none at all. And she suspected that was true.

So not letting herself do something she might well come to regret was the only *rational* way to behave at the moment. Regardless of what her heart was saying.

"Hey," Trent murmured as she forced herself to sit up straight. "You might as well be comfortable."

"Thanks, but I'm awake now. And I shouldn't have fallen asleep in the first place. There I was, telling you I'm the big expert at surveillance, and—"

"It doesn't matter. You didn't miss anything."

"No David Brown," she said, even though she knew Trent would have wakened her in a flash if the man had appeared.

"Uh-uh. And it's almost four o'clock."

"Then the odds he's coming are about zero."

"Yeah. Unless he's a real night owl. Stayed in Boston until the bars closed or something."

"Which is when?"

"I don't really know."

"But you think we should wait awhile longer?" she said. "Just in case he still shows?"

Trent wearily shook his head.

"He's not coming. Hell, if I was him, if I knew that we'd been in his apartment today, knew the cops had been there, I wouldn't get within ten miles of the place. So what were we thinking?"

"That we had to give it a try," she said gently.

"Trent, we don't know him. Don't know how his mind works. And we couldn't take the chance on not being here in case he *did* come home.

"Or Gloria might have been here. Or arrived while we were waiting. We just didn't luck out, that's all. It doesn't mean the basic idea was bad."

"Yeah," he muttered.

She wanted to snuggle close again and try to comfort him. Wanted it so badly that she almost had to sit on her hands to stop herself from reaching for him.

But hadn't she just finished thinking this whole thing through again mere minutes ago? Hadn't she decided—

"I was hoping so damn hard it would all be over tonight," Trent said. "That we'd nail him and make him take us to Amy and... I was just hoping so damn hard."

"I know," she whispered. "We're still going to do it, though."

"Yeah," he said once more.

Then he started the engine and added, "But not tonight."

CHAPTER FIFTEEN

IT WAS WELL PAST FOUR by the time they'd driven back from David Brown's and left the van in the parking garage.

Chelsea switched on the light in the tiny hallway of the safe house, then wandered into the living room and sank onto the couch, too tired to bother with the light in there.

She watched Trent lock up behind them, thinking he looked even more worn out than she felt. And she knew there was no chance of his catching anything but a nap.

He had to be at the D.A.'s Office by eight. Apparently, Matthew Blake always met with his staff first thing on Monday mornings.

When he eased himself down beside her, she began thinking he'd be lucky to stay awake through that meeting, let alone be as alert as he'd like when he began seriously going through the case against John Brown. Began seriously trying to figure out how he could ensure the man walked.

But no, her brain was getting fuzzy. What he *actually* had to ensure, initially at least, was that whoever Brown's people had in the courtroom on Wednesday would believe the outcome was going to be a verdict of not guilty.

Wednesday. The word lingered in her mind, making her wonder exactly when she'd begun to believe that the case probably *would* come to trial. That they weren't going to succeed in finding Amy before it was scheduled to begin.

She reminded herself that they still had a couple of days until then. And Trent could probably drag the proceedings out if that became necessary.

But if they eventually ran out of time…

No. That simply couldn't happen. Because if John Brown beat the rap and they didn't have Amy back…

Well, they just couldn't trust those people to live up to their side of the bargain. Which meant they simply *had* to find her.

She mentally shook her head, aware she'd had those same thoughts ten thousand times before. And right now, she knew she was so tired that she should give up on trying to think at all.

Yet she just couldn't stop herself from speculating about how things would turn out if this *did* end up in the courtroom. What would the result be?

She didn't know.

Weeks seemed to have passed since Trent had mentioned the possibility of double-crossing Brown's people, but it had been only yesterday. And nothing had changed since then—not significantly enough that he'd dare take such a risk unless Amy was safe and sound.

So, most likely, he hadn't decided what he'd do if things came down to that particular wire.

She considered asking whether he had, then rejected the idea because there were more immediate concerns.

As she glanced toward the coffee table, at the little phone book she'd taken from David Brown's apartment, Trent said, "Do you think it's worth getting a little sleep?

"I guess it is," he added, answering the question before she could say a word. "We don't want you nodding off at the wheel on your way to Boston."

She'd never in a million years nod off at the wheel. But she merely said, "You know, I've been thinking that rather than starting for Boston right away, I'd be smarter to check out Brown's apartment again."

He gazed at her in the dimness of the room, waiting for her to go on as if he didn't even have the energy to ask her to elaborate.

"If Gloria *was* in there tonight," she continued, "I could catch her first thing. Before she goes anywhere."

"*Catch* her," he repeated.

She nodded. "It made perfect sense for us not to go knocking on the door late at night. Especially when we knew Brown might show up any minute.

"But if I go over there when you leave for the D.A.'s Office—"

"I don't know, Chelsea. It seems to me that—"

"No, wait. Think about what we were saying earlier. That Gloria *has* to be able to get in touch with David. And that if we can find *her,* then we can force her to lead us to *him.*

"So here's what I'm thinking. If you drove the Mustang to the D.A.'s Office, whoever's watching us would have to follow you—to make sure that's really where you were going. And while he was doing that, I could head back to the apartment.

"And?"

"Knock on her door. Since there's no peephole, even if the neighbor gave her a perfect description of me, it wouldn't be any use until she'd opened up. So I'd just have to convince her to do that. Then I'd make her go with me to wherever David—''

"You are *not* taking her hostage and then going after David Brown without me."

"But if I—"

"No," he said firmly. "Chelsea, he'll have a gun. Hell, Gloria probably has one."

"Well, she won't have for long."

"No," he said again. "If she's there, if you *do* get to her, call me and I'll come running. Because you are *not* going one against two with those people."

"But you'll be at the D.A.'s Office. And you have to—"

"*Nothing* is more important than helping you catch up to David Brown. I'll just say there's an emergency and leave.

"Okay?" he added when she said nothing.

"Yes. Okay," she agreed.

He was right. Going one against two wouldn't be the smartest thing.

Even though she could probably handle it, there was always a lot to be said for a level playing field.

"She might not be there," Trent said quietly. "In fact, since we didn't see any sign that she was…"

"I know." She glanced at the little phone book again. "If she isn't, then it's got to be worth contacting some of the people in that book. Maybe I can learn where she is from one of them."

Trent looked skeptical. "You really figure any of them would tell you? Assuming they even knew?"

"There's got to be a chance. And the more I imagine myself wandering around Boston, checking out those Franklin streets…

"I mean, if *you* had a kidnapped child in your apartment, would you answer the door to a stranger?"

He shook his head. "That occurred to me as a problem, too. But I guess I just couldn't think of a better plan.

"What you're saying makes sense, though. It *has* to be worth checking the apartment again.

"And if you come up empty, then calling people and maybe saying you're a friend of Gloria's..."

She nodded. "I'll have to see what sort of reactions I get, then play each call by ear."

"Right. It'll be just like everything else we've been doing."

He sounded so discouraged that she didn't think for a second before resting her hand on his.

Then he covered *her* hand with his free one, and she realized a little thought would have been wise.

Her brain might be half-asleep, along with the rest of her, but she'd hardly forgotten that allowing anything to happen between her and Trent would be incredibly foolish.

He could break her heart if she allowed things to go too far between them. Or maybe he *already* possessed that power.

She was afraid that was the case, because the way she felt about him...

But letting herself get onto that subject wasn't smart. What her heart felt, what her body wanted...

"Chelsea?" he said quietly.

She looked at him.

He was so obviously worn out that she could almost feel his exhaustion.

There were shadows under his eyes. He was in desperate need of a shave. Yet—still—he was the most desirable man she'd ever met.

She tried to look away but couldn't. His dark gaze was compelling. Full of longing. Full of…

Under different circumstances, the word would be *love*. Under these circumstances, the word was *danger*.

He took his hand from hers and trailed his knuckles down her cheek.

It almost made her cry. She didn't know why, but it did.

"It's been a long couple of days," he murmured.

She merely nodded, not sure she'd be able to put words together if she tried to speak. Every fiber of her being seemed completely focused on the warmth of his skin against hers.

It made her want to feel the warmth of his touch all over.

A taste of honey, an imaginary voice whispered.

Yes, she *knew* that. She knew what she *should* do.

The problem was, it wasn't what she *wanted* to do. Not at all.

Then he leaned closer, cupping her face between his hands, and gently touched her lips with his.

That was all it took to undo her resolve, to ignite her yearning for him. Merely the prelude to a kiss.

No longer caring what was wise or foolish, she wrapped her arms around his neck, deepening the kiss.

He made an animal noise in his throat. Then, his mouth not leaving hers, his tongue playing magical games, he eased her down onto the couch with him, running his hands hungrily to her hips and back up, sliding them beneath her T-shirt and quickly helping her out of it and off with her bra.

Slowly, he weighed the fullness of her breasts with his hands.

The throbbing ache that started between her legs almost made her moan.

She reached to unbutton his shirt; he began brushing his thumbs back and forth across her nipples.

That sent hot waves of longing rushing through her. Waves that did nothing to drown the ache.

They only made it more intense. Until it became almost painful. Until her lower body was moving against his, seeking relief.

She could feel how hard he was, that he wanted her as much as she wanted him. But as she slid her hands down to his zipper, he whispered, ''Chelsea, I don't have anything.''

Blessing her mother for insisting on those pills, she murmured, ''It's all right. I mean, I'm all right. Pills.''

She hesitated, hating the fact that sex had become so potentially risky, then made herself add, ''And annual blood tests. One of RCI's rules.''

''I haven't been with anyone since Sheila died,'' he told her. ''I'm okay.''

He lowered his head, then, and began suckling one of her nipples.

Her need for him skyrocketed and she couldn't keep from crying out with desire.

Then he started kissing his way downward, undoing her jeans and tugging them lower, his mouth trailing after them.

She was writhing with a white-hot craving now, her breathing nothing more than tiny gasps.

And when his tongue found the center of her desire she began to sob with need.

She couldn't think, was aware of nothing but the sensation of climaxing. Of completely losing control and whimpering like a confused child. Of feeling as if she'd die if this ended. And die if it didn't.

Then he was inside her, climaxing with her, making them one. Making her love him more than she'd known it was possible to love.

TRENT LAY on the couch with Chelsea snuggled to him, their body heat keeping them warm.

They were no longer breathing raggedly, and he realized they must have drowsed a little. While they had, early morning had crept into the room.

Prolonging the moment, he slowly inhaled the sweetly musky scent of sex—not quite able to believe that he was really here with her like this. Not quite able to believe that what had happened actually had. That he and this beautiful creature…

Unable to resist, he trailed his fingers down the soft skin of her stomach.

"Oh, Lord," she whispered. "Don't do that. I can't take any more."

He couldn't keep from smiling. Out of this horrible situation had come…

Dammit.

For a few brief minutes he'd almost not been thinking about why they were together. But a cold shroud of reality was already settling back around him.

Making a major effort to ignore it, he kissed her shoulder.

"That's nice," she murmured.

"Nice? Is that the best you can do?"

"Wonderful," she said sleepily. "Superb. Fantastic. Breathtaking."

Breathtaking. He liked that one the most. And he liked the fact that he literally *had* taken her breath away. Not with the kiss. But before.

However, "before" was gone. And now he was aware of a chill that told him reality intended to regain complete control.

After allowing himself another few seconds to relish the warmth of Chelsea's body, he checked his watch and reluctantly said, "I'd better get moving."

"Uh-huh. Me, too. And I guess either I go first or you'll have to crawl over me."

"I guess."

After he'd given her shoulder a second kiss, she shifted around so she could see his face and said, "Trent…I hope so much that I *do* get to Gloria."

"Me, too," he said.

Then he swore silently again, remembering something about Matthew's Monday meetings.

"I'll have to turn my phone off while I'm in that meeting this morning," he told her. "The D.A. has a rule about it. But it's going to kill me. I'll be imagining you getting my voice mail while you're holding Gloria at gunpoint."

"I'll cope."

"And I'll check for messages the first second I can."

He waited a few beats. Then, when she said nothing more, he forced himself to take his arms from around her.

As he watched her walk, naked, toward the bathroom, he grew hard with wanting her again. But there was nothing he could do about satisfying his desire right now. No matter how badly he wanted to.

FOR A MOMENT, Trent lingered at the apartment's door, eyeing Chelsea.

The way she'd responded when he'd kissed her goodbye, the way she'd clung to him, had told him she didn't want him to leave any more than he wanted to go.

But already she looked barely aware of him— seemed engrossed in going through that little phone book, choosing which names she'd try if it came to calling people.

She'd gone back to keeping herself busy so she wouldn't worry as much. That was his interpretation, at least, although maybe he was only projecting his own feelings.

He told himself to get going; his feet wouldn't move. Not in the direction they should. Because what he really wanted to do was walk back across the living room and take Chelsea in his arms again.

If he did that, though, he might *never* get out of here, so he reached for the door handle, saying, "I'll see you later."

She glanced up and nodded. "I'll call as soon as there's anything to tell you."

Man, she was playing this as coolly as he was trying to. When both of them knew they were actually playing with fire.

He thought about wishing her good luck, but didn't. It went without saying that he desperately wanted the day to go well. Was praying that if Gloria *did* have a gun…

Reminding himself Chelsea could take care of herself better than half a dozen other people combined, he said a final goodbye, then left the apartment and headed down to the parking garage, his thoughts returning, once more, to what had happened between them.

He'd loved his wife. And he'd truly believed that he'd never fall in love again. Yet, with Chelsea…

Was that really where things stood? In the midst of this horrible situation, with Amy gone, had he actually fallen in love?

Of course, he'd been half in love with Chelsea practically from the first moment he'd laid eyes on her.

But even so, the timing…

He was aware of a sharp sense of… Was guilt the right word? If not, it came close.

Yet how could making love with her have been wrong when they'd both wanted to so desperately?

As for the way he felt about her…

Well, feelings weren't things people could control. And as incredibly impossible as this might seem, considering the circumstances, he *was* in love with Chelsea.

That simply *had* to be it, because there was no other explanation for why merely looking at her made

him ache with desire. Or for why, when he was close
to her, he could barely think straight.

And knowing that something awful could happen
to her today…

He climbed into his car, aware he was an emotional
wreck and getting worse with each passing hour.

But he had to hang in. Had to concentrate on the
moment and try his hardest not to worry about either
Amy or Chelsea.

He was doing everything in his power to make this
mess turn out right. He was giving it one hundred
percent, and more wasn't possible. So he just had to
devote all his attention to the role he was playing and
try not to let thoughts about anything else throw him
off.

Once he'd driven out of the garage and onto the
street, he kept a close eye on the rearview mirror.

Sure enough, a dark Taurus pulled away from the
curb and started after him.

Good. Now there wasn't any chance that whoever
was watching them would see Chelsea leave in the
van—and suspect they hadn't actually stopped trying
to find Amy.

During the short drive to One Hogan Place, he kept
an eye on the rearview mirror. Then, after he'd
parked, he got out of the Mustang and stood beside
it, faking a call on his cell phone.

He glanced at his watch several times while he
spoke, to make it look as if he might be planning to
stay at the D.A.'s Office only briefly.

Chelsea couldn't go knocking on Gloria's door too

early. That would arouse the woman's suspicions and she'd be less likely to open up.

So the best thing he could do was make that guy who'd followed him decide he'd better stay right where he was, in case his quarry headed off somewhere. Then there'd be no way he'd try to check on what Chelsea might be doing.

Finally putting his phone away, he strode into the building. It was still well before eight o'clock, which meant he had time to settle into the office that belonged to Les Masson, the prosecutor who'd met with the "accident" yesterday.

Resisting the urge to pore over the material he had on John Brown one more time, he skimmed through some of the other case files Matthew had assigned him.

Because Brown's trial was slated to begin on Wednesday, his giving that case the bulk of his attention would be only natural. Still, he didn't want anyone getting the impression that he was concerned with it and only it. Even though that was the truth.

A few minutes before eight, he gathered up the files and headed to the conference room.

Some of the people already there—and some of those who gradually filed in after him—he knew. They'd been with the D.A.'s Office before he'd left.

A couple of them asked what he was doing back; he gave them the same story he'd given Matthew.

At exactly eight o'clock, the D.A. walked into the room and closed the door.

Things apparently hadn't changed, and anyone not

already present would be subjected to a black look when he or she arrived.

"'Morning," Matthew said.

As his staff members returned his greeting, he sat down at the head of the table.

Then he nodded toward Trent and said, "For those of you who haven't met him, this is Trent Harrison. He used to be on staff here, and he'll be with us for a good part of the summer.

"Now, aside from that there are a couple of other things I should get to right off. First of all, some of you may have heard that Les Masson is in the hospital.

"He was mugged," he elaborated when several people glanced at him expectantly.

"He's going to be okay, but he'll be off work for a while. Fortunately, with Trent on board, we're not going to be in as bad shape as we would have been without him.

"The other news is that we've got one less case on the go than we had Friday. This affects you," he added, focusing on Trent again.

CHELSEA SPENT the entire drive over to David Brown's trying to force her thoughts off the subject of Mr. Trent Harrison. But she simply wasn't able to.

How could she, when making love with him had been so amazing? How could she not remember the wonderful way he'd made her feel? Or contemplate feeling that way again?

She was so deeply in love with the man that her

mother was going to be the happiest woman in the world.

No, that wasn't right. Her mother was going to be the *second* happiest woman in the world.

She was going to be the happiest one. Just as soon as they got Amy back and everything was—

You're making a big assumption there.

She exhaled slowly, silently ordering that nasty imaginary voice to mind its own business.

Then she turned onto Brown's street and began looking for a parking space.

After she'd found one, she told herself that enough was enough. She had to stop thinking about anything to do with Trent and focus entirely on the task at hand.

When she figured she was psyched up enough to manage that, she got out of the van and began walking quickly toward Brown's building.

All she needed was Gloria to be home. Given that, this would go perfectly smoothly. No catches.

Since the apartment didn't overlook the street, Gloria couldn't possibly have any warning. And getting her to open the door shouldn't be tough.

After all, what woman wouldn't jump at an offer of a hundred-dollar gift certificate from Macy's just for answering a few questions about her shopping habits?

Of course, if Gloria *didn't* cooperate…

But she would. One way or another.

Her adrenaline pumping, she climbed the front steps, very aware of Trent's Beretta pressing against the small of her back.

As she reached the top of them a man hurried out,

so she didn't even have to bother with the pressing-random-buzzers trick.

Taking that as a good omen, she headed up the stairs and along to Brown's apartment.

She listened at the door for a minute, but there was no sound from inside. Nobody talking on the phone, no radio or television turned on.

Hoping that didn't mean Gloria wasn't there, she knocked.

Nothing.

She knocked again, waited, then started back down the stairs, trying to ignore her disappointment at the total lack of response.

There was still plan B. She'd sit with that phone book and call people until she connected with someone who'd tell her what she needed to know.

Trying not to let herself think that she was making another big assumption, she headed out to the street.

She was halfway to the van when her cellular rang.

CHAPTER SIXTEEN

CHELSEA TOOK HER PHONE from her purse and checked the screen.

The *caller ID blocked* message on it tempted her to let her voice mail pick up, but thinking it might be Trent wanting to tell her he'd gotten out of that meeting sooner than expected, she answered.

Then she swore under her breath when it turned out to be Shawn Madders.

Since Trent had told him they were an item, he certainly wasn't calling to ask her out. And she had a horrible feeling she wouldn't like whatever he *was* calling about.

Her suspicions were confirmed when he said, "What's going on with your friend Harrison?"

"What do you mean?" she asked, hoping she sounded merely curious. Not worried.

"He didn't really get his little girl back, did he?"

Her heart stopped for a second, then began to race as frantically as her thoughts.

"And the two of you have been trying to find her," he added.

Oh, Lord, what should she say?

Shawn might only be guessing, in which case denying everything would be the way to go.

But if he wasn't guessing, he'd know she was lying

to him. And that sure wouldn't make him feel inclined to help.

If that was what this call was about.

Maybe it wasn't, though. Thus far, he hadn't said a word to that effect.

She tried to recall exactly why Trent was adamant about telling him nothing.

Her brain had been into overload for so long now that it was hard to remember all of the details she'd filed away, but she finally managed to retrieve the ones she wanted.

Basically, he'd said that—because Shawn was a Fed—if he learned the truth then he'd be obliged to report what was going on.

Otherwise, if Trent got caught Shawn would end up in prison along with him. So if Shawn had discovered—

"All right, look," he said, interrupting her thoughts. "Here's where we are. I didn't buy Harrison's story about Amy escaping and I started asking around.

"I know he told me to butt out, but I've got a lot of contacts in low places and I figured...

"At any rate, one of them thinks he knows who grabbed her and where she's being kept."

Chelsea almost couldn't believe he'd said what she'd heard. But there was nothing wrong with her hearing so he must have.

She warned herself not to get too excited. Then warned herself to think a little more before she spoke.

Regardless of how much she wanted to believe what Shawn was saying, she couldn't simply ignore the possibility that he was only fishing for information. Just feeding her a line to see what she'd tell him. And if she admitted Amy *was* still gone...

Why would he do anything so horrid, though?

Surely he didn't take his job seriously enough that he'd stoop to entrapment with her. Not when all she and Trent were trying to do was get his daughter back unharmed.

And didn't that mean Shawn must really believe he knew where Amy was?

Of course, he might be intending to blow the whistle on them after they had her back. Insulate himself from the potential repercussions that way.

But she knew that Trent would do *anything* to get Amy back safely. Without regard for whatever consequences might result. And so would she.

Which meant there was only one way to go. Wasn't there?

Yes.

The single important thing was Amy's safety. Compared with that, nothing else mattered.

"Your contact," she said, desperately hoping she actually *was* doing the right thing. "When you said, he *thinks* he knows where Amy is, does that mean he thinks *maybe,* or..."

"He's pretty sure. *I'm* pretty sure, given what he told me. She's still right here in Boston. So I figured you and Harrison would want to drive up."

Boston! Yes! They *knew* she was still in Boston, and if Shawn's guy had told him exactly where, then they were practically home free.

Her hopes soaring, she said. "I'll get hold of Trent as quickly as I can. Where should we meet you?"

"Take Highway 93 east when it intersects with 95.

You'll see a McDonald's on your right a couple of miles beyond that. I'll wait for you there.''

"Okay."

"Oh, and there's something I should ask about. Back in Faneuil Hall? When we were just starting to search for Amy?''

"Yes?"

"I asked if you had your gun and you said that you'd left it in Hartford.''

"I had."

"Then, did you go home and get it before you headed to New York?''

"No."

"All right, I'll bring one for you. And what about Harrison? Can he handle a gun?''

"Yes, he's done the RCI training."

"Good. I'll bring one for him, too."

Before she could say that they had Trent's Beretta, Shawn clicked off.

TRENT HAD MANAGED to regain a reasonable degree of composure since Matthew had dropped his bombshell.

Oh, he was still sick with fear, but was no longer on the edge of panic—not the way he'd been immediately after he'd learned that John Brown was dead.

At that point, he'd needed every bit of his willpower simply to remain in the conference room. And he'd felt so ill that he'd barely kept from throwing up.

But he'd been right not to go charging out of here. At least he'd known better than to do that. Had realized that until he pulled himself together, anything he did might prove to be the wrong thing.

Besides, he hadn't been able to figure out where he'd go if he *did* leave. And that had been a pretty good indicator that he'd damn well better just sit tight for the moment. No matter how tough it was.

By now, though, he'd had time to recover from his initial shock. To get his brain working more or less properly again. To reassess the situation and see that he and Chelsea still had a chance.

Only, now they were *really* racing against time.

But maybe she'd gotten to Gloria. She could be with the woman right now, holding her at gunpoint and waiting for him to call. And David Brown might not have even heard the news yet, let alone decided what he was going to do.

Actually, the more Trent thought about that, the more likely it seemed.

After all, Brown wasn't at home, couldn't be reached there. And he'd hardly have given his cellular number out to anyone on staff at Rikers Island.

But there were so many maybes. So many uncertainties. And the stakes were so damn high.

Life or death.

Amy's life or death.

He began willing Matthew to wrap up the meeting and—almost like magic—it was over.

After brushing off a couple of people who wanted to stand around and chat, he raced back to Les Masson's office and shut the door. Then he took his cell phone from the drawer he'd left it in and checked his voice mail, praying there'd be a message from Chelsea saying she *had* gotten to Gloria.

If she had, there really was still a chance. A hostage would give them a trump card to play. Otherwise…

No. Contemplating the otherwise would only make him crazy.

But he *did* have a message from Chelsea. And there was such an excited tone to her greeting that the news just had to be good.

Man, oh, man, could he use some good news.

He held his breath and listened.

"Shawn Madders called me," she said. "And he's pretty sure he knows where Amy is. So we're going to meet him in Boston."

He's pretty sure he knows where Amy is!

Those had to be the sweetest words he'd ever heard. As long as they weren't coming too late.

"But I'm assuming that the guy in the Taurus is watching the D.A.'s Office," the message continued. "So I don't want to go anywhere near it. And you should probably take a back way out and grab a taxi.

"I'll wait for you on East Houston. Just before the north ramp onto F.D.R. Drive."

Right. A back way and a taxi.

Good thing she'd thought of that, because he hadn't. Which said that he might have been deluding himself when he'd decided his brain was back to working more or less properly.

He spent a precious minute telling the receptionist he was going out to interview a witness. Then he checked Centre Street from one of the windows overlooking it.

Sure enough, the Taurus was parked where it had been earlier. And he could see there was someone in the driver's seat.

Perfect. He was safe on that front.

He headed out the rear of the building and hailed a cab, telling himself they'd be in Boston in not much more than a couple of hours. And that nothing would have happened to Amy by then. They *did* have enough time left.

Not until the taxi had almost reached East Houston was he struck by the sense that something wasn't adding up.

By the time he spotted the rental van, his anxiety level was back to where it had been immediately after Matthew had dropped the news about John Brown. Bordering on panic.

He paid the cabbie and strode over to the van.

Chelsea shot him a smile as he climbed in. He tried to smile back, but her expression said she could tell how upset he was.

"I thought you'd look a lot happier," she said. "What's wrong?"

He took a slow, deep breath, which did absolutely nothing to help him, then said, "John Brown is dead."

She simply stared at him. As if she couldn't make his words compute.

"He was killed early this morning. On Rikers. Stabbed to death by one of the other detainees."

"Oh, my Lord," she whispered.

"So they don't need me anymore," he forced himself to say. "And they don't need Amy. Unless Madders really does know where she is, and we can reach her fast enough…"

"Oh, Trent," she murmured, taking his hands in hers. "She's still all right. I'm certain she is. I can feel it in my bones. But let's get going."

She released his hands and started the van, then took off so fast the tires screeched.

"There's something else," he said.

"What?"

"Tell me exactly what Madders had to say when he phoned."

He listened while she recounted the conversation.

"That's it?" he asked when she'd finished.

"Yes. We didn't talk for long."

"And he didn't say *why* he was inviting us along?"

"Well, no. But it's obvious, isn't it? I mean, you're Amy's father and—"

"I'm also a civilian. You are, too. So why is a Fed who's going to confront a criminal involving us? Cooling his heels and not taking any action until we get there?

"Why wouldn't he handle it on his own? Save the day? Be a lone hero?"

Chelsea glanced uncertainly across the car. "I didn't think about it from that angle. But..."

She focused on the traffic once more and slowly said, "Okay, let's figure out why."

He waited through a minute that seemed like an hour, then said, "How much does he know?

"I mean, did he really just randomly ask around or did he put together my suddenly being back in the D.A.'s Office and the kidnapping? Did he learn about the plot to get John Brown off? And does he know Brown's dead?"

"Trent, I haven't got answers to any of those questions. I told you everything he said. And it was literally nothing more than that he'd asked around and come up lucky.

"But getting back to why he might have decided to involve us—do you remember what he told you on Saturday? When you refused to call the police?"

"No. Not really." A lot of his memory of Saturday was nothing more than a fog.

"Well, he said that if you wouldn't contact the authorities, then he couldn't help you. Not *officially*. But he was willing to help you *unofficially*.

"Even after you went storming out of that bar, after you'd told both of us to just leave you alone, he was still prepared to help. He said I should call him if you had a change of heart.

"So…well, he obviously decided to see if he could do something whether you wanted him to or not. But it would have been unofficially. And now that he's taking on David Brown…"

She glanced across the car again. "My best guess is that he called partly because he realized how much we'd want to be involved. And partly because he figures he might be glad of backup. Which would explain why he's bringing guns for us."

Trent considered that. It sounded logical. And it wasn't hard to buy that someone would want Chelsea as their backup. Yet…

"What are you thinking?" she asked.

He merely shook his head. He was probably being totally paranoid. Still…

"I'm just wondering," he said at last, "if his running into you in Faneuil Hall was more than a coincidence."

"You think *he* could have had a role in all of this?"

Her incredulous tone told him what *she* thought about that possibility.

"I guess it's not very likely, but…"

"Trent, aside from anything else, if he wasn't on our side he'd hardly be bringing guns for us."

"Yeah. Yeah, that's a good point."

They sped along for a few miles in silence, Trent telling himself that totally paranoid definitely summed things up. But he couldn't stop thinking how seldom people just happened to run into someone they knew in a city the size of Boston.

Finally, he said, "You didn't mention the Beretta, huh?"

"No. I was going to, but he clicked off."

"And you've got it where?"

"In my purse."

"Then humor me, okay? Don't say anything to him about having it."

As PROMISED, Shawn was waiting for Chelsea and Trent at the McDonald's on the outskirts of Boston.

Like Trent, he was wearing a suit, despite the heat. That made her think that, also like Trent, he'd left work for this.

He walked rapidly out of the restaurant, virtually the moment she'd parked, and in lieu of a greeting asked if she'd mind driving.

"Of course not," she said.

"Good, because I already told the manager I'd be leaving my car here for a little while. There's no sense in taking two vehicles."

She looked at Trent, imagining he must be thinking exactly what she was. That with any luck, this ordeal would be over in only "a little while."

They got into the van again and Shawn climbed in the back.

He gave her some preliminary directions. Then, while she was pulling out of the lot, he produced two standard police-issue Glocks—equipped with silencers—and set them down on the floor between the front seats.

"Why the silencers?" she asked.

"The apartment where they have Amy is in a pretty rough part of town. The kind of neighborhood where, when people hear shots, half a dozen cowboys grab their own guns and go looking to see whether they can get in on the action. And if this gets nasty, we're not going to want any extra complications."

She nodded; Trent turned around in his seat and said, "Before we go any further, I want to thank you. You've really gone out of your way to help, and considering I'm virtually a stranger to you... Well, thanks."

She checked the rearview mirror in time to see Shawn shrug. "All I did was talk to people. And fortunately, special agents can usually find the right people to talk to."

"So...do you know the whole story or...?"

"Don't ask me *anything* about what I know, okay?"

"Yeah. Sure. That's fair enough."

"And once you have Amy back, just forget I played any part in this."

"You've got it."

Trent started to turn back toward the front, then stopped and focused on Shawn again. "How certain are you that your information's right? That Amy will be where we're going."

"She'll be there."

Chelsea shot Trent a reassuring look.

Shawn wouldn't say he was certain if he wasn't. Which meant that barring anything terrible and unexpected, there *was* going to be a happy ending to this. And they'd almost reached it.

That thought made her feel better than anything else in the world could have.

"OKAY," Madders said to Chelsea. "It's the next street. A right turn."

Trent reached down for one of the Glocks, thinking that Madders hadn't exaggerated about the neighborhood. It rivaled the worst slums in Manhattan.

Once she'd made the turn, he pointed to a tenement and said, "That's it. Find a place to park and we'll go in."

"Just like that?" she said.

"Uh-huh. With a hostage to consider, especially a child, we don't want to start playing games. Our best bet is to be straightforward. Knock on the door, see what response we get, then take things from there."

"Do you know who's inside with Amy?" Trent said.

"You aren't asking *anything* about how much I know, remember?"

"Yeah. Sorry."

Of course, he'd only asked because he'd been hoping their Fed would tell him it was Gloria.

Since there'd been absolutely no sign of her in New York, he was back to thinking she well might be the woman here.

And he'd a million times rather it was her with Amy than David Brown. As sexist as it might be, he had no trouble imagining a guy with Brown's rap sheet grabbing a child and putting a gun to her head. Whereas a woman…

Not that *all* women would be kinder to children, but the odds had to be better.

At any rate, they'd know who was in there the minute the door opened.

As Chelsea wheeled into a parking space, his adrenaline began pumping so hard that he felt as if his arteries were about to explode.

Doing his best to ignore the feeling, he stuck the Glock into his waistband.

The silencer made it awkward, but his suit jacket would pretty much hide even the bulky gun. When it came to Chelsea, however, there'd be an obvious bulge beneath her T-shirt.

But she easily took care of the problem.

Once they'd gotten out of the van, she slung the strap of her purse over her shoulder and cleverly positioned the purse to conceal the bulge.

"Keep your weapons out of sight unless we need them," Madders said. "I'll draw mine, and that's all it should take."

As they started off, Trent's heart was pounding loudly enough that the sound echoed in his ears. If things didn't go right…

But after they'd gotten this far they simply *had* to go right.

He began repeating that like a mantra as they climbed the steps.

The front door was standing half-open—not even the pretense of concern about security here—and the stale air inside was hot and heavy. It started him sweating even harder than he already was.

He could feel a serious stream of perspiration running down his back as they followed Madders up two flights of stairs.

The Fed stopped on the third floor and silently pointed at one of the apartment doors. Then he reached under his jacket, produced his own gun and began moving forward.

Trent glanced at Chelsea, catching her gaze for a moment and seeing his own tension and fears mirrored in her eyes.

If this *didn't* go right, nothing they'd done thus far would count for squat. And Amy would be dead.

They headed along the hallway after Madders, Trent's gut aching and his chest burning as if it were on fire.

Then their Fed stopped walking and the fiery sensation turned to ice.

He wanted Madders to knock on that door but was terrified of what would happen after he did.

"Only another minute or so," Chelsea whispered.

He glanced at her again.

She tried to smile. She didn't even come close.

His gaze returned to Madders. He watched as the man raised his fist, listened to the solid sound of it banging against the worn wood.

"Yeah?" a voice called.

A man's voice. Undoubtedly David Brown's. The tension and fears grew even harder to bear.

The door opened a crack.

Quick as lightning, Madders slammed it fully ajar.

He barreled into the apartment, and even though Chelsea and Trent were right behind him, Madders had the man backed up against a wall with the gun aimed at the center of his chest by the time they were inside.

Another gun was lying on the floor nearby.

Thinking that Madders must have knocked it out of the guy's hand, Trent focused on the man.

He *was* David Brown. Looking just like those mug shots the warden's people on Rikers had provided.

But where was Amy? The tiny kitchen was empty, the doors to both the bedroom and bathroom were open and there didn't seem to be anyone in there except Brown.

As he tried to swallow his fear that his baby was lying dead someplace, Madders said, "Chelsea, would you pick up that gun and give it to me."

Sticking it into his jacket pocket, he added, "And would you shut the door and lock it."

While she quickly did that, he said to Brown, "Where's the kid?"

"She's not here."

"What do you mean? Where the hell is she?"

Brown's gaze flickered away from Madders and fresh fear seized Trent. Something was very wrong with this picture.

He was good at reading people. It was a skill honed by years in courtrooms. And David Brown wasn't happy, but he wasn't afraid, either.

A man with a gun pointed straight at him. Not afraid?

"Okay, let's try this again," Madders said. "Exactly where is the kid?"

His eyes back on the special agent, Brown muttered, "Gloria took her out. She said it wasn't right that she should be here when—"

"Wait a minute," Chelsea interrupted.

Trent looked at her.

She had her Glock trained on the other two men.

"Shawn, I've got a bad feeling here," she said.

"So I want to ask a couple of questions before we go any further."

Madders turned toward her. His gun was aimed at her now, and there was an ugly expression on his face.

"Do you," he said.

Trent's heart was pounding in his ears again.

"Well, before you ask them," Madders continued, "there's something you should know.

"Those Glocks are loaded with blanks."

CHAPTER SEVENTEEN

CHELSEA HAD NEVER BEEN as frightened in her life. Even being used for target practice on Rikers Island was nothing compared with staring at the little black hole in the business end of Shawn Madders's gun.

The silencer somehow made it seem even more deadly, and her fear was only exacerbated by her shock that Shawn was involved in this up to his ears. In fact, given the other players, she had no doubt that *he* was the brains behind the entire plan.

A shiver ran up her spine as she thought it was too bad they hadn't realized that sooner. Because now, unless they were either awfully lucky or awfully clever, she and Trent weren't going to see tomorrow.

Just the awareness of that made her throat tight and her eyes sting. She wanted to see tomorrow so badly. Wanted to see a million tomorrows. See them with Trent. And Amy. But now…

Telling herself the old saying was right, that things were never over until they were over, she surreptitiously glanced at Trent, wondering if he had any ideas about how they could get themselves out of this.

They did have one thing going for them. The Beretta in her purse had live ammunition.

But how could she get at it with Shawn watching her?

And if she did, he'd start shooting the second he realized what she was up to.

"Take their weapons," he said to David Brown.

As Brown stepped over to do that, she tried to force away her fear.

She could barely think for it, which meant she had to at least get it under control—so that it wasn't like a living thing devouring her from the inside.

"And you two sit down," Shawn said, using his gun to gesture Trent and her toward the couch.

Once they were sitting, he reached into his pocket and took out a couple of clips, saying to Brown, "The bullets in these are live. Replace the ones in those Glocks with them, then leave the guns on the kitchen counter."

Briefly, Chelsea wondered about the point of that, then turned her attention back to Shawn.

He was still watching them, but keeping an eye on Brown, as well. And the moment Brown set the guns down he said, "How soon is Gloria bringing the kid back?"

Brown shrugged, looking uneasy. "I'm gonna call her on her cell after... After we take care of these two."

"That was *not* the plan," Shawn snapped.

"Yeah? Well, it wasn't the plan for my brother to get killed, either."

"Which was hardly my fault."

"Yeah? Well, that don't bring him back, does it? And it wasn't the plan to kill the kid, either. Or these two. And Gloria said no little girl should have to see her father get shot. She said—"

"I could care less what Gloria said," Shawn practically hissed. "The plan has changed.

"I was doing everything I could for your brother. You know that. And we'd have gotten him off.

"But now that he's gone we don't need these two. Or the kid. And there's no way we can *not* kill them. If we don't, we'll end up with life sentences. Gloria, too.

"So you get her on her phone and you tell her that. And tell her to haul her ass and that kid back here as fast as she can."

Brown didn't look happy, but he merely said, "I better call from the bedroom."

"Whatever," Shawn snapped. "Just do it."

Chelsea began praying that Brown wouldn't really do it at all. Or that Gloria would refuse to bring Amy back. That one way or another Amy would be—

"And make sure she understands," Shawn added, "that as far as the law is concerned, *she's* in this every bit as deeply as we are."

Damn. There probably wasn't the slightest chance of Amy not ending up back here. And soon. But there just had to be some way…

When Brown closed the bedroom door behind himself, Chelsea was still trying to think of an idea. The only one that had come to mind was to start Shawn talking.

That was never hard to do. And although it might not help, if he was thinking about something other than the immediate present, if he got himself distracted… Maybe somehow, someway…

From the bedroom, she could hear David Brown speaking—but too quietly for her to make out the words clearly.

Then the door opened and he walked out, saying, "I gotta go get Gloria."

"What?" Shawn demanded angrily.

"I *said,* I gotta go get her. You want them back here, don't you?"

"Look, Brown, if she has any stupid ideas about—"

"She's just in one of her moods. She'll come around. Don't worry about it."

"I'm warning you, if you screw up—"

"I'm not gonna screw up. I'm just gonna get Gloria and the kid."

With that, Brown unlocked the door and walked out, slamming it shut behind him.

Still looking mad as hell, Shawn shifted the lone chair in the room around so it was facing the couch, then sank into it, keeping his gun pointed toward Trent and Chelsea.

Telling herself this was the time, she quietly said, "I thought I knew you, Shawn, but I didn't. I'd never have believed you'd be part of anything like this."

"Shit happens," he muttered.

She snuck a quick look at Trent and wordlessly tried to give him the message that he should just keep quiet and wait, that Shawn always felt a need to fill silences.

Her telepathy must have worked, because after they broke eye contact he simply sat staring at the floor.

"You know," Shawn said at last, "in my line of work, every so often you find yourself owing somebody a really big favor."

Thank heavens. Once he started, he generally went on for ages. And if they saw a chance while he was talking, if his attention wavered from them for even a second...

That just *had* to happen. Now that she and Trent...
And Amy, with her entire life still ahead of her.

But Shawn had stopped speaking, which was *not* good.

"You find yourself owing somebody like John Brown?" she prompted him.

"John Brown? Hardly. I meant the sort of man who makes sure he has friends in the Bureau. Who's got bags of money and is generous with it. Who knows that somewhere down the line he might need a guy like me."

"The sort of man the D.A.'s Office puts away," Trent said.

Shawn almost smiled. "You don't know how ironic that is. The fellow I'm referring to is someone *you* put away. Years ago."

"Oh? Really?"

Shawn nodded.

"One of those jerks who swore revenge against me? Is that it? A crime lord who figured he was too smart ever to end up in prison? But got a surprise?"

When Shawn merely shrugged, Trent said, "Since you're going to kill us, you might as well tell us exactly what this whole exercise has been about. There's nothing else to do while we wait."

Chelsea was afraid even to glance at Trent again. He was playing this perfectly and she didn't want to do anything that might disrupt the flow.

All they needed was one small lapse on Shawn's part and they'd have their chance.

"I've never done this before," Shawn said. "Never had to sit around waiting with people I'm going to kill."

Chelsea swallowed hard. She took that to mean he

had killed people before, although she certainly wasn't going to ask.

"But to answer your question," he continued, focusing on Trent, "the man I'm helping out wasn't one of the guys who went mouthing off about getting back at you.

"He has more brains than that. And he's into action, not talk.

"In any event, you'd sent him away and he told me to ruin your life. That I could figure out how. And in exchange, I have enough money to retire whenever I choose."

"Then all this has been about money?" Chelsea said.

"All this? Chelsea, you somehow managed to make that sound like nothing, when you can't even begin to imagine just how much has been involved in *all this.*"

"I think I can," she said, telling herself that with any luck that had been the right line to really get him going.

Sure enough, he was looking amused and shaking his head—a definite sign that he was about to fill them in on the details he thought she couldn't even begin to imagine.

"Who do you figure was behind your wife's death?" he said to Trent.

She felt as though she'd just been kicked in the stomach. Trent's face went pale, and she knew how much worse *he* had to feel.

"You?" he said, his voice strained.

"Got it in one. Her death, then the letter that made you so scared for your daughter you decided to leave the D.A.'s Office and hole up in that backwater college town.''

Chelsea exhaled slowly, certain that if Shawn wasn't pointing a gun at them, Trent would—right this instant—be trying to kill him. And she'd be helping.

Nobody said anything for a minute or two, then Trent cleared his throat and said, ''Well, at least now I know who I've been hating for so long.''

Shawn merely shrugged once more.

''And where did John Brown come in?'' Trent said.

Lord, how could he possibly have managed to set aside his emotions and act so collected?

But that was what he'd *had* to do. He'd realized, just as she had, that the only way they were going to get out of here alive was by catching Shawn off guard. And he sure wouldn't be off guard if Trent began ranting and raving at him.

''John Brown. Well, John Brown was kind of a sidebar. He'd become a problem, and I saw a way of solving it and doing you harm at the same time. A little more ruination, so to speak.

''See, Brown used to look after odd jobs for me. Things I wouldn't have been smart to do personally.''

''Illegal *things*,'' Trent said.

''Exactly. Most of them were related to Bureau cases, but I made the mistake of starting to trust him enough that I had him take care of a few details that related to…other interests.''

''You're losing me,'' Chelsea said. ''What sort of details?''

''Oh, for example, he bugged the phones in Harrison's house.''

''What?'' Trent said.

"I was working on ruining your life, remember? So knowing what was going on in it was kind of a necessity."

"For how long?" Trent demanded. "How long have you been listening in on my life?"

"Oh, a couple of years. A little longer, actually. That's how I learned everything I needed to plan the kidnapping.

"About the conference in Boston. That Amy and your nanny were going along.

"Of course, you threw me a curve by taking Chelsea. I expected that after we sent your nanny running off to Philly, you'd leave Amy with your neighbor.

"But here's something you'll find humorous about my listening in *on your life,* as you put it."

Right, Chelsea thought blackly. They were in the perfect mood to find something he told them humorous. They might even find it absolutely hilarious.

"The reason I took Chelsea's driving course was that, ages ago, you were telling a friend about the RCI courses. And saying you were going to take the tactical driving one in the summer. And I thought it sounded interesting, so...

"Well, strange how things sometimes turn out, huh? If I hadn't done that, hadn't gotten to know Chelsea, and if you hadn't taken her along to Boston, kidnapping your kid might not have been as easy as it was."

"You and David Brown followed us Saturday morning," she said.

"Uh-huh. Then I distracted you while he grabbed Amy."

"But why? I mean, why would you go to such extremes to try to keep John Brown out of prison?"

For a minute, she didn't think he was going to tell them. Then he said, "Because he was blackmailing me.

"When he got arrested, he knew that with his record he'd be going down for life. So he told me that if I didn't find a way to get him off he'd plea-bargain, using me as his bargaining chip. He'd tell the cops about all the jobs he'd done for me."

"I'm surprised you didn't just kill him," Trent said wryly.

"I couldn't. Not right then. He was in custody. Sitting in a New York jail cell. So I didn't have any choice but to play along with what he wanted."

Chelsea licked her suddenly dry lips, thinking that being on Rikers Island was also being "in custody." Apparently, though, it was easier to have someone killed on Rikers than in a New York City jail cell.

"And since I had to be making an obvious effort to save Brown's ass," Shawn continued, eyeing Trent, "I figured I'd involve you. The old 'two birds with one stone' trick.

"At any rate, because of the bugs I knew Matthew Blake had been calling you—that he wanted you back in the D.A.'s Office. So I figured he'd jump at the idea of letting you do some *volunteer* work.

"It was kind of a convoluted plan, but I like to keep my mind busy."

"Yeah," Trent muttered. "I'll bet you do. And if you hadn't managed to arrange for Brown to get stabbed this morning, if I'd gotten him off, you'd have killed him once he was a free man again, wouldn't you."

When Shawn said nothing, Chelsea decided his silence was an admission.

"And what about Amy and me?" Trent said. "Were you planning all along to kill us after I blew Brown's trial?"

"No, I had something else in mind for you."

"Oh? What?"

"I was going to make sure the D.A. learned that you'd intentionally let Brown walk.

"That would have gotten you disbarred. And probably sent to prison. Which would have gone a long way to ruining your life.

"But then, instead of doing what you were told and cooperating, you decided to play detective."

"How did you know we were?" Chelsea asked.

"I'm not stupid. We kept an eye on you."

"You and David Brown."

He nodded. "And we had another guy helping out. We were keeping a *close* eye."

"You're talking about the fellow in the Taurus," Trent said.

"You're observant. Although you didn't realize I was following you yesterday morning. When you went visiting people, then to Rikers Island."

Chelsea could practically see another piece of the puzzle fitting into place.

"It was you who tried to kill me there, wasn't it?" she said.

Shawn shook his head. "I wasn't trying to kill you. Only scare you.

"See, you were a complication I hadn't expected. I figured your friend here might try to find his daughter. But by renting this dump and keeping her in Boston, when he had to be in New York…

"Then, suddenly there were two of you to worry

about. And you *didn't* have to stay put. So I decided that if I made you back off...

"Killing you would have been stupid, though. Would have caused a major investigation.

"They'd have run the plates of every car that had been on Rikers Island—including mine. And the story I gave the bridge guard, about being there to interview one of the detainees for the Bureau, wouldn't have held up."

"You didn't follow us from there to David Brown's apartment, though," she said. "I *know* we weren't being tailed then."

"No, you weren't. I took off after I shot at you."

He glanced at Trent, adding, "But even though I couldn't be sure what you were doing in the admin building, I had an idea you might be checking on John Brown's visitors.

"So I headed over to his brother's apartment to tell him to get out in case you showed. I told him to drive back up to Boston and stay here with Gloria and the kid for the time being.

"Then, once he left, I waited down on the street.

"Saw you two arrive and go in. Saw those cops show up not long after. And when you came charging out of that alley, it wasn't hard to fill in the blanks."

"So it was *you* who told Brown we'd been in his place," Trent said.

"Uh-huh. And it was about then I decided that you were getting too close for comfort. That I'd have to kill you before you learned I was behind things. Which pretty much brings us to where we are now."

"And from here...?" Trent said.

For the second time, Chelsea didn't think Shawn

was going to answer. But he eventually said, "From here is a stroke of brilliance.

"When Brown gets back with Gloria and Amy, there's going to be a shoot-out. That's why I had him put live bullets in those guns.

"And when the smoke clears it'll look as if you and Chelsea caught up with the kidnappers and took them on."

"And all *five* of us will end up dead," Trent said dully.

"Right. The only five people who know what's happened. Except for me and the fellow in the Taurus. He knows a bit, but I can easily take care of him.

"So you'll be dead and I'll be long gone from this apartment," he continued. "That's the *real* reason for the silencers. Getting out of here would be a lot trickier if half the neighbors were calling the cops."

"You don't seriously think you can pull this off, do you?" Trent said. "Not considering how thorough today's crime scene investigations are. And with DNA testing and—"

"But for any of that to incriminate me, it would have to occur to someone that I might have been involved. And who would even consider that a possibility?

"You and Chelsea were trying to track down the kidnappers. Why would I have been? As far as anyone in the real world knows, I've never even met you. And I haven't seen Chelsea for weeks.

"And it's your rental out front. My car's never been here."

"Somebody could easily have seen you come in with us," Chelsea said.

He shrugged. "I guess. But people in this sort of

neighborhood have poor memories when the police ask them questions. And even if they got some answers, a lot of people in Boston fit my general description.''

She swallowed hard and glanced along the couch at Trent once more, giving him another silent message and hoping he got it as well as he had the last one. Then she said, ''Shawn, I have to use the bathroom.''

He eyed her for a moment. ''Okay, but leave the door open.''

She reached for her purse and was just about to stand up, when he said, ''Give me that.''

A bolt of panic shot from her brain all the way down to her toes.

''Ah…I need something in it.''

''Fine, but I assume that's where your cell phone is. And I don't want you taking it with you.''

''Ah,'' she said again.

She opened the purse, praying she could get away with just removing the cellular, but Shawn said, ''No, give it to me.''

This was it then. This was the only chance they were going to get. And if she blew it, they'd end up dead a little sooner, that was all.

''Sure,'' she said, her heart hammering against her ribs.

She pushed herself up off the couch. As she stepped toward Shawn, he shifted his gun so it was aimed at the center of her chest.

''No tricks,'' he said quietly.

''No tricks,'' she repeated.

Then, as he reached for the purse with his free hand, she lunged and struck the side of his gun with it.

She heard the spits of bullets, but none hit her.

An instant later Trent was slamming himself against Shawn's arm with such force that his gun went flying.

She went flying after it, grabbing it off the floor, then wheeling to face the grappling men.

"Stop!" she yelled. "This is over!"

TRENT'S HEARTBEAT was almost back to normal.

He and Chelsea had cut a bedsheet into strips to tie and gag Shawn Madders. And with him shut in the bedroom, the only thing to do now was wait for David Brown to return with Amy and Gloria—which was exactly what they were doing.

He had his Beretta; Chelsea had Madders's gun. They'd hidden the Glocks, just to be on the safe side. And now they were standing with their backs pressed against the wall so Brown wouldn't see them right away.

Since he wasn't going to be expecting a surprise, they shouldn't have any trouble with him.

Unfortunately, *shouldn't* wasn't the same as *wouldn't*. And until Trent had Amy safely in his arms, until the cops had carted away those three criminals…

Hell, he wished they could have called the police already. But the last thing they wanted was a bunch of patrol cars sitting outside when Brown got back. That would make him turn and run faster than a cat with a Bouvier in hot pursuit.

"Hey," Chelsea said softly.

He looked at her and managed to smile.

"Don't worry," she told him. "It's smooth sailing now."

He nodded. And afterward…

Well, he wasn't sure she truly understood how bad things could get after he told Matthew Blake the truth. And even if he didn't feel morally obliged to do that, he wouldn't have any choice, because Madders would certainly be talking.

To say the Fed wasn't happy that they'd come out ahead would be the understatement of the decade. And whatever he could do to get back at them, he'd do.

Trent didn't want to think about ending up in prison, but it might happen. And if it did...

Looking at Chelsea again, he began praying it wouldn't.

Not just for his sake, but for Amy's. And for the future he'd begun to let himself imagine, now that he knew he could stop constantly watching over his shoulder.

It was a future that included Chelsea. She was the most awesome woman he'd ever met, and every time he looked at her he seemed to be more in love with her.

But if he became Trent Harrison, jailbird, his foreseeable future wouldn't include much except a six-by-eight-foot cell.

The more he imagined a life locked away from Amy and Chelsea, the more his heart hurt.

"What's wrong?" she murmured. "It's almost over."

"I know."

He meant to stop there, but he heard himself adding, "When it is, we have to talk. Because I don't know how it happened with everything else that's been going on, but I've fallen in love with you."

That made her give him an utterly gorgeous smile.

"Well, that's very convenient," she said, "because I've fallen in love with you, too. So I think talking is an excellent idea."

Her words made his heart sing and cry at the same time. She loved him. But if his future proved to be one she couldn't share...

"They're coming," she whispered.

Sure enough, a couple of floorboards creaked in the hallway.

He aimed his Beretta in the direction of the door. A moment later it opened and Brown walked in.

Trent held his breath, waiting through a slow-motion second for Amy and Gloria to follow him. Then Brown shoved the door closed.

Dammit. Where was Amy?

But he couldn't worry about that until they'd taken care of Brown.

"Hands up and face the wall," he ordered, training his gun on the man.

He spun toward them, saying, "What the—"

"Do it! Now!"

Muttering something, Brown turned and slapped his hands against the wall.

"Where's my daughter?" Trent demanded.

"With Gloria."

"Where?"

When Brown said nothing, Trent felt a serious urge to shoot him.

But that wouldn't get Amy back. And every minute more that she was gone he was growing crazier.

He'd fully expected to see her walk through that doorway. And the fact that she hadn't, the fact that he *still* couldn't be absolutely certain that this was going to turn out—

Chelsea gently rested her hand on his arm and shook her head, wordlessly telling him to be cool.

Then she said to Brown, "Shawn Madders is tied up in the bedroom, but we haven't called the police yet."

"And you won't," he snapped. "Not as long as you don't have the kid."

"No, that isn't true. Gloria doesn't want anything to happen to Amy. That's why she didn't come back with you, isn't it?"

Brown was silent.

"So we *will* call the police, and they won't have much trouble finding the two of them. But…well, naturally, the sooner Amy's with her father the happier we'll be. So we're prepared to make a deal."

Brown waited a few beats, then said, "What kinda deal?"

"You take us to Gloria and Amy right now and we won't hold you for the police. That'll give you a chance to get away."

"The cops'd catch up with us. Madders would tell 'em who we are and they'd catch up with us."

"They might. But we're offering you a chance. That's the best we can do. So you decide. Either take us to Amy, or we phone the police right now and you stay here with us until they arrive."

Even though Trent knew the cops *would* catch up with them, that the odds on their getting away were one in a million, the lawyer side of him was saying that offering Brown a chance wasn't what they should be doing.

The father side of him, however, was standing up and cheering.

Nothing that would get Amy back faster could really be wrong.

"How can I be sure you'd let us go?" Brown said.

"You have my word," Trent told him.

"Yeah. Right."

"It's up to you," Chelsea said quietly. "You can decide it's worth trusting us, or we'll call the police."

While Brown drummed his fingers against the wall, Trent tried to guess what he was thinking.

Hopefully, that he had nothing to lose by trusting them. That if he didn't, the cops would have him for sure. And that even if they reneged on their promise, he'd get a few brownie points with the law for taking them to Amy.

At last, he said, "Okay, let's go."

Following Brown out of the building and down the street, Trent doubted he'd ever felt more relieved.

Then, ahead, he spotted Amy and Gloria sitting on a bench in a pathetic little dirt park. His eyes filled with happy tears.

"Amy!" he shouted, breaking into a run.

"Daddy!" she cried.

A moment later he was scooping her up into his arms and hugging her against his chest.

"I love you so much, baby," he whispered.

"I love you too, Daddy."

"And everything's going to be all right from now on. Nothing like this will ever happen to you again. The man behind it will be in prison for the rest of his life." That said, he simply held her for a minute or two, then made himself put her down.

"Hi," she said to Chelsea.

"Hi. Do I get one of those big hugs?"

He watched them hug each other, thinking he loved them both so much. More than he could ever say.

But the number of laws he'd broken to get Amy back didn't auger well for his future.

And although he'd never regret any of what he'd done, he was already trying to figure out how he was going to put his case to the D.A. Because if he didn't do a good job of it, that future would be awfully bleak.

As Chelsea and Amy let go of each other, Amy looked around and said, "Gloria's gone."

Trent nodded. Then he unclipped his phone from his belt.

EPILOGUE

"So if the trial had proceeded," Trent said, "and I'd gotten Amy back before it ended, I'd have double-crossed them."

He hesitated. However, since he was coming clean, there was no point in half measures. He'd already lied too much to Matthew Blake.

"But if they'd still been holding her," he continued, "I'd have had to let John Brown walk and hope to hell they released her. I wouldn't have been able to make myself do anything else."

He held his breath while Matthew sat rubbing his jaw.

"I wish you'd been honest with me in the first place," he said at last.

"I just didn't see how I could be. Just couldn't risk the chance that you'd say no dice. If you hadn't taken me on, they'd have killed her."

Matthew rose from his desk, then stood silently staring out the window.

This was the moment Trent had been seriously trying not to worry about for the past twenty-four hours. But he hadn't been very successful.

Once the Boston police had arrested Shawn Madders and the horror was truly over, he'd known he'd have to come into New York and talk to Matthew this morning. And his concern about how the D.A. would react had been constantly lurking in the back of his mind, sneaking forward to nag at him every chance it got.

He'd tried not to let Chelsea realize that anything was bothering him. And maybe she hadn't. Not fully, at least, because they'd both been so focused on Amy.

His thoughts drifted to how having her back had almost seemed like a dream at first—during the drive from Boston to Ridley, and when they'd picked up Pete and taken him to the park.

Not until they'd ordered pizza and eased into discussing what had happened had things begun to feel entirely real. And it wasn't until then that Amy had started talking about just how scared she'd been. How scared she still was.

Once she'd started she simply hadn't stopped. Not until after they'd driven Chelsea home.

Then she'd slept with her bedroom light on—the way she had for the first few months after her mother had been killed.

He knew it was going to take time, and more than just a little talking with Chelsea and him, for her to work through her anxiety.

But he already had the name of a child psychologist who was supposed to be wonderful. And thanks undoubtedly to Gloria, Amy didn't seem nearly as traumatized as he'd feared she'd be.

Forcing those thoughts away, he turned his mind back to the moment.

The D.A. was still gazing out the window, and Trent felt as though the silence was about to kill him, so he said, "One of the reasons I wanted to tell you all this as soon as I could is that Shawn Madders is going to talk."

When Matthew turned from the window, Trent added, "He realizes he hasn't got a prayer of getting off. There are too many of us who know what he did. And he'll want to take me down with him.

"Chelsea, as well, although she isn't guilty of anything except helping me out. I'm the one who—"

"Hold on and let's look at this objectively," Matthew interrupted. "What we've got is a special agent who's so dirty that showering for a month wouldn't get him clean.

"He's going to be charged with kidnapping and multiple counts of attempted murder. If it turns out he *did* arrange for John Brown's death, then we'll charge him with murder for that.

"I'm thinking about obstruction of justice, too, but that might be overkill when he's bound to get life sentences on the other counts.

"At any rate, if Madders *does* start talking, what we'll have is a totally immoral criminal trying to lay off some of the blame on the two people who brought him down. I don't see that there should be any difficulty working around that."

Trent exhaled slowly, almost afraid to believe Matthew was saying there wouldn't be major repercussions for what he'd done.

"Look," he continued, "if this had happened to one of my children, if I'd found myself in your position…

"Well, let's just leave it this way. You don't have anything to worry about, because only you and I really know what you said when you asked about doing some work for the D.A.'s Office.

"And if my story is that you told me the whole truth right then and there and I agreed to help you with your problem, who's to know that isn't exactly what happened?

"Madders can say what he wants, but he wasn't in this room. And he can tell people you broke into David Brown's apartment or whatever else he thinks would get you in trouble, but who's going to take his word on anything?

"Trent, if I were you, I'd just keep quiet. If people are curious, tell them the D.A. asked you not to discuss any aspects of the case. That ought to shut them up."

"Yeah, it ought to. Matthew…thanks. You can't know how much I appreciate this."

The D.A. smiled. "I have a pretty good idea."

"I…"

He hesitated, because all he wanted to do for the next little while was spend time with Amy. And Chelsea.

Now that he knew his future didn't include a stretch in prison, they could get down to that talking they'd said they'd do.

But he finally made himself say, "Look, would you like me to stay on in the department for a week or so? Until Les Masson gets back? I hate to leave you in the lurch and—"

"No. It's good of you to offer, but I'm so used to being short staffed that I've learned to just live with it. So why don't you get going."

He shook hands with Matthew, thanked him again, then strode out to where Amy and Chelsea were waiting in the reception area.

Chelsea looked at him for about half a second before shooting him an enormous smile. Clearly, his relief was obvious.

"Went well?" she said as he reached them.

"Went *very* well."

"What are we going to do now, Daddy?" Amy asked.

He ruffled her hair, still almost unable to believe the way she seemed to have come through her ordeal.

"Oh, I think we should stay in the city long enough to have lunch," he said. "And maybe a carriage ride around Central Park afterward. Would you like that?"

She nodded enthusiastically.

"You know what Chelsea was telling me?" she said, taking one of Chelsea's hands and one of his as they started for the elevator.

"No, what?"

"That she's never had a dog."

"Oh?"

"So I was thinking she should come and play with Pete sometimes."

"You were, huh?"

As Amy nodded again, he looked over her head at Chelsea and whispered, "How about more than just sometimes?"

She gave him another great smile.

It made him desperately want to kiss her right then and there.

But some things were better when you had enough time to take them slowly.

Like all night.

Every night.

For the rest of their lives.

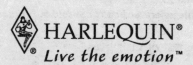

Corruption, power and commitment...

TAKING THE HEAT

A gritty story in which single mom and prison guard Gabrielle Hadley becomes involved with prison inmate Randall Tucker. When Randall escapes, she follows him— and soon the guard becomes the prisoner's captive... and more.

"Talented, versatile Brenda Novak dishes up a new treat with every page!"

—*USA TODAY* bestselling author Merline Lovelace

brenda novak

Available wherever books are sold in February 2003.

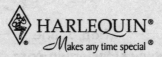

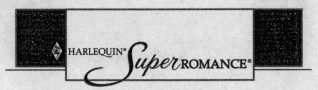

HARLEQUIN *Super*ROMANCE®

Koomera Crossing

**Welcome to Koomera Crossing,
a town hidden deep in the Australian Outback.
Let renowned romance novelist Margaret Way take
you there. Let her introduce you to the people of
Koomera Crossing. Let her tell you their secrets....**

In **Sarah's Baby** meet Dr. Sarah Dempsey and
Kyall McQueen. And then there's the town's
matriarch, Ruth McQueen, who played a role
in Sarah's disappearance from her grandson
Kyall's life—and who now dreads Sarah's
return to Koomera Crossing.

Sarah's Baby is available in February
wherever Harlequin books are sold.
And watch for the next Koomera Crossing story,
coming from Harlequin Romance in October.

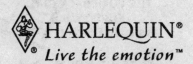

HARLEQUIN *Super*ROMANCE

presents a compelling family drama—
an exciting new trilogy
by popular author Debra Salonen

THOSE
SULLIVAN
SISTERS

Jenny, Andrea and Kristin Sullivan are much more
than sisters—*they're triplets!* Growing up as one of
a threesome meant life was never lonely...or dull.

Now they're adults—with separate lives, loves,
dreams and secrets. But underneath everything that
keeps them apart is the bond that holds them together.

MY HUSBAND, MY BABIES
(Jenny's story)
available December 2002

WITHOUT A PAST
(Andi's story)
available January 2003

THE COMEBACK GIRL
(Kristin's story)
available February 2003

HARLEQUIN®
Makes any time special ®

HSRTSS